Heist 2

Also by Kiki Swinson

Playing Dirty
Notorious
Wifey
I'm Still Wifey
Life After Wifey
Still Wifey Material
A Sticky Situation
The Candy Shop
Still Candy Shopping
Wife Extraordinaire
Wife Extraordinaire Returns
Cheaper to Keep Her

Also by De'nesha Diamond

The Diva Series
Hustlin' Divas
Street Divas
Gangsta Divas
Boss Divas
King Divas

Published by Kensington Publishing Corp.

Heist 2

KIKI SWINSON

DE'NESHA DIAMOND

Dafina
Books

KENSINGTON PUBLISHING CORP.

www.kensingtonbooks.com

DAFINA BOOKS are published by

Kensington Publishing Corp.
119 West 40th Street
New York, NY 10018

Heist 2 © 2015 by Kensington Publishing Corp.
The Last Heist © 2015 by Kiki Swinson
Caked Up © 2015 by De'nesha Diamond

All Kensington titles, imprints, and distributed lines are available at special quantity discounts for bulk purchases for sales promotion, premiums, fund-raising, and educational or institutional use.

Special book excerpts or customized printings can also be created to fit specific needs. For details, write or phone the office of the Kensington Sales Manager: Kensington Publishing Corp., 119 West 40th Street, New York, NY 10018. Attn. Sales Department. Phone: 1-800-221-2647.

Dafina and the Dafina logo Reg. U.S. Pat. & TM Off.

ISBN-13: 978-0-7582-8031-2
ISBN-10: 0-7582-8031-9
First Kensington Trade Paperback Printing: October 2015

eISBN-13: 978-0-7582-8033-6
eISBN-10: 0-7582-8033-5
First Kensington Electronic Edition: October 2015

10 9 8 7 6 5 4 3 2 1

Printed in the United States of America

The Last Heist

KIKI SWINSON

422 - 5283

1

Shannon

Dear Shannon,
  I guess the fucking joke was on you. I heard through
the grapevine that Jock turned on your ass. I had to
laugh. I guess you should've been more careful about
who you gave your pussy up to. If I had gotten out you
would've been sitting pretty right now. Instead, you are
being charged with conspiracy to commit armed robbery and accessory to murder. You must be kicking the
shit out of yourself right now. I hope you rot in jail,
you bitch! By the way, the judge put the plea back on
the table for me so with good behavior I will be out in
seven. I hope you grow old and fucking die in prison,
you grimy bitch. You will always remember the end re-
sult of the ultimate heist!
  Love,
  Your husband,
  Todd

Every night before I closed my eyes and every morning before I left my prison bunk, I made sure I took out that fucking letter from my ex-husband, Todd, and read it a couple of times. It was fuel for my fire and my daily motivation to keep going although I was in this fucked-up predicament. I needed Todd's words on paper to remind me of what I had left to live for: revenge against his sorry ass, Jock's back-stabbing ass, and a couple of dirty feds and bastard-ass cops, all of whom I wanted to see brought to their knees in the worst way.

Todd's letter wasn't the only motivation I had to keep going. I also took a look at my son's picture each day and night to remind me that, aside from revenge, I did have something positive to live for. Being locked up, it didn't always seem like life was going to be worth living, but I knew I couldn't let my son grow up and have the kind of childhood I was subjected to. I often blamed my situation on how I grew up too. My mother was a full-fledged crack-head. I mean one of those crackheads that left her kids for dead, starving while she sucked dick in the projects for a ten-dollar hit. She was once a flying-high beauty queen that all the hood niggas broke their necks to get at, but once my father—one of the biggest drug kingpins in the city—got knocked and sent to prison for life, my mother turned to sucking that glass dick and she completely forgot about me. I didn't have it easy growing up, living with my grandmother and about a million cousins in a cramped two-bedroom project apartment. The thought of my son growing up like that made me want to fight harder to get out of prison.

I can't front, Todd was the reason I had even escaped my terrible childhood. He had given me a good life, but he had also ruined my fucking life on the same token. I mean, look at me now.

Here I am, Shannon Marshall, former fashion and swag queen of Tidewater lying in a prison bunk with unkempt hair that was in dire need of a perm; broken, chipped, and unpolished nails; ashen and acne-filled skin, and dead in the water without a person in the world who cared about my ass. You could just say I didn't have any other family aside from Todd. My family was all jealous, hating-ass bitches that were probably celebrating the fact that I was locked up. They always were jealous of me and the fact that I had snagged a man like Todd and lived the high life off his money. My turn of bad luck was surely making them happy.

My life had changed drastically over the past six months and for damn sure it hadn't changed for the better. Sometimes I think the fact that I was in the same predicament as Todd right now—sitting in prison with no hope of getting out—was karma for me leaving Todd and taking up with his right-hand man, Jock. Yeah, I fucked my husband's partner and best friend, but that's a whole other story. Like I said, I think my situation is karma, but other times I think this is just a temporary situation to teach me something . . . one that I will bounce back from and come out even better than before.

No matter what, though, I couldn't help but obsess about my past life. Sometimes it made me smile, but other times it made me want to cry to even remember it all. I had the type of life bitches in my hood was dying for. Those bitches would've probably sold their kids on the black market to walk one day in my shoes. Everybody wanted to be me and everybody wanted to have Todd in their beds too.

Yeah, my life was fabulous. I had gone from shopping almost every day in stores like Saks, Neiman Marcus, and Nordstrom. And, when I say shopping, I don't mean to buy one outfit or one pair of shoes, I mean damn near shopping sprees where I was buying six and seven pairs of high-end shoes and two and three leather jackets and two and three of the newest designer bags. I was living that life and I was definitely about that life. In fact, the day my life changed for the worst, I had been in Saks shopping with my best friend Satanya—who by the way is dead now and partly to blame for the way shit blew up. But, anyway, I went from the fabulous life of a celebrity to wearing a jail-issued jumpsuit, white half-size-too-small Keds, and sleeping on a metal bed with a paper-thin mattress and threadbare blanket that smelled like twelve babies had vomited on the shit. That was a far cry from the six-thousand-square-foot mini-mansion Todd and I shared, which was decked out in the finest Italian furniture, expensive art pieces, and top-of-the-line appliances. I closed my eyes and fought back the daily round of tears that threatened to fall every day when I woke up facing the dank, gray walls of my cell and smelling the funky pussy and piss smell coming from my bunk mate. Reality was a bitch but so was reminiscing over the past.

"Yo, Queen Shan!" I heard her voice before I could fully see her. Dee, one of my prison minions, was huffing and out of breath as she rushed toward my bunk with her eyes all bugged out and shit. "Queen! Queen, I gotta tell you something," Dee said, winded.

I was still rubbing sleep and tears out of my eyes when she rushed in. I wasn't like the other inmates who got up all early for breakfast. I never left my bunk for that whack-ass breakfast they served. Nah, I ate from my commissary snacks every morning instead . . . no jail slop for me.

"What? Whatcha want this early in the morning?" I growled at Dee, seriously annoyed that she even dared to step into my cell this early. Dee immediately fell back a little bit. She knew better than to get on my bad side. She was a short, chubby girl that I had taken under my wing and used as one of my errand girls. What I had learned real fast about being locked up was that you had to command respect, either through force or through having shit. I had done a little bit of both. My first two weeks there I was weepy and real sensitive because I wasn't used to that controlling, horrible, dirty environment. But I learned real fast that bitches are ruthless and if I didn't become the old Shannon—street, ghetto bird, fuck-a-bitch-up-real-quick Shannon—I would be fucked out of the game up in the joint. So, I got with the program real quick and I fucked up a few bitches that were claiming they were running shit. Once that happened, I had solidified my spot at the top among the black crew inside. I even had them simple bitches calling me Queen Shan . . . short for Shannon. I'm laughing in my head now just thinking about it.

With sleep still clouding my judgment and an attitude that could kill a bitch, I cocked my head to the side and looked at Dee with an evil glare. My growling stomach made it easy for me to be mad and agitated that early in the morning.

"I . . . I . . . just heard something going around," Dee huffed, putting her hand over her heaving chest like she was about to faint. She could see that the look on my face was clearly telling her to get to the fucking point or else we was going to have a problem.

"They . . . they . . . saying that somebody in here got a kite from outside . . . and . . . and . . . it ain't good." Dee gulped. I let out a long, exasperated breath.

"Get to the fucking point, Dee!" I snarled. She licked her lips, something she does when she's nervous. I bit my bottom lip, something I did when I was getting ready to spaz out.

"They . . . they . . . saying that there is a hit out on you up in here, Queen Shan," Dee finished breathlessly. I let my tense shoulders fall. I rolled my eyes and inhaled like I had just gotten the most annoying news ever.

Not again, I thought to myself. What Dee was saying wasn't news to me. Todd had made several attempts to have me jumped, shanked, beaten up, etc. He was a fucking loser point blank. I stretched and yawned like I wasn't fazed at all. I couldn't let my little soldier see me sweat the bullshit. There was a good possibility that this time he could've gotten the right people to carry out his hit, but I wasn't about to let on that I was one bit nervous about it. Acting tough was one hundred percent of what got me through each day inside, so I wasn't about to change it now. I jumped down from my bunk so that I could meet Dee eye to eye.

"Dee, calm down. I ain't worried about Todd and his threats. These bitches ain't about shit. That's the same fucking kite Todd been sending since I got here. That nigga sore about me and Jock and all the shit that happened. I already told you and the whole crew, I ain't worried about his fake-ass hits. He ain't got shit and damn sure can't pay nobody to put a hit out on me," I said calmly, although my heart was drumming against my chest bone like Questlove from the Roots was hammering out a song on it. I'm telling you I should've been an actress, because the entire time I had been locked up, everything I had shown was all an act. Inside, I was a shaken, scared little girl dying to go home before somebody pulled my card up in that prison.

Dee's expression eased once I said what I had to say. She believed everything I told her, no matter what it was. I was happy about that because if not, I would have to keep explaining myself to her. As Dee and I got ready to leave my cell, I could feel my stomach was churning with a mixture of anger and fear. I knew that anything was possible and at any time the threats from Todd could materialize into some hungry-for-a-name-ass-bitch attacking me in the shower while I was wet and helpless or while I slept or when I had my back turned in the library researching my case. I had seen it happen to a few of the hardest butch bitches in here; a few of which I hadn't seen return once they were carried out by the medics.

"Don't worry about me, Dee. You worry about going to that library and getting your read on . . . I wasn't playing when I said you need to learn how to read before my appeal comes up," I said seriously, hoping that changing the subject with Dee would also make me feel better about my potential threat.

Dee lowered her gaze and hung her head slightly. She was the most loyal of the little crew I had put together inside the prison, but she was also the dumbest. It pained me to know that at almost thirty-five years old, Dee couldn't read or even write her own name. She had spent so many years in different jails and prisons and no one had ever encouraged her to even learn how to write her name properly. A damn shame, if you ask me. I had finally taught Dee to sign her name without just using a typical illiterate person's X; now I was forcing Dee to learn how to read. The fact that they had *Hooked on Phonics* in a women's prison library was startling to me, but I quickly realized why. Dee wasn't the only grown-ass woman locked up that couldn't read or write. Surprisingly, a few of the white girls in there were just like Dee, if not even worse. Growing up in the hood, I always thought all white people were rich, could read, and lived like kings and queens. Shit, coming to prison and growing up taught me differently.

"C'mon. I'm going to hit the chow hall with you," I told Dee as we made a beeline for the crowded chow hall. Her eyes lit up with excitement because it was rare for me to set foot in that place. Whenever I didn't have what I wanted or enough, I just acted like a tough girl and took from some of the weaker inmates. The power I had inside the prison, I had never felt while I was on the outside. It was all an act, but even that was about to change.

* * *

I sat down in the chow hall while Dee got her breakfast of cold hardboiled eggs, lumpy oatmeal, and stale square institutional bread that was rough enough to scrub pots with. I kind of felt like a sitting duck in that chow hall. I was very aware that all eyes were on me, but my mind was so far off in another place I wasn't thinking about those restless-ass bitches. I kept telling myself that the threat wasn't real, but the idea of it was nagging at me like a fly buzzing in my ears.

I couldn't stop thinking about the nerve of that bitch-ass nigga Todd to put a hit out on me like I was one of his street enemies. After all I had been through at his fucking hands? I had stuck by his worthless ass through prison bids, baby mama drama, cheating, and him sending me on the streets for money. I think he must've forgot that it was me who he had sent to the front line to set up a heist just so his selfish ass could get money to pay for an attorney. What real man asks his woman to be involved in crimes for his own selfish reasons? Well, Todd is obviously not a real fucking man.

I would never forgive Todd for the shit he put me through, especially because I ended up in prison behind his ass. All the years I had spent with him riding with him through it all, I deserved better than this bullshit. I had to shake my head just thinking about how many times bitches called me in the middle of the night telling me to smell Todd's dick when he got home because he had just finished fucking them. I shuddered now thinking about all the chicks that claimed Todd had fathered their babies. I had tried to keep my head up when these hoes flaunted these children in my face, but even I could see that some of them resembled Todd.

Then, to top it off, this last time Todd got knocked on gun charges, he expected me to be the same old young, dumb little girl I was when he met me. Nah, I was all grown up and I was sick of his shit. I went along with his stupid-ass plan about robbing the biggest kingpin and businessman in the Tidewater area—Bobby Knight—but that all backfired on me and it certainly didn't benefit Todd's sorry ass. He should've never gotten me involved in the first place. I was supposed to be his woman; he was supposed to be my man, my protector, my everything.

I swiped roughly at the tears cropping up in my eyes. I couldn't afford for anyone to see me having a moment of weakness. Anyway, in the end, after the Bobby Knight set-up, there was no honor among us thieves and even the fucking feds were dirty on that shit. I'm telling you, money will make niggas tie their own mothers to the fucking railroad tracks. Before I knew what had hit me, I found out that Todd's so-called cellmate Dray was a fed and he had set me up to get Bobby Knight's money for himself. His ass got set up by the Norfolk police and Jock set that up. Now I was sitting in prison shaking my head in disgust but smiling slightly because I was still proud of myself.

See, it was all me when it came down to it. The planning and execution of the Bobby Knight heist was all my handiwork. I didn't think I had all of that conniving in me, but apparently I was more talented than I thought.

It started when Todd had met that bitch-ass fed Dray in jail and Dray had put Todd on to Bobby Knight. Dray did the introduction part, but I was the bitch putting the *Ocean's Eleven*-style plan together. I'm chuckling now just thinking about how smooth I was during that time. Seducing Bobby Knight was supposed to be my biggest challenge, but shit, that was the easiest part of it, if you ask me. I had that nigga Bobby Knight wrapped around my finger in no time and everybody knew he could've had any bitch in Virginia if he wanted to; instead, he was eating out of the palm of my hand with the quickness.

Bobby Knight wasn't no slouch. I had really started to fall for him. He was a well-spoken, well-read, wealthy man that I could've gotten used to living with. Before I could really fall for Bobby, he was growing suspicious of me. He wasn't no slouch when it came to picking up on clues and when it came to protecting his shit. So, when shit started to go south because of Satanya's big-ass mouth, Bobby was on my ass like stink on shit. I remember him picking me up one night and taking me to a place where I thought for sure he was going to kill my ass. Even when I was scared shitless for my life, ride-or-die-ass Shannon Marshall was not giving up. Nope, instead of running and cowering, I called in the team I had wrangled up to rob Bobby and we got it on. I felt dreamy just thinking now about how it went down . . .

"Get to the first room and grab everything you can. There is a truck outside behind the last room on the left. There is an exit. We need to be out of here in five minutes," Bam yelled at me over the sound of small explosions erupting all around Bobby Knight's mansion.

"Okay, okay," I wolfed out, putting the gun Bobby had given me a few minutes earlier into the back of my jeans. My chest was heaving in and out. I made a mad dash for the hall-way as Bam went along door by door shooting off the locks and taking out the cameras. Although all of the power had been shut down, Bam didn't want to take a chance that Bobby had a backup generator on those cameras. I really felt like a rene-gade bitch. I wasn't leaving the fucking house without enough money to set me straight. The first room was filled with boxes. I tried to grab more than one but they were fucking heavy as hell. I started dragging one toward the door so I could get out-side. Bam and the two dudes that were still alive grabbed boxes too. I couldn't even think to ask where Black was. I just fig-

ured when I didn't see him he was a casualty of war. "Wait!"
I heard Bam scream out. He stopped and used a knife to strip
off the tape on one of the boxes. Sure enough, the shit was
filled with neatly rubber-banded stacks of cash. He wanted to
make sure we weren't wasting our fucking time.

"Go!!!" Bam screamed and we raced outside toward the
truck. I kept dragging my one box. As soon as we made it toward the front, more gunshots rang out. My legs buckled from
the sound and fear gripped me, but I kept moving. Two more
of Bam's dudes dropped. Now it was just Bam and me. I was
too fucking scared to cry or scream. I just kept ducking and
running for the truck. I had a warrior mindset going on and I
was going to get the fuck out of there alive. I had a baby boy to
pick up and start a new life with. There was a dude in the driver
seat of a black van. He got out and hoisted my box into the van.
Bam was still struggling to get out with his boxes. The driver
helped him and Bam turned around like he was going back in.

"Where are you going?!" I screamed at the top of my lungs.

"Yo, that ain't enough," Bam said greedily, and soon as he
turned around, one last security guard was there. Bam and the
guard both shot at each other at the same time and they both
dropped. I saw Bam's brains leaking onto the pavement and
piss trickled from my bladder.

"Ahhhhh!" I screamed, jumping into the van. The sight of
Bam's brains was forever etched in my brain. The driver sped
out and the van was swerving all over the road leading out of
the estate.

"Oh God!!" I screamed and cried.

"Shut up!" the driver barked. "You fucking making me
nervous!" He looked to be no older than eighteen years old. He
was shaking and could barely drive. He finally got the van to

*go straight and slowed up a bit so that we wouldn't bring at-
tention to ourselves. My nose was running, my heart was
thumping, and the tears just flowed and flowed. I appeared to
be crying for all the dead soldiers I had left at that mansion,
but nah, I was crying for other reasons. I had done it. I had
carried out the ultimate heist and I was the only one left
standing. Or so I thought.*

A searing pain crashed through my skull like I had been hit by
lightning, violently jolting me out of my daydream.

"Aggh!" I screamed out as I quickly realized what was happening. Another powerful blow caused blue streaks to flash behind
my eyelids and I felt the bone in my nose shatter. Blood leaked
over my lips and, since I had my mouth open into a silent scream, I
could taste the salty, metallic taste of my own blood. I tried to put
my hands on my head to protect my skull, but being that my guard
had been down while I relived the robbery memories, my reflexes
were slow now. I was too late. I was under attack and there was
nothing I could do to protect myself now. I was dragged down to
the floor where I took a swift blow to my ribs.

"Bitch, I heard you thought this hit was a joke? A fake?" a
brawly, flat-chested butch hissed in my ear as she wound her go-
rilla fists up into my hair. I swung my arms and tried in vain to
fight back. My hair was my weakness. I guess Todd had told the
goon bitches he hired to make sure they grabbed my hair. My at-
tacker hoisted me up by my hair so I could meet her eye to eye.
Chaos had broken out in the chow hall and I could hear cheers
from some of the other inmates . . . a few of whom I knew was
rooting for me to get my ass kicked. My eyes darted around help-
lessly and I noticed the butch's crew was holding my crew at bay. I
also quickly peeped the COs acting like they ain't see what the

fuck was going down. The Hispanic lesbian gang that ran the weed trade in the jail surrounded me, and everybody knew these bitches were built like men and loved to see blood on their hands.

"Nah, *mamita*, this ain't fake. This shit right here real. We got paid to take you down and we plan to do that, *puta*," the butch said, her Puerto Rican twang accenting her words as she increased the grasp and pressure on the fistful of my hair she was holding hostage. There was no use in being in denial: I was about to get my ass whipped or worse.

"Fuck you!" I growled, hocking a wad of spit into her ugly, scarred-up face. Even with the pain throbbing through my scalp, my nose bleeding like a faucet, and the possibility that these Spanish chicks was about to slash me open like a gutted pig, I couldn't back down now. Not only did I have a reputation to uphold in the prison, but I was just not going to let Todd win all the way. I figured if this pussy bitch-ass nigga Todd's hit was going to take me out, I surely wasn't going out like no sucker. I wanted to make sure he got the word that Shannon Marshall didn't go out without a fight.

CRACK! CRUNCH! WHAM! The next thing I knew punches, kicks, and stomps rained down on my body from every direction. I was conscious for a while and enduring the pain, but that didn't last long. Finally, blackness engulfed me.

2
Todd

I was still locked up like a fucking animal, but today I felt a little better about it. Not because I was getting out or anything like that. Nah, nothing good, but I was feeling good because I was waiting for word that my bitch wife Shannon was dead. Yeah, that's right, I was wishing death on that bitch ten times over. She was a snake bitch that didn't deserve to live.

I used the last of the bullshit commissary money Shannon had put on my books to send a kite to the women's prison and pay some Latinas to take Shannon's ass out. In my eyes, any bitch that could fuck your best friend, have the next nigga playing house with your seed, and steal all your money didn't deserve to fucking live. That was Shannon . . . a straight ghetto bird bitch. I must say I was real shocked when I received her letter telling me that she had been fucking my friend Jock for years from when I was locked up the first time. When I had gotten home from that bid, both Jock and Shannon had picked me up and smiled all in my face like shit was all good. I had put Jock on to my new gun business and all that; meanwhile, this nigga was fucking my wife all along. He and I had grown up together, got locked up together, built a business together, and I guess he thought that meant he could have *everything* that I had. Just like I did Shannon, I was planning to see Jock one of these days. Either in person or by way of messenger; he wasn't getting away with what he did to me.

I hadn't gotten the word back yet, but I was sure I would be hearing about Shannon's demise sooner or later. I just hoped that expensive-ass insurance policy I had taken out on that bitch was still in full effect. I had paid up the premiums six months in advance when I was out, so I knew that would give me some time before the shit lapsed. Locked up or not, collecting a cool million off Shannon's dead body would be a major fucking score for me.

The plan to set Shannon up came just as easily as the Bobby Knight set-up had come. My new bunk mate Hector told me his wife was locked up in the same place as Shannon and that was all I needed to hear. I had seen pictures of this butch Hector called a wife . . . shit, she looked harder than some dudes I knew, so I don't know how he thought he was wifing that bitch.

Hector's wife, Maria, rolled with a deep group of Latina lesbians that ran the drug trade in the women's jail. Yeah, that's right . . . I said lesbians. This nigga Hector was in denial, but that was none of my business. The Latina chicks were the perfect ones to hire: ruthless, desperate, and got off on violence. I set that shit up easy breezy and with the quickness.

Yeah, it may sound fucked up that I would do something like that to my wife . . . someone I had once loved and contemplated giving my life for. But what she had done to me was way worse because she might as well had killed me. You know what it is like for a nigga locked up to find out his wife had betrayed him and on top of it all was fucking one of his soldiers. Man, listen, she might as well had stabbed me full of holes and shot me in the cranium. I can't stop thinking about how sick Shannon left a nigga with his dick in the dust, all the while making me believe she was going to come through for me. She played a good game coming up here in her short skirts, fucking me by the vending machines, and making lip service promises.

I held my head in my hands now as I suddenly remembered the day that I got Shannon's letter telling me that she had been fucking my right-hand man, Jock. I ripped up the letter, but trust me, I memorized those fucking words and they still ring in my ears to this day.

I just want you to know. I knew about the whole plan all along. I knew where Jock was—he was waiting for me so he could give me the dick he has been giving me for the last two years while you chased bitches around Virginia. Me and Jock are together raising your son. Your son who calls Jock Daddy.

"Grrr!" I growled as I punched the heavy bag in the prison gym harder and harder with every passing thought. The more I thought about Shannon and Jock's betrayal, the harder I hit the bag, wishing that it was both of their faces that I was hitting. Finally, my knuckles split open and pain shot up my arms.

"Fucking bitch," I huffed and puffed as I slid down to the floor in a heap of sweat, bleeding from my knuckles. I closed my eyes for a few minutes to collect my thoughts. And, trust me, there were many thoughts swirling around in my head. Most of the thoughts were about killing those traitorous muthafuckas.

"Marshall!" Broadbent, the CO I hated the most, yelled out my name like he was losing his fucking mind. This nigga had a hard-on for harassing me on the daily. You would've thought he had something personal against me, but I didn't even know his fake ass.

"Marshall! I know you fucking hear me, you piece of shit!" Broadbent hollered, trying to play me as usual.

I slowly lifted my head, my face drawn into a tight scowl. This nigga just didn't know how lucky he was that I was locked up and trying to keep my nose clean so I would have a better chance at appeal later on. If that wasn't the case, I would've already fucked his ass up and caught an additional charge.

"Get up! Somebody here to see you . . . fucking dirt bag," Broadbent said through gritted teeth. If I wasn't looking forward to finally getting a good behavior streak I would've punched that fucking faggot-ass nigga in his face. I was sure that Broadbent wasn't shit outside on the street. He used his uniform to act like a thug behind the walls, but I had it in my head that whenever I got out, I would see his ass for sure. Once I put a hit on a nigga in my mind, I wasn't going to rest until it was carried through. Broadbent was on that list, along with Jock, Zack, and Billy—all those niggas that were supposed to be in my crew that shitted on me because they thought I was down and out forever.

Broadbent manhandled me as usual. He led me past the visit room, which caused me to raise my brows.

"Where the fuck is you—" I started to ask, but my words were cut short when I saw what was happening. I saw that white, shiny, bald head before I could protest. My stomach immediately knotted and my heart started thumping. I thought I would never have to deal with this white devil again.

"Aww shit," I sighed, shaking my head from side to side. "Yo, just take me back to my fucking cell. I don't wanna talk to this nigga here," I grumbled as I got closer to the source of my discomfort.

"Marshall . . . Marshall . . . Todd . . . fucking Marshall," Sergeant LaBeckie of the Norfolk Police Department sang, smiling like a goofy fucking kid as he made a song out of my name.

"Fuck you, LaBeckie. I don't want to see your ugly ass," I hissed. LaBeckie started laughing raucously like I had told his white ass a joke.

"Well, damn, I thought you would always be happy to see my handsome fucking face," LaBeckie said sarcastically. "I mean we got so much history together, ol' Toddy boy." LaBeckie smiled wickedly.

"I ain't none of ya fucking boy!" I spat just before I was forced down into a chair.

Sergeant LaBeckie was right, though. He and I had a lot of history, which wasn't a benefit to me at all. LaBeckie had pursued me for years while I was living large on the streets. He would grow angrier and angrier each year because he could never get at me since I ran my operations virgin-pussy tight. I remember seeing LaBeckie and taunting him on the streets because he would be following me or my boys and we would always be clean. He would look so defeated when me and my boys would roll past him and laugh at his ass, giving him the finger and shit. It was like LaBeckie woke up and went to bed thinking about catching me. I would've never suspected that day would come one day and this bastard would have his full revenge on me.

Finally, LaBeckie got the break he needed—a snitch—in the form of my best friend, Jock. Now, I'm thinking Shannon also had something to do with the shit too. She might've played the shocked roll but maybe it was all an act so shit looked more realistic to me. Maybe not. Who knows? All I know is that it was the worst day of my life so far, aside from the day I found my mother dead from a drug overdose. My life changed on both days, but LaBeckie getting his revenge was one that stuck out more.

The day LaBeckie and this unit raided my house, LaBeckie took full advantage of my helpless position. I squinted at him now, my mind drawn backwards to that horrible day . . .

* * *

"Get on the floor! Get the fuck on the floor!" Those commands were very familiar. I put my hands up, folded them behind my head, and assumed the position. I was pushed down to the floor roughly and about five of those bastard cops dropped knees in my back. My arms were yanked behind my back roughly and I was cuffed and made to lay face down on my own goddamn floor. Those fucking pigs were swarming my crib like flies around a pile of freshly dropped shit. It seemed like it was a million of them. All of them against just me.

"Punk bitches," I grumbled under my breath. I recognized one of them—a big-head white boy that thought he was the shit. A snake muthafucka named LaBeckie. He was the sergeant of the Norfolk Police Department's narcotics and gun unit and he hated my ass.

"Take out that wall! Tear this fucking place up until we find some shit!" I heard that bastard yell, as he looked down at me and smiled.

I closed my eyes when I heard them axing down walls and cabinets.

"Fuck you want, LaBeckie?" I snarled as I was roughly thrown into a hard, metal chair by that stupid ass Broadbent.

"Todd, my friend, you break my little heart." LaBeckie chuckled evilly, tapping the left side of his chest for emphasis. I bit down into my jaw and swung my legs in and out furiously. "Can't I come visit an old friend? I mean, you do know you're the reason I made lieutenant, right? Oh maybe you didn't know that I got promoted and I owe it all to you." LaBeckie laughed and I felt all of the hairs on my body stand up.

I wanted to spit in his fucking eye because I knew what he meant by saying it was me and my case that had helped him climb the ranks. LaBeckie had been working with Andre Burkett aka Dray, my former bunk mate, who also happened to be a fucking snitch-ass fed. I couldn't even control my rapid breathing right now just picturing Dray's traitorous face and thinking about how he had fucked me royally.

Man, I was so torn up and desperate when I first got locked up that I had my street guard all the way down, which led to me trusting that nigga Dray way too easily. Me, a nigga that usually don't trust a soul, let Dray into my world fast as hell, so when Dray proposed that I use my outside connections, namely my fucking wife, to set up Bobby Knight, a big hustler and wealthy businessman that had the Tidewater area on lock, I didn't think twice about it. I had tunnel vision at that time: get Knight set up, get some paper for a lawyer, and get the fuck out of prison. I wouldn't say the shit was foolproof, but it could've possibly worked if it wasn't the fucking feds all along.

When I proposed the set-up to Shannon, it didn't take that much convincing. I should've suspected that shit wasn't right, just judging from her quick enthusiasm to do it.

Shit, Shannon was down from the jump; little did I know she would set up Bobby Knight and take flight with all of the money that she got from the heist. She ain't even try to get the high-priced defense attorney I usually used to help me out . . . Nah, Shannon was too busy running with the dirty money and fucking Jock along with it. Wow, that shit blows my mind every time I think about it.

"Yo, go find your snitching-ass fed flunky Andre Burkett," I spat at LaBeckie, squinting at that bitch-ass pig, and if eyes could kill he would've dropped fucking dead.

"Well, Marshall, that's why I'm here," LaBeckie said through a yawn like he was already exhausted by what he was going to tell me. That was his little trick and I had learned that through the fifty interrogations I had had with him in the past. I knew all the cop tricks: acting unfazed, good cop/bad, and helpful cop. I was too smart for any of that bullshit LaBeckie was coming with right now.

"Burkett turned out to be dirtier than you in this whole thing," LaBeckie said. I guess the expression of shock on my face was giving away all the questions that were now swirling through my mind.

"Yeah, that's right, Marshall . . . Burkett or Dray, or whatever the fuck he wanted to call himself, played all of us. He set us all up, but I'm too fucking smart for that, so he lost in the end . . . You know why?" LaBeckie said while stretching and raising his arms behind his head and rearing back in the chair across from me like he was relaxing on a beach somewhere. I raised my eyebrows when he asked his rhetorical questions, but I quickly put my poker face back on. No way I wanted this pig to think I was interested in what he had to say.

"Why? Because I'm the smartest motherfucker in Virginia . . . that's why and you, your wife, Burkett, and your little crew were all way behind the eight ball while I was out in front of it. I knew when Burkett came to us with the idea of using you and your sweet pussy wife to set up Knight that Burkett had other shit in mind. My little dirty bastard radar was going off whenever I was around that little snake Burkett," LaBeckie relayed with a lazy grin on his ugly face. I swallowed hard and curled my fingers into tight fists just hearing LaBeckie refer to Shannon as a piece of sweet pussy. It made me start thinking if she had fucked this pig too. This smug piece of shit LaBeckie had not only gotten a promotion by standing on my fucking neck, he had caused my son to be parentless just to advance his own bullshit agenda. My nostrils flared and fire burned in my chest as I listened to him brag about himself.

"So, all in all, you helped us more than you knew you were

helping. And since I'm a nice fucking guy, I came back to thank you in person," LaBeckie said, all sinister like. My stomach knotted because I knew better than to trust this snake. He came back to rub it in my face, that much I was sure of, but what else could he want with me? I mean, he had chased me for years and finally got me where he wanted me. In my eyes our feud was over now.

"To thank me? Yeah fucking right," I grumbled, breaking eye contact with him.

"Okay . . . okay . . . maybe not to thank you." LaBeckie laughed. The sound of his laughter sent a heat wave of anger through my chest. I let out a long breath trying to keep my cool.

"But I do have an offer for you, Marshall," LaBeckie said, leaning in and getting closer to the table with a joker-type smirk painting his face. I just bit down into my lip. There was nothing this devil could offer me that I would accept. I didn't get down for no police and that was final.

"You do a little something for us and I do a big thing for you . . . what we smart people call quid pro quo," LaBeckie said snidely.

"Ain't shit I would ever do for you, pig," I fired off, leaning my body forward and staring straight into his evil blue eyes for emphasis. LaBeckie leaned back from the table as if I had slapped him in the face. He was power-hungry and a control freak so the fact that I dissed his ass wasn't sitting right with him at all. I could see the redness—either from embarrassment or anger—creeping up his neck and making its way to his face. LaBeckie closed his eyes for a few minutes, let out a long breath, and then he dug into his suit jacket pocket and pulled something out. I had my head cocked to the side and my eyebrows furrowed, looking at him like I didn't give two fucks about what he had in his pocket. What could he do to me? I was already locked up like an animal. LaBeckie smirked and tossed something onto the table, then squinted with a satisfied look on his face.

"I think if you want to ever see this face or to know that he will always be safe . . . you'll fucking hear me out, you piece of shit," LaBeckie gritted, slapping the table hard as he pushed something across the table so that I could get a better look at it. Reluctantly, I looked down and my heart immediately came to life in my chest. I glared at LaBeckie evilly as my chest heaved up and down. I couldn't control the emotions that seemed to be choking off my air supply now as I looked down at the face of my son. I was feeling Incredible Hulk strong, like I could just break those foot shackles and handcuffs now. I could feel my veins cording against my muscles and my entire body tensed up.

"Ah yes, Little Todd Marshall, how adorable he looks here. We took this picture while he played alone in the park . . . his careless caretaker off doing her own thing. But I knew that would get your attention." LaBeckie chortled. He could see my face going dark, my eyes hooding over, and my chest moving up and down so rapidly I almost hyperventilated.

"Now here is how this shit is going to go down . . ." he continued, tapping the table next to my son's picture. My ears were ringing so loud from the adrenaline that was coursing through my veins, I could hardly hear what LaBeckie was saying, but I knew that whatever the offer was, it wasn't going to be easy to turn it down, especially if it meant putting my son in danger.

3

Shannon

"Mmmm," I moaned as I came into consciousness days after the attack. I was immediately aware of every inch of my body because everything was wracked with pain. I slowly opened my eyes and painfully realized I was in the jail infirmary. The pain that shot through my skull when I opened my eyes forced me to quickly snap them shut.

"Mmmm," I moaned again, quickly feeling a fire raging in my throat. It was because my mouth and throat were so damn dry. I didn't know how many days I had been in the infirmary, but after being conscious for a few minutes, I vaguely remembered being attacked by the Latinas. I guess thinking that Todd's threat was a bluff this time was a big mistake on my part. They were definitely trying to kill me. My head was banging and I could tell there were tight bandages wrapped around it.

The constant blip and ding of the machines next to me told me that my condition was probably serious. Todd had really tried to have me killed, a thought that both hurt me and angered me. The nerve of his ass. I bet he would be fucked up when he found out I was still alive.

As I lay there in pain waiting for the nurse to come give me something to knock me back out, I heard footsteps coming toward me. Instinctively, I began to shake inside with fear gripping me tight. In prison you just never knew who worked for who. It would be just my luck if one of those goons paid one of the infirmary staff to let them in to finish me off. I'd be gone for real this time. I swallowed hard, which was painful as hell. I started saying a silent prayer in my head, although I hadn't spoke to God in a hot minute.

Suddenly I felt a cold hand touch my arm. The heart monitors began screeching as my heart rate sped up. I just knew I was about to die. I couldn't bring myself to open up my eyes and face death like a woman. Then I heard a voice.

"Shannon . . . um . . . Mrs. Marshall?" A man's voice filtered into my ear. The voice was kind of soothing and didn't have any hints of evil behind it. I felt relief wash over me, but now I was curious about who this was that knew my name and knew where to find me. I hadn't had any visitors since I'd been locked up and I wasn't really expecting any, either.

"It's me . . . Saul Kaufman, your husband's old attorney . . . you remember me?" Mr. Kaufman said, whispering lightly. "I finally got your messages and got around to coming to hear you out. I didn't think I would find you here." A jolt of excitement flitted through my stomach and even that caused me pain. He was right; I had been trying to reach out to him for a quick minute. Mr. Kaufman was an ace defense attorney that had gotten many street dudes off on their charges. He was so good, niggas on the street were willing to pay him boatloads of cash for his services. I heard it had gotten so lucrative for Kaufman that he wouldn't fuck with no other types of clients except gangsters and street dudes. I guess he came to fuck with me because he was very familiar with Todd.

I finally calmed down a little bit and struggled to open my battered eyes. I could tell by the look of terror etched on the old white man's face that I must've looked like shit. I moaned and motioned with my one good hand for a piece of paper. I couldn't speak since my jaw seemed like it was wired shut, and my right hand, which is the one I wrote with, was in a cast.

"Oh . . . yes . . . here, let me help." Mr. Kaufman jumped up so he could retrieve a yellow legal pad and a pen from his briefcase. He passed them to me and it hurt all over to even take the stuff from him.

Barely able to write with my stiff left hand, I finally managed to get my point across to Mr. Kaufman.

I have money stashed for your fee.
Need your services to get out of here.
I can direct you to the money.
Will you help me? Can I trust you?

Mr. Kaufman read my chicken-scratch note. He looked down at me with a serious look on his face and let out a long breath. Something about his look caused a flash of panic to go through my chest, but I ignored it. He was the person I had been putting all of my hope on since I'd been locked up. I wanted to see my son again.

"Sure, Mrs. Marshall, I can help you. But I must tell you, your husband owed me quite a bit of money from his last case," Mr. Kaufman said seriously. I began shaking my head from left to right and waved at him to give me the paper and pen back.

Not with him anymore. He is locked up.
I only have money for my case.

Mr. Kaufman read the note and lowered his eyes. I felt my stomach drop and it began somersaulting again. I just knew he was going to tell me that he wouldn't represent me because of Todd's debts.

"I will help you, Mrs. Marshall, but I need to get paid upfront," he said flatly. I shook my head in understanding and closed my eyes as tears began to leak from the sides. All I could do now was pray that when I sent Mr. Kaufman to my stash, I could trust him to only take what I owed him for his services and not everything I had left to my name.

4
Todd

"Ohhhh shit. Yeah, yeah . . . do that shit," I gasped, throwing my head back against the cold cinderblock wall as my legs trembled.

"Fuck! Haaaahhh," I gritted, balling my hands up into fists and biting my lip as waves of ecstasy rose in my body. The loud slurping noises were making it even worse for me to control myself. I felt like I was about to lose my damn mind.

"You like that?" Laila Dugan, the CO I had been fucking and getting head from asked me in a sexy, vixen voice. She knew just what to say and do to take care of me and that's why I fucked with her like that.

"Shhh," I hushed her as I grabbed her head and guided it back to my rock-hard throbbing dick. I didn't have no time to be talking to her like we was in some porno, this was about getting my nut off. She ain't know it, but she was the reason I had stayed sane for so long. Niggas locked up were also backed up and that made them restless, violent, and trouble.

Dugan went back to slurping and sucking my dick like an expert. This chick was all a locked-down nigga could ask for—she sucked dick good, she had a county job and her own paper, and she was willing to do anything I asked her to do. Shit, Shannon ain't never give me head this good. Shannon never held her own when it came to having her own money and Shannon damn sure didn't cater to me like I thought she should have, being that she was living off of me.

"Agggggh!" I growled as I nutted. My body tensed and then relaxed. I felt damned good.

When I was done busting my nut down Dugan's throat, I readied myself to tell her the bad news. Well, it was bad for her, but it was good for me. I knew she wasn't going to take it well. As a man who had fucked a whole lot of chicks, I knew when they were in love with me. There was just something about the way they looked at you, even when you were down and out, that told you that they loved you. Dugan was definitely in love with me. She didn't have to tell me with her words. Shit, I could get her to bring me anything in prison and risk her job doing it, that's how I could tell how much she loved my ass. So far, I had gotten a cell phone, weed, porno magazines, and cigarettes from her. All of those things were like having millions of dollars in prison. You could trade that stuff for anything you needed. Niggas would've sold all of their belongings for a nick of weed and something to roll that shit up in. Thanks to Dugan, I was in business behind bars.

"Yo, I need to tell you something before you lock me back in," I said somberly as Dugan rinsed her mouth out in the mop sink. I closed my eyes, dreading the reaction that was coming next.

"What? What you got to tell me, sweet dick Willie?" Dugan joked. "You wanna marry me?" She chuckled after she spit the water out of her mouth.

In the darkness of the janitor's closet, Dugan didn't look so bad, but I knew the truth. She was one ugly-ass chick, so when she said was I going to marry her, I wanted to say something mean, like *Hell no, I would never marry you*, but I didn't.

"Nah, baby, I want to tell you that I'm getting out of here," I said, tentatively trying to give her the news as easily as I could. Dugan whirled around on her feet as if she was a ballerina doing a dance move. Even in the dim light I could see the terror in her eyes. She let out a funny noise like a squeak. I couldn't tell if she had started crying or what.

"Stop playing, Todd," she said, shoving me in the chest lightly. After the initial shock of what I said, I think Dugan thought I was really playing with her. I knew this was the calm before the fucking storm that was coming.

"Laila . . . I'm getting out in two days. I've been put into a special program and I'll be living on the outside while they try to work with me," I said, telling half truths. "Dead ass . . . I wouldn't joke about something like this." Dugan moved closer to me. Her eyes hooded over and she drew her lips into a snarl.

"That's bullshit! The only way you'd be getting out is if you snitched or struck a deal with the cops!" she said, her raw emotions causing her to raise her voice. I quickly cupped my hand over her mouth.

"Shhhh! You trying to get us caught? You trying to lose your fucking job," I said in a harsh whisper, pressing my hands roughly over her big-ass mouth. She quickly realized what I was saying was true and quieted her tone. I slowly removed my hand from her mouth.

"I didn't snitch. I have been selected for this program, but I can't say much more about it," I lied. Even I knew that in jail, outside, in the hood, and anywhere in America, being a snitch was lower than being a child molester.

"Will you be around here . . . in the state? Will we still be able to see each other? Where will you live?" Dugan shot question after question at me, tears streaming down her plump cheeks.

"Nah . . . you know they ain't letting me stay in the area," I lied. "These programs don't work like that. How they gon' rehabilitate me if I go back to my old stomping grounds," I continued deceptively.

"Well, I have to tell you something too," Dugan said through her tears. "I was going to wait and just show you, but I guess I have to tell you now," she said, all cryptic and shit. I looked at her strangely, my face crumpled in confusion.

"I'm pregnant, Todd," she cried. I moved my head to the side and looked at her like she was crazy as hell.

"And it's your baby," she finished. My knees got weak. What the fuck else was going to go wrong in my life? "So you better try and find a way to make it back to the state because I'm definitely keeping this baby."

LaBeckie and his pig cronies picked me up on the low two days later. I had not been able to sleep, eat, or think straight since Dugan told me she was pregnant. Between that news and this so-called mission LaBeckie was putting me on, my nerves were fried.

The night they came through to get me, I was whisked out of my bunk and out of the prison in the dead of night. They ain't want niggas behind bars to know where I disappeared to and start sending kites to the streets that the cops took me out. Any street nigga worth a damn would know right away that it meant I was on some snitching shit. We all know how much the streets talk and how fast shit gets back. I couldn't afford for that to happen because the street niggas I knew wouldn't think twice about blowing my cap back.

LaBeckie made it seem like what he wanted me to do was easy breezy and shit. He would say that I had a simple assignment: set up the Russian muthafucka that I had been getting all my guns from and turn him over to the pigs. I don't know what made this pig LaBeckie think it was going to be that easy. I guess he had gotten spoiled working with that nigga Jock. See, Jock was able to give LaBeckie and Dray and the feds my name, my movements, and all that, but I had never put Jock on to my connect, Abraham Klitnicov, or Abe, as I called the nigga, so they were never able to get the main source of the guns. Having me locked up apparently wasn't enough. I guess they saw that the guns was still making it to the streets, which told me, there was just some new street cat to contend with that had taken my crown and started wearing it.

When LaBeckie offered me the deal to get out if I agreed to set Abe up, it wasn't like I could refuse. LaBeckie was threatening my son's life. Lil Todd was the one person I still had to live for. Basically, I was blackmailed into becoming a snitch. Some people would just suffer their fate rather than snitch, but me, I wasn't willing to have my son suffer because I wasn't willing to snitch. I would've died for my son and that was the God's honest truth.

As we drove from the prison ground and made it to the city, I could not stop thinking about Dugan telling me she was pregnant. I knew I didn't love her, but the one thing about me a nigga should know is if I had any seeds anywhere, I was going to take care of them *all*. I had it in my mind that I was going to get at her whenever this LaBeckie muthafucka stopped breathing down my neck. I was going to make sure I made a way to see Dugan and keep her up while she was carrying my seed. It was the least I could do.

LaBeckie had his driver pull up to a small one-family house in the Church Street section of Norfolk. I ducked and weaved my head around so I could see just where the fuck they was gon' have me laying my head. I mean, anywhere was probably better than prison, but a nigga had to make sure it was gon' be safe and secure and decent. So far, from what I could see, the neighborhood looked like any suburban neighborhood with similar houses equal distance from one another, fences out front, lawns and driveways with regular cars parked on them.

"This is going to be your home from now on. You do right by us and you may never see the inside of that prison cell again . . . You fuck this up . . . you *will* never see the light of day again," LaBeckie threatened me, in true LaBeckie fashion. He was such a dick rider for power that I realized he couldn't help himself: being a dick was what kept his ass alive every day. I had long ago realized that LaBeckie was hiding behind that badge like the coward that he was.

We all exited the heavily tinted Impalas that had transported us to the house. I was still shackled and shit. What did they think I could do to the ten of them with no ass gun?

The inside of the house was cool. I mean it was nowhere close to how I was living at the time I got locked up, but it wasn't a hole-in-the-wall roach-ridden project apartment like what I thought they were going to put me in.

The house was simple. It had light hardwood floors, beige standard cabinets in the kitchen with those cheap, bottom-barrel counter tops. There was a small family room area off the kitchen with a dark brown suede couch, a small glass coffee table, and a forty-two-inch flat-screen hanging on the wall in front of it. The TV was a plus since it had been almost a year since I had been able to watch what the fuck I wanted to watch on TV.

Shit, it wasn't the mini-mansion I had lived in before I got knocked, but it damn sure was better than a hard metal bunk and a dank, pissy, roach-infested prison cell. At least in this house I wouldn't have to inhale the stink of another man's balls all fucking day long.

After LaBeckie's flunkies unshackled and uncuffed me, LaBeckie immediately started with his rules, regulations, and lectures. There were more rules to becoming a confidential informant than there was being a fucking prisoner. But I listened because there were a few things I had in mind that I was going to benefit from being out. Number one, I was going to see my son in the flesh. Not a muthafucka alive was going to keep me from doing that. I wasn't going to let Lil Todd see me and start crying and shit, but I was going to creep and see him. I need assurance that he was alive and well before I went through with this mission for LaBeckie. Wasn't no use in snitching if they had already did some shit to my son.

Number two, all the niggas that had shitted on me while I was inside were going to get a visit from me. That meant those bitch niggas Zack, Billy, and most important of all, Jock. And, last, I was going to find Shannon's heist stash and I was going to take every single nickel of that shit. I knew my wife well enough to know that she had taken some of the Bobby Knight money and put it away. What I had to figure out was exactly where she had stashed it. I had a few places in mind. I also knew that she had been trying to get in touch with my old attorney, Mr. Kaufman, because when I called him his secretary had said, "Oh, Mr. Marshall, I told your wife yesterday that Mr. Kaufman would get back to her." That let me know that my snake-ass wife was trying to hire Kaufman to get her off, which also meant Shannon had money somewhere that she was going to use to pay him.

It would take me some time to get my bearings being out of prison, but as hood rat and predictable my wife was, I knew it wouldn't be long before something came to mind about where she might have hidden her stash. That bitch thought she had pulled off the ultimate heist, but this nigga here was about to pull off the last heist.

5

Shannon

I was fucking sick when I finally recovered from my injuries and returned to general population and heard that Dee had been stabbed to death trying to save me from those Latina bitches that Todd had put on me. None of the other bitches I had in my crew had even dared to step up, but my main bitch Dee had lost her life trying to save mine. It depressed me to no end because Todd was trying to kill me, not Dee. She was innocent in all of this.

I had lain in my cell three days, refusing to leave for yard, chow, shower, nothing. It was all my fault that Dee was dead. I kept picturing her face and all of the things she had done for me while I was locked up. I could've never imagined that she would've given up her own life for me, though.

The depression had hit me so bad that the prison psych came by to speak to me and even that soft-spoken, mousy-faced bitch couldn't get me to utter a word. She kept whispering my name and asking me if I was okay or if I thought I needed to see a doctor. What the fuck did she think? Dee was like my little protégée and my family. I didn't know what I was going to do without her, because the rest of the bitches in my so-called crew wasn't about shit.

I hadn't said two words to those weak-ass bitches since I had been back and I had something special in mind for each one of them too. Them bitches all stood around while I was literally getting the shit kicked out of me and they ain't do shit.

., When it was all said and done, I had landed in the infirmary with three broken ribs, a small fracture in my skull, two or three subdural hematomas, both eyes swollen shut, six missing teeth in the front, a broken nose, a broken collar bone, two busted knee caps, a shattered ankle, and five broken fingers on my right hand. I heard I had pissed and shitted on myself during the beat-down and blood had leaked from my pussy too. I probably could never have babies again. It was really a wonder that I was still alive. Even the doctors and nurses in the infirmary couldn't believe that I had made such a miraculous recovery. I chalked it up to God wanting me to get my revenge . . . or else why would I have made it through that beat-down alive. Especially now that I walked with a limp and one of my eyes never opened back all the way. Yeah, I was all messed up and I refused to look in a mirror to see just how ugly I had become. I could feel the raised scars still on my neck and left cheek—remnants of the slicing I had taken from those Latinas. I felt like the hunchback of Notre Dame when I was going through physical therapy to learn how to walk all over again. It was apparent without even looking in the mirror that I was not the same flawless Shannon as when I had arrived. Whoever made up that saying beauty is in the eye of the beholder was full of shit. Either your ass was beautiful or you wasn't. I would never be considered beautiful again and that was final. I was used to being drop-dead gorgeous and getting what I wanted because of it. That's how I had snagged Todd in the first place . . .

"I never seen nobody as gorgeous as you, ma," Todd said,
sidling up next to me at the skating rink where everybody hung

out on Saturdays. I didn't look or smile at him; instead, I
rolled my eyes at his corny-ass game. I was so used to niggas
pushing up on me with whack game that I had already formu-
lated a plan to dismiss them. I was that stuck up.

"Oh, it's like that? A'ight, ma, you got it. I just wanted to
let you know that your face is flawless," Todd had continued. I
sucked my teeth, ready to say something smart to his ass. That
was until I turned all the way around and noticed the huge
diamond-encrusted Jesus piece dangling from his neck, his
iced-out Rolex, and the crispest pair of white Gucci sneakers I
had ever seen. I couldn't even look in his face because I was
already feeling ashamed of myself by just what he wore. Dollar
signs rang in my head and right away I felt inadequate.
Finally, I shyly looked up at him with my heart racing a mile
a minute. I was screaming his name in my head because I
couldn't believe he even took the time out to say something
to me. Shit, everybody in the hood knew who Todd Marshall
was . . . kingpin of the south.

Me, I was hardly on his level at that time. I was the
daughter of a crackhead mother and a father who was doing
life. I lived with my grandmother and twelve of my cousins in
a two-bedroom project tenement where I slept on a pissy mattress with two other cousins and didn't have shit to call my
own. In fact, I shared shoes, clothes, and even a book bag with
my cousins: that's how poor we were.

"See now, you actin' like the cat got ya tongue. You must
like what you see," Todd said smoothly. I felt a flash of heat
come over my body and I felt like my feet had suddenly been
planted in cement blocks on the floor.

"What's your name?" Todd asked, licking his lips like he
always did. Blushing and about to faint, I opened my mouth
to tell him, but I didn't get the chance.

"My name is LaShell. La first, then Shell," my older cousin called out from behind me before she rudely cut in front of me, smiling with her yellow-ass teeth and big-ass gap. I sucked my teeth and just moved aside. I wasn't going to get on her bad side and have to deal with her wrath later on at home. Besides, little ol' virgin me ain't have nothing on my cousin. LaShell had a reputation around town for sucking dick and being fast in the ass so I just knew Todd was going to love her. To my surprise, he pushed LaShell aside.

"Excuse me, though," Todd said, dismissing her. "I was talking to this beauty right here." He smiled, grabbing my hand and kissing the back of it. I swear flashes of fire engulfed my body at that moment. That was it. I belonged to Todd Marshall from that day forward. I was with Todd every day after that. I didn't remember life without him after that. One day I asked him what would have made him choose a bummy girl like me when the skating rink was filled with gorgeous girls. He told me that my face was so beautiful that he'd never even looked at the holey sneakers, dirty jeans, and ripped sweatshirt I was rocking. He couldn't see anything but my gorgeous face. My beauty had snagged one of the richest dudes in our neighborhood.

"Marshall! Visit!" one of the COs yelled into my cell. I slowly sat up in my bunk, feeling too depressed to even care. I was wondering why she was even fucking with me because it was common knowledge in the prison now that I was mentally fucked up.

"I don't want no visitors," I grumbled, killing my own nostrils with my breath. I hadn't brushed my teeth in days.

"It's your attorney, so let's go. You ain't got no choice," the CO told me.

I forced myself up from the bunk. I could smell myself, which meant the CO and anyone else I passed could too. I didn't give a fuck, either. I dragged my bad leg as I walked to the attorney/client visit room. When I saw Mr. Kaufman, the look on his face gave me chills. I didn't know why right then, but something in my gut just wasn't feeling right about him. As usual and just like with Todd, I ignored my first instinct about Mr. Kaufman. One of the many mistakes I made that would come back to haunt me.

6
Todd

I had convinced LaBeckie that I needed to go see one of my former workers in order to get my connection back to Abe. I had to work hard to convince LaBeckie that putting a wire on me would be a big mistake because Abe and the dudes I ran with were pros at finding those shits. When I was on the streets and I didn't trust a nigga wasn't snitching, I would even have one of my flunkies glove up and feel around a nigga's asshole looking for wires. LaBeckie finally agreed, but of course he had mad warnings about if I didn't do this and if I didn't do that. They provided me with a whip—one of my S Class Benzes that they had seized when I was arrested. Crazy, right? But I guess it was the only way to convince niggas in the hood that I had gotten my shit back and I was out for good. LaBeckie had his tech guys strap a small tracking device to the car and then came more verbal warnings about coming back and reporting everything to him. In my head I was laughing at LaBeckie because he thought he had me under pressure, but really, I had his stupid ass under the most pressure. I wasn't stupid and everything I do always has a plan B.

I drove the S Class to my old car garage and the code on the gate was, surprisingly, still the same. I thought for sure that nigga Jock would've changed all that shit. I knew LaBeckie and his crew was watching the GPS monitors so being there wasn't going to raise any red flags. They knew that on some level I had to make my old crew think I was back in business. What they didn't know was that I was two steps ahead of their asses. I parked the Benz inside the garage and went into my old office. I stopped for a few seconds, inhaled and exhaled and shook my head. "It was all good just six months ago," I said to myself. Being there made me reminisce on how large I was living at one time. Now here I was scrambling for revenge. I quickly shook it off, raced over to the desk, moved the office chair, and pulled up a loose floorboard.

"Jock ain't find this shit," I whispered excitedly as I retrieved two stacks of cash totaling three thousand dollars and an old .40-caliber Glock I had stashed in there for emergencies. The money and the gun were all I had left to my fucking name. I turned back to the desk, picked up the phone and, again to my surprise, it was still operational. Things seemed to be going perfectly. I called a cab and told the dispatcher to have the cab pick me up in the alley behind the garage. LaBeckie would think I was at the garage all night and even if he had a tail on me, they would all be looking for the Benz. My first stop was to see a little nigga that came up under me named Zack. As I rode to the address I had for him, I thought about what Shannon had told me about how the nigga had shitted on her when she came to collect from him. I could see the whole shit taking place.

Shannon said there was a bunch of niggas out there, gambling and standing around waiting for their customers. She was disgusted and scared because although she had grown up there, she hadn't been to this side of town in a long time. All the run-down buildings and crack fiends running up and down the streets made her nervous. Even though some of those crack-heads were her relatives and she grew up around there, it was a place she had wanted to forget.

Shannon pulled the E Class Benz I had bought her right up to the corner where she spotted Zack.

"Zack!" Shannon called out of the window. She said all of the niggas in front of the trap turned around like they were ready to flex. They were all staring at her like she was crazy. Zack put his hand up to his eyes and moved his head in and out like he was having a hard time recognizing Shannon. She said the nigga looked confused and shit, even though he had stayed at our crib and seen Shannon a bunch of times. Shannon called out to him again, this time bending her head down a little so she could be sure he could see her face through the window. Her face wasn't one niggas in the hood could for-get, either. Shannon said that she knew damn well Zack knew just who the fuck she was, but she played it cool while he played his little game.

Finally, he bopped over to Shannon's car.

"What's up?" she asked, giving him a dirty look.

"Oh, damn, Todd's wife—Shannon, right?" Zack asked, putting a little phony-ass smile on his face. Shannon said the way he was playing all dumb and shit she could've slapped the shit out of his skinny ass.

"Yeah. You don't remember staying at my crib when you first got home?" Shannon asked him, reminding that nigga just who took care of his ass and got him back on his feet when he was hungry.

"Nah, I'm saying I remember and shit, but you look differ-ent and shit," Zack said, all cocky like.

"A'ight, well I'm sure you heard about my husband, right?"

Shannon asked Zack, not even giving him time to answer because the way the streets of Norfolk was, she knew he already knew about me getting locked up.

"Well, Todd sent me here," Shannon started again.

"Oh yeah, I heard he got locked up on some ol' life sentence shit," Zack said with more cocky boldness behind his words. Shannon told me that Zack's words kind of gut-checked her and she felt like doubling over like he had actually punched her.

"Nah, that's what niggas might think. He gonna get out as soon as I collect from all the dudes that owe him so I can pay his attorney," Shannon had said with an attitude. "That is the reason I'm here. You owe Todd twenty thousand, right?" Shannon asked Zack, giving him that eye that said she already knew what he owed. Right away Shannon wasn't getting a good vibe from the nigga at all.

"Ummm. I thought me and that nigga had settled that," Zack said dismissively.

Shannon was a little shocked by what he said but she wasn't having it. "Settled it? Well, that ain't what Todd told me. I really need to collect that as soon as possible," Shannon shot back at him. She was not trying to hear that nigga right then.

"I'ma see what I can do," Zack said, starting to back away from the car like he was dismissing my wife.

"When should I check back?" Shannon yelled out the window, but Zack had moved away from her car fast as hell.

"I'll get back to you. You don't have to look for me. I'll get at you," Zack called out, turning his back and returning to his little group of corner boys, leaving Shannon sitting there looking like some bum bitch begging for money.

* * *

I snapped out of my thoughts of the story Shannon had told me about Zack just as I made it to the address I had for him. Trust me, I had a renewed fever to get at this nigga thinking about how much paper he owed me and how he didn't even try to help my wife get up the attorney fees. ✔

When I pulled up to the spot where Dugan had told me Zack was staying now, my jaw dropped. Zack had gone from little flunky corner boy and runner to the big leagues. Seeing how he was living just infuriated me more, knowing that when Shannon came to Zack to collect money he owed me to help me get a lawyer, this nigga played the fool and dismissed her like he never owed me shit. I squinted my eyes at the house as jealousy and anger cropped up in my mind. Zack had bought a crib bigger than my old crib. He was living large over in Emerald Green Estates, which was a ritzier neighborhood than where I used to live. I bit down into my jaw and curled and uncurled my fists as I sat outside and watched the house for a little while. This nigga had big huge columns outside of the house with a beautiful beveled-glass front door. I guess my mentoring had done Zack some good. I had always told my crew to buy things like property and invest some of their money so that they always had a backup plan. I guess my words of advice and mentoring wasn't good enough for Zack to look out for a nigga while I was locked up. I had been hearing that loyalty among these young niggas was dead, but seeing was believing. How did Zack think that that shit he had done to Shannon by not giving her my bread was going to come back and bite that nigga in the ass?

I waited and watched the house about forty minutes before I finally saw the front door open up, and from where I stood lurking, the female that exited looked pretty damn hot. She kind of reminded me of Shannon back in the days. This chick walked with that sexy switch of the hips and her stilettos clicked on the marble front steps. Zack was definitely living like I used to live—hot-ass house, hot chick, and hot cars—what I like to call the hood rich formula.

I watched closely as the chick slid on a pair of oversize shades, which I can only imagine was either Gucci, Christian Dior, or Prada. Those were all of Shannon's favorite brands of shades. The chick switched her ass to the driveway and opened the door to a little red sports car. The car had to be a Ferrari or something fast like that. It was smoking fucking hot. It was one of those 0-to-80-in-a-minute joints that made men into bitches when they drove them.

Zack's bitch looked hot as hell behind the wheel of that whip. I can't front: I felt my dick getting a little hard for her too. I had a thing for beautiful, well-dressed women driving expensive cars. Damn! I was already starting to miss my old life, which I had promised myself I would dwell on when I got out. It was real hard not to think about it, though.

I kept watching Zack's chick but she was so busy on her cell phone and doing something else she didn't even see me creeping. The distance from where I had been watching to Zack's front door wasn't that far. I had told the cab driver to wait and under no circumstances was he to leave. The nice wad of cash I had given him would insure his loyalty, because I knew it was more money than he would make in one day running fifty fares.

Depending on how shit went with this nigga Zack, I figured I might have to hightail it out of there and would definitely need a ride back to the garage. The green-eyed monster in me wanted to just take one of those high-priced luxury cars Zack had in his four-car driveway.

I crept up on Zack's front door like a thief in the fucking night, just like I wanted to. Catching a nigga slipping was the best way to get at him. I played the perimeter of the mini-mansion real close and since Zack had the most beautiful Roman columns out front along with expertly cut bushes that were in the shapes of animals and the most beautiful flower beds and grass, it wasn't hard to find somewhere to hide. It was hot as hell outside though so by the time I made it up to the front door, I was dripping with sweat. I figured that would just make me look even more evil when I confronted this nigga. I took a deep breath and gave myself a pep talk: "Don't take no pleas from this dude. You know the truth," I said to myself. With my courage on 100, I was ready.

I rang the bell all bold and shit like I was a Kirby salesman or some friendly little Boy Scout selling caramel popcorn. Whoever came to the door was about to get it, so I was silently hoping that it would be Zack. I didn't really want to have to deal with no other niggas or no bitches and especially no kids.

My heart was pounding in my chest and sweat poured off my body, but I had my gat in hand ready for whatever.

"Yo . . . what you forgot . . ." Zack was complaining as he yanked back the door. He was standing there in boxers and a wife-beater, and when the reality of the situation set in on him, his eyes almost popped out of his head.

"I ain't forget shit but obviously you forget a nigga when I was locked down and you thought I wasn't coming back," I snarled as I put the barrel of my gun right to his left eye. Zack looked like he was about to shit on himself. He immediately threw his hands up as a sign of surrender. None of that meant shit to me.

"Oh shit . . . Todd . . . man . . . um . . . what . . . what's up . . ." Zack stammered, stumbling backwards as I advanced on his ass.

"Oh, now that's 'what's up, nigga?' You wasn't worried about what was up when you skirted on the money you owed me while I was locked up," I growled, pressing the gun harder into Zack's eye socket. I was feeling Incredible Hulk angry at that moment. It's so funny to me how niggas be all scared and shit when you confront them, but when they think you never coming back, they living it up like tough guys.

"Na . . . nah. It wasn't even like that, man." Zack stumbled over his words. Hearing the fear dancing around when he spoke made me feel even more powerful. I had so much pent-up anger and emotion to let out, Zack was the most unlucky nigga in the world to be the first on my list. I ain't even let him finished coping his sorry-ass pleas. I raised the gun and brought it crashing down on his skull. Zack dropped to the floor in a heap, holding his head and moaning. "Agh, man! I ain't do shit!" Zack cried out, looking wide-eyed at the blood on his hands.

"You ain't do shit, huh? Yeah, that's my point, nigga! You ain't do shit for me when I needed you after I fed your little bum ass when your moms was out there sucking dicks for crack and not feeding your little scrawny ass," I barked with feeling. Niggas really killed me with their logic.

"How much money you got up in here, you little bitch-ass nigga?" I asked, hitting Zack again to let him know not to fucking lie to me. I heard bones crack in his cheek when the butt of the Glock connected with his face.

"Yo! Please, man! Stop! I . . . I . . . got," Zack hollered. I smiled wickedly. I needed this power rush like nothing else. I was feeling high off seeing this nigga grovel.

When he said he only had about five G's on him, I forced his bony ass up from the floor, stuck my gun into his spine, and made him take me to the money. Turns out that five G's all of a sudden turned to twelve. See how niggas try to play you even when they are getting fucked up? How he telling me he only had five G's but really had twelve. I hit his ass again for lying. I can't front, that nigga face looked like a bloody mess by the time I was finished. It didn't even matter, though. I took the money and then turned my sights back to Zack.

"There was one thing I always taught you when I was showing you around the streets and the business . . . What was that?" I asked him with fire flashing in my eyes. He was moaning and trembling like the little bitch that he was.

"Um . . . um . . ." Zack stuttered. I could tell he remembered but he wasn't trying to say it. I slapped him across the face with the end of my gun again. This time a bigger gush of blood and two of his teeth shot from between his lips. He was crying now and he pissed on himself.

"Tell me what the fuck I taught you, bitch-ass nigga," I growled. "Or else all of your teeth gon' be laying on this floor by the time I finish!"

"To be loyal to those that are loyal to you. All you got is your loyalty and good name in this game," Zack repeated the exact words I had taught him when he was a young'un.

"Well it was something you should've always lived by, nigga," I snarled with my face curled into a scowl with an evil Joker style grin on my lips.

BANG! BANG!

I let off two shots into Zack's dome without hesitation. I watched as his body spun around, did a little jerk, and collapsed to the floor. I had a few more stops to make. LaBeckie just didn't know he had let a beast out of prison.

7

Shannon

With reluctance I sent Mr. Kaufman to my first stash spot where I had seventy thousand dollars of the Bobby Knight heist money stashed away. He had told me his fees to represent me was going to be fifty thousand from the first court hearings until the trial. Instead of paying him a little bit here and there and since I didn't have access to the money myself, I instructed him to take the whole seventy G's. I told Mr. Kaufman to keep the other twenty thousand so that I could have that when I got out. He agreed to put the money in an escrow account in his law firm's name and promised me that I would have the twenty G's plus interest once he got me off the charges. It sounded like a good plan to me.

The money should've been easy enough for him to find. I called it hiding in plain sight because the cops and the feds would look everywhere except places that were right under their noses; I knew that from my experiences with Todd. He was the one who'd given me the idea about different stash spots in the first place. So, using one of the ideas I had learned from Todd, I had rented a gym locker at the sports club and I had paid it up for the year. I had put my own combination lock on it so that no one would fuck with it. It would just look like someone working out had put their stuff in and put a lock on it, especially since the fees were paid a year in advance. It was a place the feds and the cops would've never thought to look and I knew that. I didn't have to worry about Todd either because he was in the same boat as me: locked up.

I prayed for days after I revealed my stash spot to Mr. Kaufman that he would just take the money and come to court and work his magic for me. With the depression that had set in on me and the lifelong injuries I had acquired since being locked up, I didn't know how much longer I could survive inside the prison. I had already contemplated suicide a couple times. Every time I thought about killing myself, I had to work real hard to picture my son's face and think about how his life would change forever if I was gone.

"Let's go, Marshall," a new female CO named Dugan yelled at me. It was time for me to lock out for court. I looked at the ugly CO and something about her was fishy. She was always extra rough when it came to me and she was always staring at me on the low. It was like she thought she knew me from somewhere or like she had something against me. I guess you could say my feelings about Dugan and about Kaufman was like a sixth sense I had about them. Kind of like what I felt when I spoke to Kaufman the day I gave him my stash information. It was the same nagging gut feeling that something wasn't right.

"Move your ass!" Dugan screamed as I dragged my bad leg, moving to assume the position so that she could cuff me for movement to the bus. It took everything inside of me not to cuss her ass out. But I didn't want any infractions keeping me from going to court, so I kept my mouth shut.

I was loaded into the prison transport bus that took inmates to court. I was feeling kind of good being dressed in regular clothes and seeing sunshine for a change. I hadn't realized how much keeping myself inside the prison and not taking yard time had worked on my mood and had contributed to the onset of the deep depression I felt. The clear sky and bright sun was doing wonders for lifting my mood. Thoughts of Mr. Kaufman walking up in that courtroom all sharp and ready to defend me helped to brighten my mood a little more too. For the first time in months, I was feeling much more hopeful about my situation than I had since I had been locked up.

The prison bus was musty and the air was hard to breathe in, but I was trying to keep my mood light. I told myself it was all temporary. This whole shit—the stinking bus, the harassing-ass COs, and the lack of freedom—was all temporary now that I had one of the best lawyers in Virginia representing me.

It was noisy inside the bus with chicks yelling to each other across the aisle, talking about their situations, their kids, and their bids. I would never understand that shit—inmates who didn't know each other from a hole in the wall feeling so comfortable telling each other all of their business. Fuck that, I didn't trust a soul, especially a fucking convict bitch who might be jealous of me or, worse, who would try to screw me just because she needed something to do. Why would I share my personal struggles with these bitches? Not me. I sat there silent as a mute. Their back-and-forth banter was grinding my nerves.

There were about six other inmates aside from me on the bus all yelling to each other about how they hadn't seen or heard from their court-appointed attorneys and how they hoped their family members showed up so they could at least get a glimpse of their kids. Listening to them speak about those horrible court-appointed attorneys made me feel kind of good inside, since I had had the pleasure of telling my court-appointed attorney to get lost. I felt superior to those other inmates because I had been smart enough to save money for a situation like this. It's not like I was planning on getting locked up, but after the ultimate heist we pulled on Bobby

Knight, I stashed away money just in case Jock had ever tried to
front on me or if I had to get out of Dodge because of Todd. One
thing my grandmother always taught me was to keep that "get
mad" money stashed some place that the man didn't know about.
It was a lesson well taught and definitely well learned.

The stories these chicks were telling were sorry as hell. One girl
said she had never met her court-appointed attorney. Another one
said all her attorney ever did was tell her to hurry up and take a
plea deal that would leave her in prison for ten years. She said he
was always in a rush and didn't care if he took a loss on a case. It
was sad but I can't front, I was smiling to myself and saying in my
head, *Y'all bitches couldn't afford a high-priced attorney like I got.
I'm getting the fuck off on these charges.* I knew that Mr. Kaufman
prided himself on winning cases and so far he'd had a perfect ac-
quittal record. He had been in the newspaper so many times that
they called him "front page Kaufman." That was the type of attorney a bitch needed standing at the table with her.

Once we got to the courthouse in downtown Virginia Beach, we
were pulled off the bus, searched again, and loaded into the courthouse through the back doors. I had crazy butterflies in my stomach and for some reason my heart wouldn't stop pounding.

Those bitches were still talking shit about how they couldn't
wait to curse their attorneys out and yada, yada, yada. They were
giving me a straight headache for real.

We were all placed in the court holding cell that is located behind the courtrooms. These cells were much cleaner than what we
were used to in the prison. I found a spot in the corner and just sat
and waited. My nerves were on edge because I knew from coming
to court for Todd so many times that these hearings all depended
on the judge and the defense attorneys.

One by one the court officers started pulling us out to go see the
judge. Two chicks went ahead of me, one had come back kicking,

spitting, screaming about fuck the crooked-ass system and the other one had come back in tears saying something about not being able to see her kids like that.

I can't front, their reactions were scary for me. It was like nobody was coming out of that courtroom with good results. There were rumblings inside the holding cell about how the judge was a bitch that wanted to make an example out of people. I was a little shook inside, but I was putting all of my hope into Mr. Kaufman. I said a quick little prayer before I heard the call.

"Marshall, Shannon!" The court officer finally called my name, sending a jolt of nerves and wave of nausea through my stomach. "Marshall, let's go!"

I jumped up like my legs were suddenly on springs. A cold feeling shot down my spine and I swallowed hard.

"Now or never, Shannon . . . you got this," I whispered under my breath as I was led toward the little door that led to the courtroom.

When I stepped through the door, I couldn't believe how crowded the courtroom was. It was my first time being on the other side. I was usually a hopeful spectator in the back waiting for the judge to show a little leniency. Not this time . . . I was the spectacle today for everyone to see. It was like all eyes were on me. With my eyes almost bulging from the sockets, I looked over at the judge. Terror choked off my air supply and suddenly I felt light-headed. Everyone was right: the judge looked evil as hell. She was a severely wrinkled white woman with a bird's nest of white hair on the top of her head. Her cheeks sagged and she had a permanent angry dip between her eyes right above the bridge of her nose. She reminded me of a witch from a children's fairy-tale book, and just like a child, I was terrified.

I was led over to the oakwood defendant's desk and I immediately noticed that there were two seats and both were empty. I crinkled my eyebrows a little bit but I still wasn't worried yet. I knew that one seat was for me and one was for Mr. Kaufman. I looked down at the desk and noticed there were no papers on it. I knew from experience that defense attorneys usually walked with huge files containing briefs from previous cases so that they could prove what judges in other districts did and allowed. So no papers, no Mr. Kaufman. Suddenly a cold sweat broke out all over my body and I felt like I would throw up.

This has to be a mistake! He is probably running late. Or he went to use the bathroom. My mind raced with a million possibilities about Mr. Kaufman's absence. I whipped my head around frantically thinking he had to be somewhere in the courtroom . . . that maybe he had sat at the wrong seat or had run out to his car to get his folders. Something had to be wrong if Kaufman wasn't there and he had probably already collected my money from the gym locker.

"Miss Marshall, it is my understanding that you've fired your court-appointed attorney," the judge said in a disgusted tone, her voice wet and filled with phlegm. I looked at her dumbfounded, too shocked about Kaufman's absence to get my words together. Finally the judge's words sank in. She wasn't asking me, she was telling me that she already knew I had let my court-appointed attorney go and replaced him with Mr. Kaufman.

"Um . . . yes . . . um . . ." I stumbled over my words.

"Well, with no attorney on record for your appearance, your case will be put down for eight weeks," the judge said perfunctorily. "If you want to represent yourself, you'll have to file that motion with this court, Miss Marshall," the judge continued in a dull uninterested tone.

"No! Wait! I hired an attorney! Saul Kaufman is my attorney!" I belted out as I saw the court officers heading in my direction to take me back. I was being dismissed just like that. The judge looked at me over the rim of her wire-frame glasses, her eyes flashing with fire.

"Miss Marshall! You will not have outbursts in my courtroom. No attorney has put himself on the record for you. Certainly not Saul Kaufman, who I saw make an appearance earlier today. He may be your dream attorney, but he sure hasn't recognized you as his client. Now I will not allow you to waste this court's time any longer. Next outburst, you will be held in contempt," the judge growled.

With that, the court officer rushed over and roughly grabbed me as he tried to cuff me.

"I have an attorney! I paid him! Let me call him! Please! Mr. Kaufman is my attorney!" I cried as the officers manhandled me and began dragging me back toward the door that led to the cells. I could feel the hot tears welling up in my eyes, but the anger that was flashing in my chest was more overpowering. I truly felt like I had the strength of ten men at that moment. I had lost all hope and when that happens it seems like something inside of my mind just snapped loose. Miraculously, at that moment it seemed like all the pain I had suffered from my attack previously had gone. I went straight in attack mode.

"Get the fuck off of me!! Get off of me!" I screamed, bucking my body and dropping down to the floor. I flailed my arms and legs like a crazy woman and started spitting and kicking too. Within seconds there were about six court officers surrounding me and roughly putting their hands on me. Some of them slapped and punched me as they tried to grab me and I would get a kick in. I saw one of the officers drop to his knees as my foot connected with his balls. I didn't give a fuck at that point. I was kicking, spitting, screaming, and trying to bite them. Even if it meant they would beat my ass to a bloody pulp . . . what else did I have to live for.

"Ahhh!" I screamed when one of them finally had enough sense to spray me with pepper spray. "Aggg!" I coughed and wheezed as that shit set my entire face, throat, and chest on fire like I had swallowed a flaming torch. I was choking and gagging, but I was still trying to fight. Another blast from that potent spray and I finally collapsed. I felt pain coursing through my whole body once again so I finally gave up. My head was pounding and my heart was broken. Mr. Kaufman had got me.

"Take her to psych holding now!" one of the court officers screamed. They were still surrounding me but I didn't have any more fight left in me. They hogtied me with flex cuffs and carried my ass through the cell block. I could hear hushed murmurs from the chicks in the other cells talking about me. The officers took me to a small, padded holding room, but not before they got their rocks off with a few punches and slaps and rough slams into walls. I deserved it. I had put them through unnecessary bullshit that day and I knew it, but fuck it, at least I didn't go back to the regular cell crying and shit like a weak bitch.

Once the door to the padded room was locked, all I could do was slide down to the floor and scream at the top of my lungs. I kept screaming until my voice box could no longer make any sound.

It was crystal clear to me that Mr. Kaufman had pulled a heist on my ass. He had probably snatched my stash money as repayment for Todd's debt with no intentions of ever representing me.

After exhausting myself with screaming and crying, I lay perfectly still on the floor. My mind raced with ways to get Mr. Kaufman back. He had just added himself to my shit list along with Todd, Jock, and those cops. I was Shannon Marshall and I was going to get the last laugh and the last heist on all of them.

8
Todd

The next nigga I went to see was Billy, another one of my old
partners that had thought I was going away for life. Billy and I had
been boys since we were young. We didn't go back as far as Jock
and I did, but I had considered Billy a pretty good friend before I
got locked up. In fact, I was the one that had put Billy on to the
game and helped him out of the hood. When I heard that nigga
shitted on me, I was hurt but not surprised. There was no loyalty
in our business. I had something a little different for Billy's ass.
His betrayal was different than what Zack had done. I wouldn't
say one was any worse than the other, but Billy had gone to a whole
different level of disloyalty. His betrayal was the type that got niggas killed on a regular day because there were certain rules and one
of them was never disrespect the next man's wife. When Shannon
told me the story about what Billy had done, I could picture the
whole shit happening like I was sitting right there. I could picture
it every time I thought of Billy's name. Even now I could see it
clearly.

*Shannon said she rang Billy's bell and within minutes he was
at the door. She was kind of still distraught from being dis-*

missed by Zack so she was kind of out of it. She said Billy pulled back the door and was standing there in his wife-beater and boxers.

"Wassup, Billy? I'm sorry if I woke you up but this is an emergency," Shannon said, on the verge of tears.

"Nah, I'm good. I heard about T . . . are you a'ight?" Billy asked her like he was real concerned about me.

Shannon said she felt like breaking down but she held her head up and got to the point, something I had taught her to do.

"I'm good. Todd asked me to come by and check for some loot that you got for him," she explained to Billy as he let her inside his crib.

Shannon said Billy's eyebrows went down and his face changed. She said he got a dark look over his face like he was about to scream on her. He told her she could sit down on the couch. Shannon didn't want to be rude but she wasn't there for all that sit-down bullshit. She wanted to get to the point. Did Billy have the money or not?

"Yeah, yeah. I owe him a few dollars. Whatcha need?" Billy had asked.

"I need all of what you owe Todd. For real, shit is crazy right about now and I just need to get up some money for his lawyer," Shannon explained, feeling like she was doing way too much explaining for a nigga who owed the money. Shannon said she felt like she had to cop a plea to those niggas that owed her fucking husband money!

"Hold up," Billy said, disappearing toward the back of his house.

Shannon said she got a little leery, but as she looked around, she could tell by the flat screens, the expensive furniture, and artwork that Billy wasn't doing too bad financially.

He came back with two plastic bags in his hands with some money in them.

"Here is a little something," he said, tossing the bags at Shannon, then he plopped down on the couch beside her. Shannon's eyes immediately lit up, thinking the nigga was paying up. She was happy to see that he was coming up off the money, unlike Zack.

"How much is this?" she had asked Billy.

"That's like two G's. I'ma have to work on the rest," he explained.

Shannon's face went dark. She told me she wasn't trying to be ungrateful but she was thinking what the fuck is two G's gonna do? She still wouldn't be able to pay for that lawyer.

Unlike that little punk-ass Zack, at least Billy came up off of something. Shannon decided not to argue. She put the money in her bag and was getting ready to bounce. The next thing she knew, this nigga Billy had moved real close to her on the couch. She said his movement had shocked her and then when he put his arm around her and got close to the side of her face she was totally frozen with shock and fear.

"Yo, if you need a nigga to take care of ya pretty ass, all you gotta do is holla," Billy said, breathing on my wife's cheek like he was an animal in heat.

"What the fuck is you doing?!" Shannon screamed, pushing him away, trying to stand up. Shannon told me her heart was racing so fast and she was in such shock she didn't even know what to say.

"Don't be acting like you too fucking good for a nigga," Billy growled, holding onto Shannon's arm so tight she could feel the bruises coming as she felt a sharp pain.

"Get the fuck off me!" Shannon screamed again, yanking her arm away, which hurt her even more.

"I could take ya pussy right now and nobody would know. Ya fucking man ain't getting out no time soon. You betta get with a nigga that can take care of you without getting his ass locked up every other year," Billy said cruelly.

"Fuck you, Billy!" Shannon spat, twisting her arm out of his grasp and pushing him away from her.

Shannon said she was scared as hell but mad as hell at the same time. Billy didn't take it any further, but he could have and he had tried it, so that was already the violation. Shannon said she was so scared she rushed toward the front door to get the fuck out of there. She said Billy looked like he was liable to rape her right there. Once she was back in the car, she cried and cried. She had felt so betrayed by Billy, knowing that he was supposed to be one of my closest soldiers.

I pulled up to Lola's, the strip club that Billy always hung out at with the hopes that I would find him inside doing what he loved to do best—being a pervert. I drove my Benz to the club to make it more realistic that I was attending a meeting that would get me closer to Abe. It was the story I had been selling to LaBeckie every day that I went on the streets in pursuit of my revenge.

I saw LaBeckie's crew of pigs tailing me, but I didn't care. I had already had everything set up inside of Lola's to go the way I wanted it to go.

When I walked in the club, I moved like my old self. My swagger was on a hundred and I played it cool as a fan. I saw mad girls that I knew from my days out there giving me the eye, and a few dudes, both past friends and enemies too.

I found Billy and his new crew of young heads in one of the VIP sections of the club. Of course they had some of the baddest chicks that work at Lola's up in there with them. I can't lie, if I wasn't in there handling business, I might have stopped and got some pussy or at least a quick blow job, but I decided against it.

"Ohhh, shit! My nigga!" Billy sang out when he finally moved his face from a Spanish chick's titties and spotted me. "I thought you was down for the count, my nigga!" Billy continued with a wide, phony grin on his face. He got up so he could greet me with the customary street pound and shoulder bump. I plastered a fake smile on my face like shit was all good too. I was better at playing the game than niggas gave me credit for.

"Nah, only weak niggas go down for the count," I said, returning the fake gesture of love. "You know a nigga like me always lands on my feet. Shit is sweeter than ever, my dude," I said, faking right along with Billy.

"Yo . . . sit down. Have a drink. Get some ass. Live it up with a nigga. You know we missed you," Billy invited, spreading his arms like a game show host over the nice array of expensive bottles he had on the table in front and pointing out the beautiful strippers that were taking care of them in the VIP section. I was thinking, *Yeah, nigga, it must be nice to pop bottles . . . spending money that could've helped me out. You gon' learn, though.*

I played it cool, though, and kept my anger at bay. I had a much more important mission rather than jumping on the nigga and wilding out. I sat down and took Billy's invitation while he poured me some Ace of Spades. I looked around at all of the beautiful women in Billy's company and that same pang of jealousy that flitted through my chest when I saw Zack's girl and his big fancy house came back even stronger with watching Billy waste thousands of dollars on bottles, bitches, and bullshit. This was what these dudes were doing on the outside while I suffered on the inside. I was the one who'd taken all of them out of the hood and showed them how to be businessmen in the street, and betrayal and abandonment was how they decided to repay me. Loyalty was bigger to me than anything . . . even bigger than money.

"Yo, Todd, man, shit ain't been the same since you been inside. Niggas all went off on their own and nobody stayed loyal to our original crew," Billy told me. I nodded my head up and down, but couldn't help the sneer that had taken over my lips.

"I had to look out for myself, man. You gotta understand that, right?" Billy said, a quiver of fear lacing his words. I nodded again.

"I know you was looking for niggas to come together on your defense attorney, but after you left, there was no harmony among us. Niggas wasn't trying to stay together so nobody took the initiative. I was trying to get niggas together several times and shit. I even gave Shannon some paper towards that," Billy copped his plea. My jaw rocked feverishly and I took my drink to the head. I needed something to calm the eruption happening inside of me.

"Listen, man, it's all good. What matters is I came through for myself and I'm back and even better than before," I lied, cracking a halfhearted smirk.

"Yeah, see. I knew shit would work out. And word . . . I was about to ask how you got that paper up," Billy said with a surprised look on his face. "I heard your wife was playing that grimy role and bounced out with Jock and shit . . . a shame. I always did think Shannon was loose like that. Beautiful girl, but she used to flirt with all us niggas," Billy said, like he felt sorry for me. His conversation had just took a turn that it shouldn't have. I was going to let the nigga enjoy his entire night, but now it was time to put shit into play. I had had enough of his lip service and his lies. In my book niggas like Billy didn't deserve second chances because there was always going to be a need for a third . . . a fourth . . . and so on. He was one of those can't-give-a-nigga-an-inch type of dudes.

"I think any one of us could've tapped that shit out here, man. I was real mad when I found out she was with Jock . . . I'm saying how she gon' leave you sick like that?" Billy went on, rubbing it in. His words felt like open-handed slaps to my face.

I bit down into my jaw and put my glass on the table. My ears were ringing and suddenly a cloud of red shaded my vision. It took everything inside of me not to jump up and fuck Billy up. I gave the eye signal to the chick from the club that I had hired. She sauntered over and grabbed Billy by the hand. I was smart enough to get at Billy with something I knew he couldn't resist: pussy.

"Aye, papi . . . you told me you would have a private . . . just me and you," the chick named Emmy said, licking her lips seductively. "I've been waiting for you all night, papi . . . I'm not that patient. C'mon," she pressed Billy with a sexy groan bubbling up from her throat. Emmy resembled Shannon a lot. They both had that Halle Berry mixed chick thing going on. I chose her because she had the kind of beauty that made me want to fuck her myself.

"Mmmm, damn, mami, I would but my manz just got home," Billy said, licking his lips like he wanted to fuck her on the spot.

"Nah. Don't turn down this beauty for me, nigga. I'll be around. Shit, I would leave yo ass sitting here in a minute if she was trying to get at me," I said, laughing. "Go on get ya shit taken care of, man. This beauty is not to be passed up," I urged. Billy seemed glad that I was letting him off the hook. He had probably grown tired of copping pleas to me about why he didn't assist me anyway.

"A'ight, man . . . I won't be gone all night," Billy said as Emmy pulled him up from the couch by his hand. She was leading him away and I was thinking, *You heading to your last piece of pussy ever.*

As Emmy and Billy both turned their backs and headed into one of the private champagne rooms, Emmy turned around and winked at me. I guess the ten stacks I paid her was appreciated. In my assessment that kind of paper kept her off the pole all night and would be a lot of money for what was going to be slight work for her. I loved a ride-or-die chick like that. Emmy was the kind of chick I thought Shannon would be.

I eased myself back on the leather couch in the VIP section and took advantage of Billy's high-end liquor stash with a satisfied grin on my lips. It was about twenty minutes before I heard the eruption of screams and watched the award-winning acting that took place after. Emmy should've won an Emmy award for her acting. Hah! The irony in that statement.

"Oh my God!!! He had a seizure or a heart attack or something! Help me!!" Emmy screamed, running through the VIP section and out into the club, holding her bare breasts. She had what appeared to be real terror etched on her face and she even made herself cry for good measure. I was loving every minute of it. I was definitely going to see Emmy again. I had it bad for her.

Pure pandemonium erupted everywhere. The lights came on abruptly and people were running, screaming, scrambling. Dancers were scrambling to get out of there before five-o rolled up because some of them had warrants for prostitution. The club owners and bouncers were trying to run damage control so that they didn't lose all their night's money. It was just like I had imagined it to be.

"Call the fucking ambulance!" one of Billy's little crew members shouted. Those boys looked frantic. I guess Billy was the kind of boss that fed them from his hand instead of teaching them the business so they could all learn to eat on their own like I did. Without Billy, I could tell his crew would fade away and become those little niggas that have to go crawling back to all the people in the hood they shitted on when they thought they had made it—including their mothers and grandmothers, most of the time. I sat back calmly just looking on and feeling a warm sense of satisfaction filling my belly like a good meal.

"Yo! The nigga is dead!! He ain't got no pulse!" a big, brawny, sweaty bouncer screamed, panic blazing in his eyes. I tried to look concerned but it was hard as hell. With all of the commotion, no one saw me slip out just like I had never even been there. I didn't know Billy's new crew so I didn't matter to any of them anyway. Their leader was dead . . . from what they thought was a seizure or heart attack, but what I knew was a lethal dose of potassium chloride that had just stopped his heart from beating. Easiest revenge plan I had ever hatched. Emmy's sister worked in anesthesia at some hospital so she was able to get a syringe filled with enough of the drug to stop Billy's heart in an instant. I was still a traditional street nigga that loved the shoot-'em-up bang-bang type of shit so I wish I could've tortured Billy a little before his death, but I figured I'd save the torture for Jock. Besides, when you're getting the last word, it didn't always have to be loud.

9

Shannon

There were a few awkward glances exchanged as I sat down at the prison visitor's table. I felt just as strange as my visitor, but still, I had to play it off.

"What's up, Shannon? Really funny coming to see you here," LaShell said as I looked at her strangely from the other side of the visitor table. "I thought it was a prank when I got your letter requesting me to come see you."

She had a self-serving smirk on her face that made me feel like pure shit. She knew I needed her, so now she was going to do everything in her power to remind me of who was the one that was down and out right now. And my dear cousin LaShell had made it a point to wear some of my old high-end designer clothes and shoes that I had had to sell when Todd first got locked up. I know it made her feel real good to rub that in my face, but I was humble enough to act like I didn't even notice. It was a lesson I had learned since being locked up.

"Well, thank you for coming, Shell. I wouldn't have asked you to come if I had anybody else to turn to," I said sincerely, lowering my gaze to my hands, which were wringing against each other seemingly involuntarily.

"That's the thing, Shannon—you acted all fucked up towards your family when you was living large with Todd, but look now. You calling me for help," LaShell reminded me cruelly. My jaw rocked and I wanted to tell her off so badly, but I needed her, I swallowed hard and rocked a little bit in the chair. "When you started living like a rich chick, you ain't even come to the nursing home to see Big Mama. You sent flowers? Flowers, really? That lady raised you from a child and she may not have had a lot to give you, but she kept you out of foster care," LaShell continued her verbal assault. My heart was breaking in my chest and my stomach knotted. I inhaled deeply and fought against the tears welling up at the backs of my eyes.

"I know, Shell, but it's not like we all had the greatest relationship growing up. Our family always been jealous of each other and we were taught to be in competition with each other instead of being like a close family," I told her honestly. "If you remember correctly, after I got with Todd Big Mama told me not to come back to her house and Poochie put me on a restricted list at the nursing home. Y'all tried to even keep me from the funeral, even though I was paying for it. It wasn't all my fault," I said with feeling. The tears finally fell from my eyes. Reliving those painful experiences is something I had tried not to do over the years, but I was not going to let her turn me into the bad guy all by myself.

LaShell seemed to contemplate what I was saying. She twisted her lips and shook her head up and down.

"You right, Shannon. We did have a fucked-up childhood and I can't really blame you for getting out. I guess we all played a role in being fucked up towards each other. Let's just move on. I still think of you as the only sister I ever had," LaShell said, cracking a small smile. My shoulders slumped with relief that we could make amends.

"So, what's up? What's so important that you needed me to come?" LaShell asked, her eyes filled with curiosity. I leaned in to the table so no one else could hear what I was telling her.

"I need you to get at this attorney for me. His name is Mr. Kaufman—the one that Todd always used when he got locked up. I had the last seventy stacks to my name stashed away and I told Kaufman where it was so that I could pay for him to represent me. He fucking stole my money and never showed up to represent me. He thinks he got away with my money, but I want somebody to show him that he didn't." I laid it all out. LaShell was all ears, her eyebrows dipping low with concentration when she heard about the money.

"If you find him and get him set up, I'll make sure you get some money. Whatever you take from him during the robbery is all yours to keep. Right now, it is about revenge for me," I said somberly.

"Damn. I gotta think about what niggas I got that would fuck with this. You know niggas don't wanna fuck with robbing no white muthafuckas," LaShell said, rubbing her chin like she was thinking hard.

"Trust me, Shell . . . it'll be worth your while. I have a little something more out there but I just need to make sure this traitor bitch Kaufman is taken care of first," I confessed. It might've been a mistake to let her know I had another stash, but I was desperate.

"Well, if you got more money stashed somewhere, you better hope that nigga Todd don't get to it before you," LaShell said with a chuckle. I crinkled my eyebrows and cocked my head to the side. I didn't think I had heard her correctly. I was staring at her blankly.

"What? Say you ain't know Todd beat his case and got out?" LaShell asked. "Been out for the past two weeks or some shit."

I squinted at her to make sure I was clearly hearing what she was saying. I couldn't even speak. I had literally lost my voice and my tongue and brain would not cooperate to even formulate a sentence.

"Shannon . . . Todd is fucking out on the streets of Tidewater. He is driving a fat Benz and moving like he used to. First niggas was saying he was snitching and got out, but I heard he just finally got up the cake to get a lawyer that fought his case. Word is he got off on a technicality . . . something to do with the illegal search or arrest or some shit like that." LaShell ran it all down. My body was suddenly burning up hot and I felt dizzy. All I could do was stare at LaShell with my jaw hanging down. It felt like the walls were closing in on me.

"Shannon? Shannon? You a'ight?" I heard LaShell say before I felt the sharp pain crash into my head. The next thing I remember, I was waking up in the infirmary again.

I found out from the nurse that I had fainted. I guess the bomb LaShell had dropped on me had caused an explosion in my head. I couldn't take hearing that Todd was back on the street. *How could that be?* Everything that had happened to me was his fault, including me being locked up, and he was out on the street living large again? Where the fuck was the justice in that? When LaShell told me that Todd was out, I kept thinking about the last word I had gotten from him where he promised me that he would make sure I never had another red cent. I felt like the joke was on him because he was locked up for good and I still had one last stash of cash. But now that he was out, I was sick with worry because my last stash spot with all of the remaining money I had to my name was one Todd had shown me early in our relationship. I knew how Todd operated and I also realized that he knew me very well. I was one hundred percent sure he would figure out that I had put some money away. It had always been my style. Even if it was a small bit of money, it would be something. Todd was far from stupid so it wasn't going to take him long to check all of the possible stash spots before he found mine. I closed my eyes as the tears leaked from the edges. I had to think quickly before Todd ended up pulling the last heist on my ass.

10
Todd

"Yes! Fuck me! Harder!" Dugan screamed out as I went to town slamming my hips into her pelvis, devouring her pussy.

"Yeah, right there!" she panted and I flipped her over and slammed it from the back. I hadn't seen her in the month since I had been out, but I had made sure to stay in touch with her. I wanted to find out how the pregnancy was going, but more important, I had convinced Dugan to put in for a transfer to the women's prison where Shannon was, to get information. Initially my plan was to send another hit out on Shannon, but then I figured getting updates on how miserable Shannon was would be good enough revenge for a while.

Dugan lived a little minute from the house LaBeckie had me staying in. It had taken me a whole lot of dipping and dodging to get away from LaBeckie and his crew to meet up with Dugan, but when she told me she had information to share with me about Shannon, I made the meet-up happen with the quickness.

"I love you so much, Todd! Yes! Do it to me, baby!" Dugan screamed as I grinded into her from behind harder and harder with each stroke. "I love you!" she hollered again. I slowed down the pace of my thrusts and let out a grunt of frustration. She almost made my dick go soft with what she said. I leaned on her back, reached around and covered her mouth roughly with my hand. It was either that or let my dick get limp. I hated when she started talking that love shit. That's the shit I was talking about with these chicks, they never knew how to just play their position. She was cool for fucking in prison and now for using to get information but that love shit had to go. Dugan couldn't understand that I wasn't trying to love her or wife her or play house with her with no fucking baby, either. Ours was a relationship of convenience; I didn't know when she was going to get that shit through her hard-ass head. Pregnant or not, I wasn't about to marry her ugly ass. I would take care of my seed after I got a DNA test to make sure it was even mine. Other than that, Dugan could forget me settling down with her.

After I shut her up and kept pounding her out, the pussy started getting good to me. I was more worried about satisfying her, though. I wanted her to have a good nut so I could make sure she told me everything I needed to know.

"Aghhh!" she finally screamed, her legs buckling under her until she fell onto her stomach. I felt her pussy walls pulsing and closing around my dick as she climaxed. I was next. It wasn't all that good for me . . . but a nut was a nut to a nigga who had been locked up. I rolled over onto my back breathing hard and this chick wanted more.

"Hold up. Hold up, ma. I need a breather. Plus, we need to talk real quick before you-know-who starts looking for me and shit. I'm on borrowed time. He thinks I'm at some important meeting with my connect; that's the only reason I was able to give him the slip," I huffed, pushing Dugan off of me. This chick was like a dog in heat. I closed my eyes so I didn't have to look at the soup cooler lips and the big-ass gap between her teeth. *Why the ugly ones always the loyal ones?* I asked myself silently.

"Awww, daddy, I missed you. Plus, fucking you in the bed is so much better than that dirty mop closet," she whined, trying to move her mouth down to my dick. I closed my eyes, trying to stay patient. I pushed her away and tried to put on a voice that wouldn't let on that I was annoyed as shit with her.

"So c'mon, tell me what's up?" I said, getting to the point.

"With what? Me and our baby? My health? Maybe you'd like to know how I am doing these days?" Dugan snapped sarcastically. I could see in her eyes that she was getting upset.

"Awww, here you go getting all emotional. You know I care about you and the situation . . ." I started, reaching my hand toward her to try and calm her down.

"It's your fucking baby, not a situation!" Dugan snapped, jumping up from the bed before I could touch her.

Fuck! I screamed in my head. *She better stop fucking playing!*

I didn't have time for the bullshit and Dugan was wearing down my last good nerve. I needed the information she was holding and she was playing games. I got out of the bed and followed her into her master bathroom. I tried to put on my sympathetic face and soften my voice. Dugan just didn't know how much I wanted to curse her ass out.

She was sitting on the toilet holding her head in her hands sobbing like someone had just told her the world was ending in ten minutes. I took a deep breath, bit down into my jaw, and bent down in front of her. I touched her hair softly and cleared my throat so I could make sure my words came out softly.

"Listen . . . I'm trying to eliminate all of the problems I got out there so that we can just be together. I care about you that much,

Laila," I lied, using her first name to try and make her feel that I
was serious.

"I don't mean to seem abrupt with asking you the questions,
but I don't have a lot of time. It's not going to be long before
LaBeckie figures out that I haven't made contact with that gun
connect and that I don't have any intentions on doing it. If I don't
play these cards right . . . shit is not going to work out. We are not
going to be able to leave Virginia and run away together like I plan.
I'll be right back in prison and you'll be left out here on your own
with the baby and maybe even without the job. It's a fine line we
walking and all I'm saying is let me get the information, take care
of business on the streets, get rid of all of the threats to us, and let's
live happily ever after," I lied some more. I couldn't believe how
convincing I was myself.

Dugan was sobbing like she was at a funeral or some shit.
Maybe it was the pregnancy making her so emotional, but my patience was wearing thin.

"Shhh, don't cry. Let's try to talk or else I'm going to have to
leave," I comforted. I started to hear a little annoyance under my
words so I cleaned it up right quick.

"Okay," she sniffled, raising her face from her hands. "I'll tell
you what I heard," she said as she rolled off some toilet paper and
blew her nose loudly. My heart jerked in my chest with excitement
when she said she would tell me. I was looking at her with antici-
pation dancing all over my face.

"Okay so . . . Shannon had a visit from her cousin LaShell
and—" Dugan started.

"LaShell?! You sure?!" I cut her off.

"Yeah, LaShell," Dugan answered, looking at me like I was
crazy. I realized that I did look and sound crazy, I just couldn't believe my ears when I heard the name LaShell.

"I'm sorry . . . it's just that Shannon hates her family so I can't see her cousin LaShell just coming to visit her," I explained. My mind was racing a million directions now. I knew my wife was a calculating bitch too.

"Well, this cousin visited her and I heard Shannon telling her she wanted LaShell to help her set up some lawyer named Kaufman that stole Shannon's money from a stash spot and never came to be her defense attorney," Dugan went on.

I sat back on my butt on the bathroom floor with my mouth slightly open because I couldn't believe what I was hearing. So this bitch Shannon actually did try to hire my old defense attorney, Mr. Kaufman!

"Shannon told her cousin that she has another stash spot somewhere and that they would split what was there if the cousin got Kaufman set up, robbed, and maybe killed," Dugan went on. I perked up when I heard the words *another stash spot*.

"Did she say where the stash spot was?" I asked with urgency in my voice.

"No, but when the cousin told Shannon that you were out of prison, Shannon fainted," Dugan said with disgust in her voice. "She busted up her head and I had to be the one getting her help. What the fuck was so crazy about the news of you getting out that the bitch fainted?" Dugan complained.

I sprang up from the floor like a jack-in-the-box. I knew why Shannon had fainted. I grabbed Dugan's face and kissed her deeply. I let her go and raced back into the bedroom so that I could slip into my clothes. I knew there were only a few places Shannon would stash money. Shannon thought I was never getting out so she figured using my old stash spots was going to be safe. I had news for that bitch. My heart was beating with excitement now.

This was just the thing I needed to get back at Shannon's ass. That bitch liked to send me letters but looked like she was going to be getting a letter this time.

"Wait! Where are you going?!" Dugan ran after me sounding like she was going to cry again.

"I gotta go. I'll be back," I huffed. "I promise to hit you up later," I lied again.

"But . . . I have the information about Jock's whereabouts in the witness protection program too," Dugan announced. I froze dead in my tracks and turned around slowly as I buttoned up my shirt. Dugan sat down on the bed with a smile on her face. She knew she had me at least for a few more minutes.

Dugan laid it all out for me. At that moment, I think I could truly say I loved Dugan's ass. I wasn't in love with her like but I had mad love for her for real. From the time I had gotten locked up until now nobody else had came through for me like she had.

11

Shannon

"So, Ms. Marshall, where is the money?" Dray the crooked fed asked.

"I don't have it here," I lied. I was shaking all over.

"Well, you don't fucking have it in a bank, either," Dray barked, lifting his gun up menacingly.

"I have it put away," I said sarcastically; shit, at this point if he was going to kill me, he was just going to kill me.

"Okay, well, I'm waiting to hear where that is," Dray said snidely.

"I bet you are," I retorted.

With that Dray pointed his gun at Jock and shot him in the leg.

"AHHHHHH!!!" Jock let out a screeching animal-like scream, his head falling in to his chest as he tried to catch his breath from the pain. Blood was pouring out of Jock's leg. I started crying when I heard Little Todd start crying upstairs.

"Please! Let me get my son," I pleaded with Dray, looking him in the eye to appeal to any mercy he may have.

"Baby girl, all you got to do is tell us where the money is so we can get the fuck up out of here. See, I don't have beef with *you, I had the beef with Bobby Knight so his money belongs to me . . . you know, payback, restitution,"* Dray growled, his eyes looking all fucking crazy. He was a DEA agent but obviously he wasn't sticking to no fucking code of honor right now.

"The money is in a safe in the closet." I surrendered because my son was screaming and I was so scared he would open the door and run downstairs and see what was going on. It wasn't worth it.

"Go," Dray said, nodding his head to his partner. The man left. I heard his gun go off as he shot the fucking lock off the safe. I jumped hoping he didn't try to hurt my son.

"There's no money in here!" he called out.

As soon as Dray turned his head to the side in response to his partner telling him there was no money in the safe, the next sound I heard was voices screaming, *"POLICE!!! POLICE!!! Drop the weapon, drop the fucking weapon!!!"*

My jaw dropped when all those cops came trampling up in my apartment. I was really confused as hell now. Dray turned toward the cops that were rushing in and raised his gun. Before he could get a shot off, like ten of the cops that were filing in the door let off shots on his ass. I heard Little Todd crying louder at the top of the steps. All of the screaming and chaos must've scared my baby almost half to death.

"Oh my God!!! Please don't shoot my son!!!" I screamed, closing my eyes as tears flowed out of them like a river. The other guy that had been with Dray came running out when he heard the shots, and the police officers shot him too. The remainder of the cops came rushing in and started barking orders.

"Call an ambulance! Untie them! Get the kid!" I was glad they had an ambulance called for Jock, because he looked like he had lost a lot of blood. The cops finally untied me and started

asking me questions. One of the cops that walked over to me I recognized from Norfolk. He was one of the fucking cops that was always after Todd. "Ms. Marshall, we followed you all the way here and you're lucky we did or you'd be dead. Andre Burkett was an undercover DEA agent that was not satisfied that you'd gotten away with the money he felt he was entitled to. When he didn't get his way, he went AWOL from his team. Luckily, Jock led us to you and we figured out that Agent Burkett was coming after you," the cop said. He noticed the look on my face.

"I am Sergeant LaBeckie from the Norfolk Police Department gang and narcotics unit. Ms. Marshall, you have the right to remain silent, anything you say can be used against you. . . ." I just stared at him in shock. When Dray's partner said there was no money in the safe, I knew immediately Jock had turned the tables on me.

I jumped out of my sleep soaked with sweat and with my heart racing like I had been running a marathon. I looked around my cell and realized I was still in prison and had just woken up from reliving the nightmare of the day I got arrested and the day I found out Jock had betrayed me. The dream was so real, it was like I was back on the scene all over again. I could still feel the pain in my chest when those cops told me I was under arrest and the pain in my heart when they said there was no money in my safe.

"Yo, Shan, you a'ight?" Lady, my new bunk mate, asked. Lady was cool. She and I had gotten close since I had cut my old crew off after Dee's death and my beating. Lady was locked up for beating the shit out of her lesbian lover and another chick she found her lover in bed with. Lady carried herself like a dude, but she had the softest heart. She always wore her hair in cornrows going back and she used Ace bandages to flatten her chest. But Lady couldn't hide that pretty face of hers. She acted like a dude but she didn't look like one. She had smooth caramel skin, beautiful slanted eyes, and perfect heart-shaped lips: a real feminine face. She acted hard, but I had heard her crying hard more than once. She had confessed to me how she had really loved this last chick and thought the chick loved her. I could totally relate to Lady's heartbreak. So far, Lady had shown herself to be loyal, which was important inside.

"Shit, I had a crazy dream . . . nightmare rather," I huffed, swiping my hands over my face to get some of the sweat off. "I hate when I put myself back at the scene of some shit I've been through because really, it's living that shit all over again," I grumbled.

"I know how that shit is. I always picture me walking in on my girl with the next bitch's head buried between her legs and I feel the same anger I felt all over again . . . like I could almost kill them both all over again," Lady said through her teeth.

"Let's change the subject, man," I replied. I couldn't have Lady getting all riled up because every time she did, she ended up getting into some shit. She was the one holding me together lately; I couldn't afford for her to get thrown in the hole.

"Yeah, you right. No sense in dwelling on the fucked-up-ass past," she agreed.

"Any word from your cousin?" Lady asked. Damn, I wanted her to change the subject, but not to that. I had lied and told Lady I was waiting on a visit from my cousin to tell me how my son was doing. I didn't trust anyone enough to tell the truth about why I was waiting for LaShell's visit.

"Nah . . . not yet," I replied, my voice trailing off. I had tried not to get anxious all day every day waiting to hear from LaShell. I knew from experience that any good plan needed time, but my nerves were wrecked waiting. ✓

It had been almost three weeks and today was the day I was expecting the visit from LaShell about the progress of our little mission against Kaufman. If LaShell could bring me pictures or proof that the job had been done, I was going to tell her where my final stash spot was. It was one of the many storage companies in Virginia Beach, but I wasn't going to reveal which one until I was sure I could trust LaShell. I had hidden one hundred thousand dollars of the heist money at the storage place among some of the things I had salvaged or managed not to sell from my old house. I had paid up the rental of the storage for two years so I never worried about them auctioning off my shit for non-payment. Of course I didn't anticipate being locked up with no possible idea when I would get out, either. It had already been eight months that I had been locked up. Two years would be up in no time so I had to get my money out of there before it was time to pay for the rental again. All I could do was pray that LaShell could be trusted and that she would get everything done as we had discussed.

"Here this bitch go," Lady growled, nodding her head toward our cell door. I was so busy lost in thought about the money and LaShell that I hadn't seen CO Dugan standing there with a crazy-looking smirk on her face. This was becoming an everyday occurrence with Dugan. She was always lurking around me. When I showered, when I ate, when I had visits, in the yard, and when I was in my cell. Shit, you would've thought I had personal security with the way she seemed to be so obsessed with hanging around me. When I saw her this time, I smiled back. *Two can play her little game,* I thought to myself. I quickly grabbed my prison shirt and shrugged into it, making sure I buttoned up all of the buttons. I jumped down from my bunk and glared at Dugan as I buttoned the last button on my newly issued shirt. I tilted my head to the side, exchanging a knowing glance with Dugan.

"Yo, why is you always coming up in here every day smiling and snickering and shit? You got something to say to one of us?" Lady snapped, standing next to me like my bodyguard. Lady despised Dugan and had told me she would fuck Dugan up for me if I wanted that. Everyone knew Dugan had something against me . . . *everyone*.

"Shut the fuck up, dyke," Dugan spat, talking to Lady but keeping her eyes on me.

I could tell Lady was about to go ham on Dugan and I couldn't let her do that. I stepped in front of Lady with my arms spread and pushed Lady back a few steps. I wasn't about to back down from Dugan's punk ass though. I was sick of her always staring at me and lurking around me anyway.

"I think her beef is with me," I said snidely and I struggled to keep Lady from attacking Dugan. I knew more about Dugan than she could ever imagine and so did quite a few people that were interested.

"Oh yeah? You think so. And just why would I give a fuck about a lowlife inmate like you enough to have beef with you?" Dugan sneered, her eyes going into little dashes. "You ain't shit to me," Dugan spat. But I knew she was fronting. She clearly saw me as a threat. Even with my scarred face and limp I was still better looking than Dugan. She had huge lips, short nappy hair that she attempted to cover up with bad weaves, and her skin was like a rocky road of acne and dark marks. Not a pretty sight at all.

"I think you're jealous of me. You see me as a threat. You want what I've already had," I snapped, hopefully enough to provoke Dugan to run her big-ass mouth. She started laughing raucously like I had made a joke.

"I think it's the other way around, inmate. I already have what you used to have and it's real good to me too. It stays with me every night and loves all up on me. Matter of fact, it sends its love and this," Dugan said, dropping an envelope at my feet. I didn't even look down at the envelope; instead, I kept my eyes squinted and glared at Dugan. We probably looked like two snarling dogs ready to attack each other because that is certainly how I felt.

"So you proud that you fucking my husband Todd? A fucking jailbird that wouldn't even give an ugly bitch like you the time of day unless he could use you?" I came right out. Lady sucked in her breath like she was shocked. Dugan let out a short burst of air like I had kicked her in the chest with my words. She sucked in on her bottom lip and curled her face into a frown.

"Yeah, I'm proud, bitch, and when I have his baby and we run away together, you'll be sitting in here rotting away. Happy reading, bitch. I guess you weren't as smart as you thought you were, huh?" Dugan hissed, rubbing her stomach for emphasis. Lady stepped from behind me, about to get in Dugan's face but I pulled Lady back again.

"She's not worth it. She'll get hers," I chortled confidently. "Bet that bitch will get hers."

We both watched Dugan turn on her heel and saunter out of the cell like she had just won a prize. I knew better than that. In my world what goes around always came around. Karma was a bitch and I was a living testament to that fact, but I also meted out my fair share of karma too.

I picked up the letter and knew immediately it was from Todd. I looked at Lady pitifully and the letter could barely stay in my trembling hands. I could only imagine what he had done while he was out in the world. My biggest fear was that he would get my son and I would never see Little Todd again. My heart thumped wildly now just thinking about the reality.

"You gon' open it?" Lady asked softly. I could see the sympathy on her face.

"I don't know if I want to. It can't be nothing good," I croaked out, my voice trailing off. Lady took the letter from me and tore at the envelope. I slumped down on my bunk and closed my eyes. I didn't know if I was ready.

12
Todd

"Mmmm! Mmmm!" Jock moaned through the bandana I had stuffed in his mouth. His battered body was going limp against the chair I had him tied to. I guess he was finally weakening from the blows I had been inflicting on him. Blood, piss, and shit leaked down his legs and the smell of raw meat gone bad and shit was giving me a stomachache. I guess all these years when I was thinking Jock was one of my strongest soldiers, I had been wrong. This nigga was the weakest of them all after all.

"My main man Jock. Damn, man, I missed you while I was locked up," I said snidely, walking over to him after picking up the bloodstained knife again. I could see him start shaking and his eyes went wide as he stared at the knife in my hand. I ran my fingers over the blade menacingly. "Did you miss me, partner?" I asked, an evil smile curling on my lips.

"You used this to fuck my wife, right?" I asked cruelly, pointing the tip of the knife to his dick.

"Huh? You rammed this up in my fucking wife?" I growled as I made another slice on Jock's dick with his own kitchen knife. Five deep gashes in total is all it took for his dick to look totally shredded. Guess it wasn't that big to begin with. I laughed as Jock's head flew back and the veins all over his body popped up against his skin. I cut him again, this time a little deeper.

"Grrrrrr!" he let out a muffled howl behind the gag. His head rocked and his eyes rolled into the back of his head. He bucked his body, making the chair thump slightly against the floor. I laughed at him when I saw more piss spilling from his bladder. I didn't know one person could hold that much piss inside of them. It was like a small pool on the floor now.

"Damn, nigga, I didn't know you had a bad bladder," I said evilly. Then I got close to his left ear and spoke directly into it.

"You were the last person I had to see, Jock. My man . . . my ace . . . my homie since fifth grade. You really fucked my wife and ratted me out to the jake . . . mmph mph mmm. If niggas in the street would've told me it was you, I would've shot them mutha-fuckas dead defending you. But, when those feds and five-o told me and showed me, I had to believe it. A fucking snitch . . . damn, man, was you that jealous of me all along that you became a fuck-ing snitch?" I whispered harshly in his ear. Then I took the tip of a carving knife and swung it across his earlobe, cutting off an inch of it. Blood squirted out of his ear like a running water faucet. Jock's body bucked and he made a sickening wheezing noise.

"That must've been real painful. Maybe I should do the other ear?" I asked in a maniacal voice. I was starting to enjoy torturing Jock. Now I see why these crazy-ass serial killers keep killing peo-ple: it was a rush that no drug could give you.

Jock was moaning and shaking his head from left to right like he wanted to tell me to stop.

"Urgh!" I growled as I jammed the knife into his kneecap this time. "I should cut your fucking tongue out and make you swallow it. That's a fitting punishment for a snitch . . . don't you think."

"Mmmmm!!!" Jock moaned loudly, which I knew would've been a full-out scream if he wasn't gagged. When I saw the tears running down from his eyes I finally felt a tiny bit of satisfaction. I had inflicted enough pain on that nigga to satisfy the pain and hurt I suffered when I learned about his betrayal. I smiled at him one last time.

"So tell me, was Shannon's pussy worth dying for, son?" I asked through my teeth. "Nah, I won't even ask that because I could care less about that heartless bitch. I don't want you to think I care enough about that bitch to kill you over her bird ass. I'm going to fucking kill you for setting me up. The way you did that shit was smooth, I gotta admit. You knew I would do any fucking thing for you, so you called me to come get that HK and then you led LaBeckie straight to my crib. You told them where I stashed my shit. You told them everything. You was so jealous that you took my entire life away from me just by being a fucking snitch. That's a violation of every street code there is, nigga," I growled, feeling a wave of emotion welling up in my chest. With my nostrils flaring, I used the knife to slice the bandana from Jock's mouth. I figured even a snitch deserved to defend himself before I sent him to hell.

"Any last words before I mirk your sorry ass?" I said through clenched teeth.

"It's . . . it's . . . a . . . set . . . set-up," Jock said through labored breaths. Blood dribbled over his lips and fell onto his chest and stomach.

"What, nigga? What the fuck is you talking about?" I growled. "Your game ain't gon' work, nigga . . . you good as dead. Nothing can save your ass but the cavalry right about now."

"They . . . they . . . use . . . used you to . . . to ki . . . kill me," he croaked. "They . . . they . . . know," Jock gasped.

"What? Who?" I asked. I didn't even give that nigga a chance to answer my question.

"Yeah, right, muthafucka. You can say what you want, nothing can save your ass," I growled. Then I walked over to him and swiped the knife across his neck with the precision of a surgeon.

Jock started making a sickening gurgling noise and gasping. I swiped the knife again in the other direction this time. I had no idea slitting a nigga's throat was so hard. They made that shit look easy on TV.

Blood spilled from Jock's mouth, the slit in his neck and maybe even his eyes. It was so much blood I couldn't even tell anymore where it was coming from.

"Rot in hell, traitor-ass nigga," I spat, hawking a wad of spit onto Jock's dead body.

I walked over to the money I had made Jock take out of his safe before I tied him up and picked up the duffel bag filled with the cash. Even working with the feds and being in witness protection, Jock had still managed to get away with at least a hundred G's of the heist money. He was crafty like that. The money belonged to me now. It was enough to get me out of the country. LaBeckie would be waiting for me to signal him to bust in on the fake meeting he thought I had set up with Abe. By the time LaBeckie figured out that I wasn't going to call or signal and that there was no meeting, I would be on my way out of the country on a nice little single-engine plane I had chartered for me and my son. In my world, money always talked and bullshit always walked.

I guess in the end, I was the nigga pulling off the last heist. So far, I had gotten Jock and Shannon for their paper and I had gotten the cops for my freedom, or so I thought.

13

Shannon

Dear Shannon,

I hope you enjoyed the pictures I sent you. I just wanted to show you better than I could tell you that I was the one in the end that pulled off the last heist and got the last laugh. I also sent the pictures of Kaufman to the prosecutor so he could add those charges to your case.

I must admit, your betrayal with Jock had me fucked up for a minute, but I guess karma is a bitch and then you die. Jock asked me to send you his love before he went to hell. Oh, and don't think you'll ever see Little Todd again. I guess he won't be calling Jock daddy after all. By the time you get this letter we will be somewhere unknown living happily ever after without you. I know I put you through a lot over the years, but I also took good care of you. I didn't deserve what you did to me, but you deserved everything you got in the end. I hope you get raped by a million lesbians while you do your fifteen to twenty. I'll make sure every time I make it rain in the strip

clubs with the money you had stashed in the storage place, I
think about grimy bitches like you.
  Have a nice life, bitch,
  Todd

This was my third time reading Todd's last letter. I looked at
the pictures again too and just like the first time, my heart felt broken all over again.

Dugan had dropped the envelope with the letter and pictures at
my feet a few days earlier and it was Lady who had opened it and
read it to me. Then Lady had helped me sit down to look at the pictures of LaShell all battered and beaten and of Todd sitting in my
storage room surrounded by the last of my money.

The day I saw those pictures I had thrown up about six times. I
had made Lady read the letter at least two more times, although
each time she did, I got sick all over again. Today I was able to read
it on my own without feeling anything. I don't know if I was numb
from all of the pain I'd suffered over the past year, or if I was numb
because I knew that it was going to be all good in the end. Either
way, at the moment, I couldn't feel shit.

Revenge came in waves and I knew that. One good hand always
washed the other is the saying, but bad hands do the same too.

Right after Dugan dropped the letter on me, I got myself together and headed into the deputy warden's office, where I had
met with him a few days before Dugan's visit to my cell. I sat down
in front of the deputy warden and looked him straight in his beady
little eyes. He leaned into his desk as far as his fat gut would allow
and, with his eyes trained on me, he grunted.

"What do you have for me, Marshall?" Deputy Warden Skaggs
asked me, his tone both serious and concerned all at the same time.

"I have exactly what I told you I would get: her confession," I said calmly, proudly sitting up straight in the chair.

"And just how did you manage that?" Skaggs asked.

"I told you before, she was always hanging around me, so it wasn't that hard. Once she came to my cell that morning, all I had to do was provoke her with a few words. It worked like a charm and she started wagging her tongue. The little button wire your internal affairs investigators put on my shirt recorded that bitch admitting to sleeping with Todd and giving him inside information too. So my suspicions and all the prison rumors turned out to be true," I replied, pushing the balled-up shirt with the small button microphone still attached toward Skaggs. He leaned back in his chair with a serious look on his face like he was lost in thought.

"What's going to happen to her now?" I asked, breaking up the eerie silence that had settled around us.

"Officer Dugan will be handled. I will not tolerate any dirty COs working in my prisons," Skaggs replied. He looked me dead in my eyes after he said that. A funny feeling flitted through my stomach, leaving me feeling weird. It was like my sixth sense was telling me Skaggs was flirting with me on some level. I played it off like I didn't catch the vibe he was sending.

"This was good work you did, Mrs. Marshall," Skaggs complimented. "Things like this don't go unrewarded around here. I'll see to it that the prosecutors know how you've helped us here," Skaggs promised. I cracked a weak smile. Even if it didn't help my case, at least I would've gotten my revenge. I figured out that it was Dugan who had more than likely told Todd about my visit with LaShell. Why else would Todd even think to go after my cousin? Before I left Skaggs's office I told him about what Todd had said in his letter about leaving the country with my son. I knew Dugan probably knew all of the details. Skaggs assured me that Dugan would be arrested that day and that if she didn't give up all of the details on Todd, she would be facing some very serious charges.

"He won't get away, Mrs. Marshall. I think the police are already a few steps ahead of him. He only thinks he was smarter than them . . . Trust me, it was all planned out from the beginning," Skaggs assured. I couldn't get any more details out of him and I didn't need to. I would just wait to hear about it later. I guess you could say from the ultimate heist to the last heist, nobody won.

14

Todd

"Fuck is she at?" I huffed as I looked at the clock on the wall inside of the small airport where I had been waiting for the past hour. Sweat dripped down the sides of my face, my stomach was in knots, and I was pacing. I looked at the clock again, which had become a habit over the past hour.

"It shouldn't take her this long. I fucking told her dumb ass what time she needed to be here," I mumbled to myself. Out of frustration I kicked the two bags of money I had at my feet.

"All this shit might be for nothing," I spoke to myself again. I knew that I didn't have a lot of time to wait. I was on borrowed time—LaBeckie's borrowed fucking time at that.

Dugan was supposed to meet up with my cousin Tarsha, grab Little Todd, and meet me at the chartered plane hangar. I probably had one less hour now before LaBeckie would be calling in the fucking cavalry and putting that all-points bulletin on my ass. He was a stupid ass for trusting a career criminal like me, but he was far from stupid altogether. It wouldn't be hard to tell that I had been bullshitting him.

I had called LaBeckie and told him the meeting with Abe was going down in northern Virginia at a big warehouse three hours away from Virginia Beach. LaBeckie was convinced that he would be seizing thousands of illegal high-tech weapons and putting the head of the entire gun operation behind bars today. LaBeckie had probably already bought himself a plaque for his desk that read "Captain."

LaBeckie and his entire squad should've been heading in the opposite direction from where I was right now. This detour and distraction was supposed to be my head start to get the fuck out of Dodge, but this bitch Dugan was fucking all of it up right now. She was going to be dead weight, I could already tell.

"Shit!" I huffed. I had probably made a mistake including Dugan in this shit. I had felt like it was the least I could do for her instead of just bouncing on her ass. Besides, there was no way I was leaving my son behind just like that. I knew how it was growing up without parents; I wasn't trying to let my son suffer like that. Nah, he would go with me wherever I went.

I had agreed to take Dugan with me. I figured wherever we settled down at, I would let her have the baby and then I'd break it to her that I didn't really want to be with her. I would make sure she was financially set and then I would bounce and take both of my kids with me. Women were too much trouble to settle down with. Fuck it, once I got to some exotic island someplace, I would just fuck a bunch of different bitches. I wasn't wifing nobody ever again.

"Yo, dude, we gotta get out of here," Carlos, the pilot of the little plane, said as he looked at his watch with concern etched on his face. He shook his head side to side and twisted his mouth.

"We don't want to get held up by the bad weather that's coming our way. Those feds don't play when it comes to aircraft safety," Carlos said. I shook my head in disgust and pursed my lips. *I'm about to bounce on this bitch. Nah, I can't leave my son like that. Fuck!* All kinds of thoughts swirled through my mind until I was really starting to make myself dizzy. I stopped pacing for a minute to think. I inhaled and exhaled a windstorm of breath.

"Yo, can I use your phone?" I asked Carlos. He looked at me suspiciously as if to say *Why the fuck don't you have a cell phone in this day and age?* After staring at me for a few uneasy seconds, Carlos reached in his pocket and gave me his cell phone. He wasn't trying to go too far away from his shit, either. I played it cool when really I felt mad uncomfortable under the heat of his gaze. I didn't need this dude to start asking me a whole lot of questions so I just acted like it was no big deal. If he found out I was a criminal trying to get him to take me out of the country, I'm sure he would've balked at the idea. He seemed like the straitlaced type that would have the cops on his cell phone speed dial and shit. I gave him a weak smile, turned my back a little, and started to dial the number.

Using a cell phone was against my better judgment, since street niggas like me knew the phone was always a fucking bad idea, but I had no choice: I needed to find out what was up with Dugan. I was praying it was something like she was stuck in traffic and nothing more serious than that. I didn't trust many people, so I also said a little prayer that Dugan's ass hadn't turned on me too. My nerves were raggedy with all kinds of thoughts keeping them that way.

I dialed Dugan's number, and after six rings she finally answered.

"He-Hello," she stammered. Right away I could tell she sounded different. I shrugged and chalked that up to her seeing a strange number pop up on her phone. First instinct always the best instinct, but I ignored mine once again. Mistake.

"Yo! Laila! Where the fuck you at with my son?" I barked into the phone. She needed to know I was fucking disgusted. "I ain't got all fucking day sitting here like a lame fucking duck! You know what's up, so where the fuck are you?"

"I'm . . . I'm . . . on my way, baby," Dugan said, with that same leery-ass voice she had answered the phone with. I let out a long sigh.

"I'm really close, just please wait for me. Todd, please . . . don't leave me," she said, sounding like she was on the brink of tears. A cold chill shot down my spine at the sound of her voice. I scrunched up my face. Something just didn't sit right with me.

"Yo, for real, Laila, no fucking around, if you ain't here in ten minutes I'm out. No ifs, ands, or buts about that shit. A nigga on the next bird flying. You got that?" I snapped and hung up the phone without even giving her the chance to respond.

I looked down at the two bags of money I had with me—the one from Shannon's stash and the one from Jock's stash. Another chill went down my spine. Was that a sign? I don't know but I ignored it again. Every single dollar of that money was blood money and I knew it. Mad people had died behind the ultimate heist and the last heist and I was the one with the bloody money at my feet. Maybe I should've known that it would come with the most severe karmic consequences, but when you got tunnel vision you can't see shit else. And at that moment, all I could see was that I had gotten the last laugh on Shannon, Jock, and LaBeckie.

I had my back turned when I first heard it. A little bit of piss escaped my dick in response to it.

"Police! Police! Don't move, motherfucker!" I heard the loud commands and immediately recognized the voices. I closed my eyes slowly and held my breath once again. This shit was like déjà vu. Within six minutes of my call to Dugan, the police were rushing at me with guns drawn. All I could come up with at that moment was that that bitch Dugan had betrayed me!

"Marshall! Let me see your fucking hands!" LaBeckie screamed. I turned around slowly and could see his ugly face turning stop-sign red. I laughed but it wasn't because anything was funny. I laughed because I knew, and LaBeckie should have known too, that I was not planning on ever going back to prison. No matter what. As I stared LaBeckie right in his icy blue eyes, I reached into my waistband with the quickness of a cowboy on the draw at a duel.

"Gun! Gun!" I heard one of the officers scream. "He got a fucking gun!"

I drew my Glock but I didn't get a chance right away to pull the trigger. Those fucking cops were good with their response time. "Drop it now!" was the last command I heard before it sounded like a bomb had exploded in my ears.

Tat, tat, tat, tat, tat, tat . . . Rapid-fire shots rang out and resounded loudly off the hollow walls of the airplane hangar. I felt my body jerking and dancing as the bullets seared through my skin and made me feel like I had been set afire. Still, I would not drop my weapon.

"Drop the gun!" LaBeckie screeched over the sound of his officer's gunfire. I could hear something in his voice that resembled concern, but I still wasn't falling for it. I held onto my gun. It was the only thing I had left.

Although I could feel myself slipping from existence, with great effort, I still managed to slip my finger through the Glock's trigger guard.

"Drop the fucking gun, Marshall!" LaBeckie screamed again. This time he stepped from behind his cover, giving me a clear shot at him. I guess he thought since we'd played cat and mouse over the years, we had built up a rapport. What LaBeckie didn't realize is that I would never have a relationship with no pig-ass cop. I would've rather die first.

With my eyes halfway open and my body riddled with bullets, I sucked in my last breath and fought to use the last ounce of strength I had. With the tiny bit of energy I had left and with malice in my heart, I lowered the gun in front of me and used my pointer finger to squeeze back on the trigger.

BANG! BANG!

Two shots left the end of the Glock before I was done for good. I never got a chance to see who or what they hit before my body crashed to the floor in a bloodied heap.

Suddenly, I was hovering above the room. I used to always hear people say when you first die you hover above your body and was still conscious of what was going on around you. Well, now I know that to be true. I saw myself down on the cold, gray concrete bleeding profusely. I was lying flat on my face and the deep, burgundy pool of blood under me grew wider and wider each second.

I could see a swarm of officers dressed in black moving frantically around me. From where I hovered they looked like ants scrambling. After watching for a few minutes, I realized they were passing right over me. They weren't rushing for me or to save me; instead, they were surrounding someone else. I couldn't see who it was because my view was obscured by the many officers trying to provide aid to the other person. I hoped it was that fucking bitch-ass LaBeckie.

A few of the officers were screaming, "Call the medics! Officer down! Officer down!"

After a few minutes I couldn't hear anything and I was no longer hovering above the scene. I couldn't see myself or the officers anymore. A shroud of black came down over me and I knew I was gone from this life. Dead, just like that.

All I could do is hope that my story was told correctly and with all the street props I deserved. I hope the headlines read:

Gangster Todd Marshall Kill Police Lieutenant Before Being Taken Out in a Hail of Bullets.

15

Shannon

"*It is with great sadness we report that Lieutenant Austin LaBeckie, who headed up the gang and gun unit at the Norfolk Police Department, was shot and killed today by career criminal Todd Marshall. A police spokesperson told us that Marshall, who had been released from prison as a confidential informant for LaBeckie, had gone rogue while participating in the highly sensitive and very closely monitored CI program. When police found out Marshall's whereabouts and confronted him earlier today, Marshall opened fire, hitting LaBeckie. LaBeckie died on his way to the hospital and is being hailed as a hero by his fellow officers. Marshall was also killed, but not before he shot and killed Lieutenant LaBeckie. Police say Marshall, who had been on the streets for about three weeks, was trying to escape the CI program and leave the area. Police say Marshall had help from a corrections officer he had been having a sexual relationship with. That officer is now under arrest for aiding and abetting a criminal and other charges.*"

I sat rocking back and forth in front of the TV in the prison day room. My head pounded and my ears rang. At first, I thought maybe I was dreaming again since nightmares had been plaguing me from the time I'd gotten locked up. I blinked a few times and knew that I was really awake and that I had heard the reporter correctly.

Tears rimmed my eyes as I listened to the reporter's every word. I didn't know if I was crying for Todd, for Little Todd, for myself, or for the cop that had been killed. It was a mixed bag of emotions that flooded my brain and my heart. I felt partially responsible for what had happened to Todd and the police officer.

The day I turned over the recordings of Dugan admitting to her affair with Todd, internal affairs arrested her on the spot. When they questioned her, she admitted that she had planned to quit the job that day, pick up Little Todd, and meet Todd at the small charter airport near Virginia Beach so that they could leave the country together. Dugan had snitched without any hesitation. She wasn't as ride-or-die as Todd thought, I guess.

The internal affairs officers who had Dugan in custody had gotten right in touch with LaBeckie and put him on to Todd's little plan.

LaBeckie and his crew had been heading to northern Virginia to a bogus location Todd had given them. They quickly turned around and headed to the airport where Todd was.

The way I got the story from Deputy Warden Skaggs was that as soon as those cops charged in, Todd had opened fire on them. They say LaBeckie was the hero who jumped in the line of fire to save his other officers. They said Todd was shot over sixty times and even after he was down the officers were still lighting his ass up. I guess when you live by it, you die by it.

As for me, I was given a decrease in my sentence for my work in bringing Dugan down, which also ultimately kept Todd from getting away. I didn't have any plans about what I would do when I got released, but at least I could say I was alive. None of it was worth it in the end. The ultimate heist, the last heist, and all of the revenge plots against each other had all failed for me, Todd, Jock, and LaBeckie. I guess in the end God has the final say on who gets the last word.

"You a'ight, sis?" Lady came over and touched my shoulder after she'd watched the news about Todd. She was such a good friend to me. I looked up at her and I could no longer hold it back. Tears poured from my eyes, my shoulders quaked, and I let out a roar of sobs. I didn't even care that I was in the day room where all of the other inmates could see me having a weak moment. I finally let my guard down and let it all out. There was nothing left to hide behind. Lady stayed with me every minute after that to make sure I didn't do anything to hurt myself. I was cool, I started to feel better after a few days. Deputy Warden Skaggs even let me plan Todd's small funeral and see him get buried in the poor man's graveyard. After all of the riches Todd and I had shared, who would've guessed his final resting place would be among the nameless, homeless, and destitute. Such is life, I guess. I couldn't hope for much more. What did I really have left? Nothing but a little boy that I loved more than life itself.

A week after they let me tend to Todd's funeral, I was in my bunk and Lady was in hers when our new CO walked into our cell.

"Aye, Marshall, mail," the CO called out to me. I looked at Lady and Lady looked at me, both of our eyebrows up in arches on our faces. I grabbed the envelope and examined it. There was no return address, just my name and the prison addressed typed like it had been done on a computer.

"Shit, you sure you want to open that?" Lady asked, her eyebrows still arched.

"Can't be no worse than everything that has already happened. Fuck it," I said, tearing at the back of the envelope.

Dear Shannon,

I mailed this the day I was scheduled to leave the country so by the time you read this I will probably either be halfway around the world or dead. I definitely won't be back in that hellhole. I know you thought I was the worst scumbag on the planet when we were together, but I did love you at one time. Even if I fucked with chicks for sport, I never loved them. In fact, you were the only woman I ever loved. With that being said, I wouldn't leave you completely fucked up in the end. I know that the reason you're where you are today is all because of me and my shit. So, I used some of your stash and paid Laura Schiffler from Kaufman's office to be your defense attorney. I also left you a little something at the third stash spot I told you about when we first got together. All you have to do when you get out is go get it. It's all set up for you. If I'm alive, I have Little Todd with me and he will contact you when he's old enough to ask about you. If I am dead, use the money and make sure my boy goes to college and never becomes a street nigga like his daddy.

Peace,
Todd

I fell to my knees and sobbed. Lady jumped down from her bunk in a panic.

"What? What is it? What did it say?" she asked, frantically snatching the letter from my hand and reading it.

I couldn't even open my mouth to say a word. After all that I had done to him, Todd still looked out for me in the end. I felt like a piece of shit. All of this and in the end it was me who had come out on the winning side of it all.

Caked Up

DE'NESHA DIAMOND

Prologue
Harlem

Huddled in a darkened table at our favorite bar, Sparks, my life-long friend and partner-in-crime, Isaiah Kane, drops a bomb on me.

"You lost all of your money?" I repeat, in shock. "Again?"

"I know. I know, Harlem. Don't lecture me this time. Can you help me or not?"

"I don't know. How much do you need?"

He swallows. "About ten?"

"Ten thousand?" I sigh in relief. "Sure. I got you on that." When my boy shakes his head, I tense again.

Isaiah leans forward and whispers. "Ten *million*."

"Are you crazy? I can't come off that much money."

"What are you talking about? You're loaded. I know that you got your shit stashed somewhere. You probably haven't used twenty percent from that big cyber heist we pulled two years back."

"That's my retirement money. We're both supposed to be getting out of the game at thirty-five, remember?"

Isaiah rolls his eyes. "Yeah. Yeah. I remember. My retirement is going to be delayed for a little while longer." He tilts up his glass of whiskey.

Feeling a sense of panic sink in, I ask, "Who do you owe that much money to?"

Isaiah ignores me for a few seconds to signal to the bartender for another round.

"Isaiah?"

He sighs and cuts me a look. "Kingston West."

Shit. I grab my glass and drain the whiskey in one gulp. The whole reason that I'm even in this heist business is because my uncle Jonathan Banks inspired me. He and his crew worked for decades for the Guzman Colombian cartel, leading a crime team called The Jackal.

There wasn't shit Uncle Jonathan, Rawlo, Mishawn, and Tremaine couldn't jack. They were never caught and never served a single damn day behind bars. If that ain't some boss shit, I don't know what is.

In the underground world, my name carried its fair amount of weight and respect—and I extended it to cover my boy Isaiah. At thirty-three, we've been in the street game since before we hit double digits—that's a long fucking time. Unlike my famous uncles, we're more jacks of *all* street trade than specialists in just one. We deal. We gun run. We jack. We do whatever it is that needs to be done to stack our paper for our thirty-five-year-and-done plan. As kids we knew that we didn't want or believe brothahs could be running the streets with a head full of gray hair—mainly because the shit ain't never been done. There's always someone younger, faster, stronger, or smarter to enter the game and the fastest way to the top is take out the old guards. And so it goes. A vicious cycle.

My mind shoots back to when Isaiah said that he was going to start working for the notorious crime boss. Isaiah was looking to make some extra money. He's always looking to make more money, especially since I was agreeing to less and less big heist jobs. There's no need. I'm thirty-three and I have nearly twenty-five million in cash saved and stashed out of reach of the federal government. My buddy here hasn't been as smart. Money burns through his hands as fast as he snatches it. I've always known about him having a gambling issue, but clearly it's more of a problem than I've ever realized.

"So can you loan me the money or not?" Isaiah asks.

"Loan implies that you can and are capable of paying me back," I tell him.

Isaiah's head jerks back as if I'd punched him.

"Oh? It's like *that* now?"

I shrug, not wanting to come off that much cash. It would delay my getting out of the game at least another five to seven years.

Isaiah twists up his face. "Get the fuck outta here. I'm gonna pay you back."

"Can't do it. Sorry, bruh."

"Damn! At least I asked you. If I was some real foul nigga, I could've just snatched it from you. You ain't slick. I know where you keep that shit *buried*—with Grandpa."

My stomach dropped. "What?"

"But look. We're *boys*," he says like he didn't just casually hint that he could rob me at any time. "We're *always* going to be boys. If the situation was reversed, I would come through for you."

"But the situation *isn't* reversed." At his awkward laugh, I start my interrogation. "What the hell happened with Kingston?"

Isaiah sucks his teeth and shrugs. "This nigga is tripping because I lost one of his shipments. I told the man that I was jacked, but he ain't trying to hear that shit. He says if my ass is breathing, not locked down and don't have something like DEA report in the newspapers that my ass is lying. Can you believe that shit?"

I bob my head. "Of course I believe it. Ain't nobody going to just take your word on something like that. Plus, why are you running drugs? You're a thief."

"Not drugs. Weapons."

"You lost ten million worth of weapons? How is that even possible?"

"Okay. So I lost a *couple* of shipments."

"Oh, my God." I toss back my second whiskey as soon as the glass hits the table. "Bartender, another round." I shift my attention back to Isaiah. "Why did you ever agree to work for him?" I ask. "You know Kingston West is bad news."

Isaiah sighs. "I was in a fix. I owed this cat, Gold Dawg, down in Atlanta some serious cheddar."

"Gold Dawg? A poker guy?"

"So? Big deal. I recently had a bad streak at the tables. It's no big deal. Shoot me."

"I'm not going to shoot you. Kingston West is going to do that—if not worse."

"What's that supposed to mean? You're seriously not going to loan me the money?"

I'm shaking my head before I can even get the words out. "Can't do that. That's almost *half* that I got saved up. I have a one-year-old daughter I got to support. My grandmother is getting older."

"And you're trying to impress that new bougie chick that you're still seeing from that club," Isaiah tosses in.

"She has nothing to do with this."

"Uh, huh."

"When do you have to pay Kingston?"

Isaiah hems and haws, but he finally says, "One week."

He might as well have thrown a brick at my head.

"Look, if you don't just want to *loan* me the money, then maybe you can help me with this one job I have lined up for tomorrow. You can get your hands dirty with your old childhood buddy, can't you?"

"What kind of job?"

"I have another shipment to deliver down in Memphis. I don't like doing these runs by myself."

"So I'm going to hold your hands every time you do a shipment?"

"Damn. You act like I've never done shit for you before."

The more whiskey he tosses back, the hotter he gets.

"Another shipment?" I ask dubiously.

He waves me off. "Hey, it's easy money."

"How much?"

"The job pays a million. It's not all I need, but it's a substantial down payment. You down?"

I hesitate, for good reason. "Am I even going to get paid for this job?"

Isaiah looks ready to explode.

"Never mind." I toss up my hands in surrender. "Forget I asked."

"C'mon. You're going to do me like that? At the end of the day, we're still homies, right?"

"Yeah. Yeah." The second the bartender sets down my third drink, I snatch that bitch up and drain it as fast as the first two.

"So you'll do it?"

"Fine. I'll ride down with you."

"Great!"

My cell phone buzzes.

We both glance down as I scoop my phone from out of my pocket and see Johnnie's name splashed across the screen. "Hold up," I say, and step back to answer the call. "Hey, princess. What's up?"

"Me. You still rolling through like you promised?" Johnnie asks in her sexy voice that gets me so hard. "I got everything ready for you."

"Oh? Is that right?" I glance down at my watch. "Give me about thirty minutes."

"All right. Don't be a minute late or I'll have to put away this homemade pie I got baking for you."

My grin spreads from ear to ear. Johnnie knows how much I love her homemade blackberry pie. "Twenty-nine minutes," I promise her and then disconnect the call.

"Humph. Looks like the side piece is tightening the noose," Isaiah grumbles.

I laugh at his obvious jealousy. "You know that you're going to have to see someone about that shit. That color of green never looks good on no damn body."

"Whatever, nigga. You do you and play on the wrong side of the tracks all you want. Don't come running to me when the shit blows up in your face."

A muscle twitches from the left side of my face but before I can calm down I bark back, "What the fuck is your problem?"

"Problem?" he says, like my question is out of line. "I ain't got a problem."

I eyeball him hard as shit. "No? Could've fooled me. Ever since me and Johnnie hooked up, it's been one cheap shot after another. I don't remember ever having this much to say about any of the females you dip and dabble with. Clearly, you're feeling some kind of way about the woman I might marry one day."

"Marry?" he echoes. "Since when the fuck your ass been thinking about marriage?"

I shrug, amazed that I confessed the shit myself. "Not that it's any of your business, but I've been bouncing the idea around in my head for a few minutes."

Isaiah laughs, but when he sees my ass is dead serious, he sobers up. "Shit. You're for real."

"What can I say? Bae got me all up in my feelings and I can't see me riding out into the sunset without her."

"Bae, huh?" He snickers. "Does *Bae,* the New York state attorney's daughter, know what the fuck it is you *really* do yet?"

I swallow hard. "Not yet."

"Have you introduced her to your one-year-old daughter that your last side piece dumped on your nana's doorsteps?"

"Damn, nigga. What the fuck?"

Isaiah tosses up his hands like his ass ain't tryna start shit. "I'm just saying—"

"You're just saying what, bruh?" Heat rushes up my neck.

"I'm saying, as your friend, that maybe you should pump your brakes a little on this one. You up here talking about maybe putting a ring on it and you haven't even introduced ol' girl to the *real* you yet."

What the fuck am I supposed to say when I'm smacked with the truth?

Sensing that he's hit a nerve, Isaiah takes another swing at my fantasy of snatching a good girl from the one-percent crowd. "Nigga, you better wake the fuck up and get out while you still can."

"I don't remember you talking all that bullshit when you were trying to throw game her way." I stiffen when I see that same hardness flash across his face again. *Anger? Jealousy? What the fuck?* That kind of shit ain't never gone down between us. We're bruhs from the cradle to the grave. That has always been our motto.

Isaiah smiles and those emotions disappear once again. "Don't get me wrong. Johnnie Robinson is as fine as they come—and she got the nerve to have a damn good head on her shoulders. *But* for two gutter rats like ourselves? She definitely falls into the hit it and quit it column. Fuck. You shouldn't have even given her your real *first name*, Harlem. Let alone be sitting up here thinking about giving her your real *last name* in front of some damn preacher."

"Whatever, man. I'm out."

"A'ight." We exchange daps.

"See you in the morning?" he double-checks.

"Bright and early." I pound him on the back and then head out. "Text me the address." The whole way toward the door, I can feel my boy's eyes follow me. But as I climb into my gray Range Rover, I tell myself that I'm fucking tripping. Isaiah ain't never done anything to me *personally* to look at him sideways. There have been plenty of times in our past when Isaiah came through for me. He has every right to wave warning flags when I'm talking about big life changes. I'm supposed to do the same shit for him if I see him going down a questionable path.

But is Johnnie a questionable path? Not according to the hard-on I still got since her ass called. Baby girl is my fucking everything since we met at the hot new Brooklyn club, Throb. Every bad bitch in New York rolled through there that night. Brothahs flocked to Johnnie's ass like flies to the last starving kid in a Third World country. My boy Isaiah picked his lip off the floor first and stepped to her, but she shot his ass down before he got a complete sentence out of his mouth. I play the shit cool: bought her a drink without stepping to her, danced with a girl that had sat right next to her for like three or four songs, and then bought a few other girls drinks that were standing around her. The shit sparked her competitive side and she ended up speaking to me before I made a move to go back on the dance floor with someone else.

From there, she was doing the most to keep my attention. Those Coke-bottle curves and juicy, fat ass kept me in a trance all night. Despite her ass having a body for sin, a brother only had to take one look in her eyes to know the girl had a brain as fat as her ass. Most niggas don't like intelligent, independent women. Ain't nobody got time to listen to all that rah-rah about how they don't need a man for this or for that but then get all thirsty when they want a real dick instead of some battery-operated bullshit. Independent women are more than a headache, but baby girl worked me so good on that dance floor that I was ready to change up my whole damn program.

Now, rolling up on our one-year anniversary, why not think about putting a ring on that ass? In eighteen months, I'll be thirty-five and getting out of the game anyway. Johnnie don't ever have to know how I cake up. All that matters is I'll have enough to take care of her *and* my daughter for the rest of our lives. I smile all the way to my girl's crib.

I practically skip my way up to Johnnie's home forty minutes away in Greenwich, Connecticut. When I enter the house with the key she'd given me, I'm surprised to see the entire place lit with candles—but Johnnie is nowhere in sight.

"Baby, you here?" I call out, smiling.

There's a slight pause before she shouts, "In the bedroom."

My smile doubles in size. "Somebody is anxious." I toe off my shoes at the front door, peel out of my jacket and t-shirt as I tread my way toward the bedroom, following the trail of rose petals.

The second I walk into the bedroom, Johnnie greets me from the center of her California king-sized bed, wearing nothing but a smile. Meeting my gaze from across the moonlit room, she leans back among the red silk sheets while allowing her long ebony legs to fall open east to west. "Hey, baby. I've missed you."

The smile on my face stretches as I watch her walk her fingers down the center of her body and over the black turf of hair covering her pussy.

My dick hardens and tries to Hulk its way out of my jeans.

Smiling, Johnnie dips a finger inside her pussy and twirls it around so I can hear its squishy wetness. "Mmmm," she moans, grinding her hips. Her free hand lifts to her full breasts so she can squeeze and pinch the nipples.

In a trance, I walk toward the bed, stripping as fast as I can. I nearly lose it, when her fingers ease out only so that she can glaze her pretty, pink clit with her body's natural honey. Now that she has my ass worked up, she flutters open her eyes and asks me, "Are you hungry, baby?"

"You know it." I crawl my muscular six-foot-three body onto the bed. My gaze is locked onto my target. There's nothing sweeter than my baby's honey-glazed pussy. *Nothing.* I'm addicted to its touch, taste, and smell; and her ass knows it.

"Come on, baby. Let momma feed you."

I settle down between her firm thighs, spread those fat lips wider and dive in. *Delicious.*

"Ooooh, baby," she groans. Her knees spring around my head while her fingers rake and pull on my hair.

That shit doesn't stop my flow. I grip her juicy ass while my tongue drills down into her homemade pie like it's the nectar of life. Smacking and slurping, I'm on a sugar high out of this world.

"Aww, *fuck*, baby!" Johnnie sighs and pants, trying to catch her breath. "I'm coming!"

She didn't have to tell me. I can tell by the way her legs tighten and her clit swells to the size of a gumdrop. Seconds later, her legs tremble and she tries to buck her way off my tongue.

"Wait. Wait."

I ain't waiting for shit. Johnnie always cries that wait shit when her building orgasm gets too intense. Locking her down with one hand, I slide my thumb in through the back door of her wet ass and watch her whole body bounce up and down. I hang on like a rodeo clown. Her orgasmic screams are reaching octaves only an opera singer can hit—but I keep going, making her shit sensitive. Johnnie redoubles her efforts to shove my head away, but I ain't going nowhere until I hear my baby pop off at least two more times. Panting and quaking beneath my tongue, Johnnie edges up the bed, tryna get some relief. When her head hits the headboard, one last orgasm detonates and she damn near snatches me bald at the top of my head.

Chuckling, I pop off that pie and flip her ass over before she can even breathe. Ass up, face down, I ease my ten inches inside her sopping pussy through the back and have to fight to keep my eyes from rolling out of my head. It ain't easy because my baby stay on those damn Kegel exercises. This pussy is tight as a damn drum.

No doubt, Johnnie hears how my breathing changes up. She flips her hair over her right shoulder and glances back at me with the sexiest damn smile that puts me on the verge of nutting before I even get to the second stroke.

"What's the matter, baby?" she asks, wiggling her ass and then throwing it back on me to steal my breath.

"Wait. Wait."

She laughs. "Wait? Fuck that." She throws that fat muthafucka back again and my damn toes curl. Johnnie gives me a taste of my own medicine as she boss her ass all over my dick and I can't do shit but hang on for the ride.

I don't know how she does it, but each thrust, her muscles tighten. Hands down, this is the best shit ever. But I ain't no bitch-ass, one-minute nigga; I grunt and growl my way through this until I finally gain control of my body. Once that's done, I'm smacking and pounding her ass into submission.

"Damn, baby. That's my spot," Johnnie moans. "Ooooh."

Ego swoll, I drill deeper and fist Johnnie's long hair. I pull her head back so that I can see her nasty sex faces. If Johnnie knew who the hell she was really fucking with, she'd have building security toss my ass out of the damn window. Our asses are from two different worlds.

Johnnie and her family rub elbows with the New York political elite. Both the governor and the mayor are her father's close friends. Johnnie herself slaves away at a prestigious law firm, stacking a high six-figure income every year.

"What took you so long to come out here and see me? Hmm?" she asks, purring like a kitten.

"Ahhh. Ahhh."

"You missed this good pussy?" With my free hand, I smack her onion-shaped ass until I see my handprint on her brown skin. "I know you ain't slinging this good dick to other bitches when you're on your long excursions."

"Oooh. Ahh." My eyes roll back as I listen to her slick way of interrogating me. Every nigga likes to keep a spark of jealousy in their woman. For one, it shows that they care, but it also makes them work that much harder to keep you in place.

Johnnie tosses her hair the other way and glares back at me over her left shoulder. "Goddamn. Cat got your tongue?" she asks, pounding hard back on the dick.

"Damn, baby. You're going to fuck around and make me come too soon."

The booty claps around my shit, giving it a standing ovation. My fat cock glistens in and out of her ass. A beautiful sight that wets up my eyes. There's nothing more beautiful than two black, sweat-slick bodies making love.

Then she stops and expertly locks her pussy muscles. "I asked you a question."

My nuts shoot up and my ass start stuttering like a muthafucka.

"Nah. Nah, baby. You know that there's nobody but you." Her pussy tightens again and I lose brain cells. "Ahh. Ahhh. Ahh."

"You ready to come?" she asks.

I can only nod.

Johnnie releases me. "C'mon, Harlem. Give me all of that nasty candy you got in that muthafucka."

While the booty keeps backing up on my shit, my breathing comes out hard and choppy. That shit can only mean one thing.

"I'm coming," I announce, pulling her hair back harder.

"Then come on, baby. Give me all you got."

"Yeah? Are you ready for daddy?" I grit my teeth because ready or not here it comes. "Ahhhh." I whip my dick out and hose her ass down with an explosive nut. The shit is so intense that my shit keeps gushing like champagne. "Oooh. Yeah." I rub and squeeze my cock's fat head so I can get every drop out. After that, I rub my still-hard cock in the warm semen on her ass and back and paint myself a Picasso. Shit so good that I get lightheaded and tip over the side and crash into a mountain of silk-covered pillows.

I don't know what the hell happened after that. My ass is knocked the fuck out. When my ass comes to the next morning, the California king is empty and the crib smells like coffee, bacon, eggs, and sausages. *My baby is definitely wife material.*

Smiling, I peel myself off of the jizz-stained sheets that are sticking to me like glue and make a beeline toward the adjoining shower. Forced to use my baby's smell-'em-good soaps, I kick off a couple of good notes from Al Green's "Love and Happiness." If my niggas saw me now, they'd take away my playa's card. No questions. But at this moment in time, I give zero fucks.

So wrapped in my fantasy, I don't hear Johnnie sneak back in this bitch to jot *I luv u* on the stained-glassed shower door. When I shut off the shower and see it, I fly higher on cloud nine. I grab a towel and step out of the shower smelling like raspberries and crème. I grab the black velvet box out of my pants pocket from off the floor and then thread my way into the kitchen.

"Morning, lover," Johnnie greets, smiling in her sharp lawyer attire: black pencil skirt, white blouse, and hair piled in a high neat bun. But it's those damn black-rimmed glasses that make me want to grab her by her hair and drag her back into the bedroom, caveman-style. "How did you sleep?"

"Don't front. You know you put a nigga in a coma." I slap my hand on her juicy-round butt and give it a hard squeeze before stealing a morning kiss.

"Mmmm," she moans, trying not to spill her pitcher of orange juice.

I don't give a damn about messing up her clothes. My dick is hard as fuck. Yet, when I reach for one of her pearl buttons, she pushes my hand away and steps back. "No, no, no. Sorry, baby. I got a big case this morning. We have just enough time for a few bites and then I gotta go."

I don't want to hear that shit and unbutton two buttons anyway.

Giggling, Johnnie sets the pitcher down and tries a little harder to get me to stop. Less than a minute later, the towel is on the floor, she's up against the refrigerator, my dick is in her pussy, and she's clawing my back with her stiletto nails.

By the time we're done, the last batch of bacon and sausages are burnt to a crisp and the damn fire alarm is blasting.

Laughing, I'm yanking the batteries out of all the alarms when Johnnie picks up the velvet box from off the floor.

"What's this?"

I stop and grin at her stunned expression. "What do you think it is?"

Eyes wide, she pops open the box and gushes. "Ohmigod!" She looks over at me with tears making her brown eyes glisten. "Is this? Are you?"

Knotting the towel around my hips, I walk over to her and kneel on one knee. "Johanna Robinson, will you do me the honor of becoming my wife?"

She squeals so loud that I've got to wiggle a finger in my ear to make sure that she hasn't punctured the muthafucka.

"Yes! Yes! Yes!" She drops down onto the floor with me and wraps her arms around my neck so tight that it chokes off my air supply.

Happy as shit, I plant another fat kiss on her. By the time we leave her apartment, we're both late as shit. I turn my celly back on after exiting her driveway to see my man Isaiah has already hit me up ten times.

When I arrive at the texted address, Isaiah is pacing like a caged animal outside.

"Nigga, where the fuck you've been?"

"Don't start, man. I'm here, ain't I?"

He huffs and tosses down his cigarette and smashes it with his foot. "C'mon. Let's make this money."

I follow him to a van duped to resemble a famous delivery company and climb in. However, we don't even make it out of the parking lot when we're suddenly surrounded.

"What the fuck?"

SWAT and DEA vans appear out of nowhere.

Isaiah slams on the brakes in time. "Damn, nigga. Did the muthafuckas follow you out here?"

"What? Me?"

My door is jerked open and I'm snatched out of the vehicle like a fucking cartoon character and slammed into the concrete. Mutha-fuckas keep yelling, "Get down," even though I'm down as far as I can go with two or three boots threatening to crack my spine.

"C'mon, assholes. You two are under arrest for arms smug-gling!"

1

Harlem

Five years later

We're at it again.

Johnnie tastes so good.

Better than I remember—and up until twenty minutes ago I thought that I remembered everything. Her skin is softer. Her thighs are firmer. And her pussy is tighter. How can that be? It's been more than five years since we last been together. It was a night filled with so much promise and yet so much regret.

"Oh, baby. Yeeesss," Johnnie sighs like the seductress she is while squirming almost in rhythm to the sexiest slow jam in her head.

"I fucking missed you, baby," I confess, high off my own emotions.

"Oooh," she moans instead of telling me that she missed me, too.

My high is knocked down a notch, but on her next sigh I'm lost in the mix once again. Sweat drenches our bodies, causing these cheap cotton sheets to paste to our bodies. It's no worse than this old-ass mattress and flat pillows. We block this shit out and just concentrate on what our bodies do naturally: fuck the shit out of each other.

"I'm coming, baby," she pants, digging her nails into the grooves of my shoulder blades.

"Yeah? Then c'mon, baby." My hips pick up speed as I watch her toss her thick hair back and forth. A rosy glow stains her normal peanut-butter complexion. Her long legs tighten around my hips while the tight space between her pink walls gushes with more honey.

"Oh goddamn. You feel so good," I moan as my toes curl and that good feeling shoots up my entire body.

Johnnie's pants climb up the music scale. Her nails become talons across my back. We're going to come together.

"That's it, princess. Come for daddy." My grip locks on her waist.

"Oh." Her legs try to slice me in half. "Oooooh!"

We're in the zone, ready to blast off. Three strokes later, she's screaming up at the ceiling and I'm roaring like a lion to an epic climax.

Drained, I roll to her right and collapse at the same time, saving her from the brunt of my six-foot-three, two-hundred-plus-pound body.

"Oh God. That was incredible," she praises with a smile stretching from ear-to-ear.

"Yeah?" My chest expands a couple of extra inches.

She nods and manages not to look at me.

"HARLEM BANKS, FIVE MINUTES," a man's voice blares with static crackling over an old intercom box.

Damn. I slam my eyes shut as Johnnie rolls over to the opposite side of the bed.

"Wait. Wait." I reach for her, but she's already out and scooping up her clothes from the floor. "What's your hurry? We still have five more minutes." I push up onto my side.

"More like four and a half," she says, stepping into her panties and still avoiding eye contact.

I get an uneasy feeling in my gut. Something is up and I'm not too sure that I want to know what. "All right. You got four minutes. Spit it out." I climb out of the bed with my ten inches swinging as I go in search for my own brand-less white undies.

Johnnie slips on a matching lace bra to support her voluptuous D-cups.

"I'm waiting."

She pulls in a deep breath and then blurts the shit out. "I'm getting married."

Those words hit me with the force of a wrecking ball. "You're what?"

She shrugs like we're fucking discussing the weather. "You heard me. I'm getting married."

"Didn't I just have my dick inside of you less than a minute ago? What the fuck are you talking about?"

She doesn't respond.

I abandon my search for my underwear and storm across the small room to snatch her by her arm. "I don't hear from you the entire five years I've been locked down and then you finally write to request a conjugal visit so you can fuck me and then drop that shit on me?"

At last her twinkling brown eyes meet my gaze. "I figured, what's one *last* fuck for old times' sake?"

After a second to let that process, I hiss, "You fucking bitch." I push her up against the concrete wall.

She laughs. "Careful. You wouldn't want me to scream, now would you?"

"The fuck?" I release her and then assess her with new eyes.

"Don't give me that look," Johnnie says, reaching for her red dress. "It's not like you didn't get anything out of it."

Since I don't want to turn my dime bid for arms trafficking into a death penalty, I step back and order myself to keep my hands off of her.

"It doesn't feel too good when muthafuckas use you, does it?"

"I never used you," I say.

She slips the dress over her head. "Yeah. Sure. Whatever makes you sleep better at night." Johnnie attempts to move away from me, but I block her path toward her bags.

"I didn't use you," I insist. "I just didn't tell you *everything*. There's a big difference."

"Everything? You mean like your real *full name*? Or what you did for a living? How about that you had a kid? Or even a wife?" she snaps.

"We were divorcing," I bark back. "Not that it was a real marriage anyway. The papers were in process by the time I proposed to you."

"Whoo-hoo! Aren't you a real catch?"

"Give a muthafucka a break. You think a brother like me could just step up and tell you that his ass is a criminal and think you'd give him the time of day? Damn. Your father was the damn state's attorney. Now he's the governor."

"That's right! A brother like you should have *never* wasted my time, filling my head with a bunch of lies." Bitterness seeps into her voice.

The hurt I've caused her still runs deep. Believe it or not, the shit gives me hope. Bitterness is an emotion—and any emotion from a woman is a sign that she still cares.

"Johnnie." I close the gap between us with one step. "I'm sorry I hurt you. It was never my intention. I love you and as soon as I get out of here I'm going to make it up to you. I got some money waiting for me on the outside. It's enough to take care of us for a *very* long time." I slide my hand gently against her right cheek. "Just wait for me, baby." I plant a kiss against her full lips. "Can you do that?"

Johnnie is quiet for a long time—and then she breaks the spell by laughing out loud. "Wait for you? Negro, please." She shoves me away just as the door's metal lock makes a loud click and an annoying buzzer sounds off.

Two prison guards step inside the room. "Okay, you two lovebirds. Playtime is over." They stop and look at a fully clothed Johnnie and me with my dick still swinging before cracking the hell up.

"Damn, Banks. What's the damn hold-up?"

"I don't know about him," Johnnie says, "but I'm ready to go." She snatches up her bag and marches toward the door.

"Johnnie, wait." I start after her, but this time *my* path is blocked.

"Hold up, Casanova. Get dressed. We ain't got all day."

I can't let this shit end like this between me and my girl. "Johnnie!"

She stops at the door near the other guard. "Thanks for the lovely time. I'll be sure that the maid of honor drops you a thank-you note in the mail." She winks and then is escorted out.

Ain't that a bitch?

2

Harlem

One month later

Nana Gloria sits iron-straight with her coarse hair raked back into a tight bun at the top of her head. Her square, black-rimmed glasses slide to the end of her nose as she continuously looks around. It's the middle of the summer and yet she's in her favorite sweater with her arms about her like she's fighting off a chill.

When I enter the room with my fake smile, she looks up and sighs.

I know that sigh.✔

I grew up with that sigh. It's tiredness and disappointment rolled together. *I'm tired of this, Harlem. I'm disappointed in you, Harlem. When are you going to start making smarter choices, Harlem?*

Gliding my long body into the uncomfortable plastic chair, I prepare for this month's tsunami of guilt she's about to unleash my way. After taking our measure of each other, we reach for the phone at the same time.

"Hey, Nana. You're looking good."

Nana Gloria's groomed left brow shifts an inch higher than her right. "I look like shit and you know it," she counters, tersely. "I haven't slept in over forty-eight hours, the electric company won't give me another extension, the hospital keeps calling about their bill, the insurance company keeps coming up with excuses why they can't pay the bills while the doctor insists that Tyler needs another operation." She pauses to suck in a dramatic breath. "I could go on, but the list would take up all of our time."

"All right, Nana. I get it."

"No. I don't think that you do," she says, her bottom lip quivering. "I'm so tired of this mess that you dumped on my lap that I don't know what to do. I'm at the end of my rope." Her grip on the phone tightens. "Something has got to give."

My head drops a few inches as her every word carves another piece right out of my heart. "I know things are hard right now—and I'm trying to work a few things out to get you some cash."

"Some cash?" she asks. "I'm not asking for gas money, Harlem. I could lose the house. You know how hard your grandfather worked to buy that house." Nana glances around and then leans closer toward the Plexiglas. "Why can't you just tell me where you have the money stashed? I'll only take what Tyler and I need to get by."

Now I tighten my grip on the phone.

"Don't tell me that you don't trust *me*."

"Of course I trust you," I say. "That's not the issue."

"Then what?"

"Nana, I told you. There are eyes everywhere. I can't risk you winding up behind bars, too."

Another sigh. "So what in the heck am I supposed to do? Huh?" Her red-stained eyes implore me. "Am I supposed to just toss up my hands and let them take everything and put me *and* your daughter out on the street?"

"No. Of course not." I shift around in my seat.

"Then what? Tell me something, Harlem."

"What about Uncle Jonathan?"

Nana Gloria's anger changes into confusion. "And where in the hell is your uncle supposed to come up with that kind of money? He's an old man living on a pension just like I am."

I shake my head because she still refuses to believe me when I tell her that Uncle Jonathan is, in fact, The Jackal. "Nana, talk to him. I'm sure that he has a few dollars saved up."

"I will do no such thing. I'm not harassing that man for his little taste of money. You should be ashamed for even suggesting such a thing." With her bottom lip trembling, she blinks a fresh wave of tears away.

I shake my head, erasing my smile. I've lost count how many times I've tried to tell her that Grandpa's baby brother is not the wide-eyed innocent she thinks he is. She's in complete denial that he and his childhood buddies—Rawlo, Tremaine, and Mishawn— are the infamous Jackal from decades past. Hell, I had a hard time believing it, too, when I found out years ago.

"Honestly, I don't know why I keep coming up here," Nana complains. "We have the same conversation every month. First it was your mother and now it's you. It's like you two were put on the earth to punish me for God only knows what. I know in my heart that I've tried to do my best by you two. I really did." She rocks in her seat as tears crest her eyes and then skip down her face.

Shame explodes within my chest. I've never wanted to hurt this petite woman of God, but so far, that's exactly what I've done.

"I'm going to fix this, Nana. I promise."

No longer able to look at me, Nana Gloria hangs up the phone and climbs to her feet. According to the clock on the wall, we still have another thirty minutes, but I can't bring myself to tap the Plexiglas to call her back.

She's had enough.

Sighing, I hang up the phone and watch her go. When she doesn't glance back, I feel like the biggest pile of shit in this whole damn prison.

"Bruh!" Kick! Kick! "Bruh!" Kick! Kick! ✔

RaShawn kicks the bottom of my thin mattress hard enough to jar me from the past. *Shit.* I shove my dick back into my undies and jump down from the bed. "What the fuck is your muthafuckin' problem, brothah?"

This oil-slick-looking-ass muthafucka blinks up at me all shocked and shit. ✔

"What? Bruh, what? Say something," I bark, heated.

RaShawn unfolds his short, tree-thump ass from the bottom bunk to flash me his fucked-up teeth. "You were talking and moaning in your sleep," he says.

"So?"

More blinking. "Well, it was keeping me up."

"So?"

"Look, bruh. There ain't no need to get swoll. I thought that you were doing a little too much up there. I know that you miss your girl and all," he says, gesturing to Johnnie's pic on the wall. "But I shouldn't be getting all hard, listening to you rub one out. That's all. Shit ain't right."

Looking at RaShawn's twisted-up face and rock-hard hard-on, I can't do nothing but laugh at this fresh-in-the-joint brothah.

"What?" He shifts around on his feet. "What's so funny?"

"You, bruh." I grab his pillow and throw it at his face. "You better loosen up around here before that stick up your ass get your ass fucked up—and I'm the muthafucka that's going to do it the next damn time you interrupt my private time with my lady, you feel me?"

"But—"

"Naw. Ain't no damn *buts* about it. Take what I'm telling you for the warning that it is—and I'll return the favor when you're hit with a severe case of blue balls and you're whacking li'l Shawie. We understand each other?"

Silence. But this got to be the most blinking-est muthafucka in the world. I turn my back to him to wash up at the small metal sink in the corner of the cell. But no matter how much cold water I throw on my face, it's not helping ease the ache for my princess, Johnnie. Hell, memories are all I got left of her.

"Sooo . . . you got a kid?" RaShawn asks out of the blue.   ·

I glance back to see him studying all of Tyler's crayon pictures. "What's it to you?"

"No—nothing. I—I got a kid myself," he fills in quickly. "I—you know. We're gonna be sharing the same cell for a while, I just thought . . ."

"What? You thought that we're going to be best friends or some shit?" I chuckle at his stupid ass.

More blinking. "Nah. Nah. I ain't saying that. You know, I'm . . . I thought we could, you know, look after one another."

I turn, straightening my full body so that he could get a good look at how I tower over him. Not only that, but I clearly have more muscle mass than his ass. "I don't need anyone looking out for me," I tell him. "I take care of myself."

RaShawn backs up. "Yeah. Yeah. That's what I heard."

"What you heard?" My curiosity piques as my eyes narrow on him. "You've been talking about me with other brothahs up in here?"

"No. No. Not me." His mouth moves so fast his tongue gets tangled. "I didn't mean to make it sound like that. I just heard out in the yard—"

"So there's a whole yard of you gossiping bitches?" The muscles on the side of my face twitch as I lift up my jaw.

Sensing an ass whooping ain't too far away, RaShawn pushes up his hands like two stop signs. "Whoa. Whoa. Okay. Maybe I misspoke again." He takes a deep breath. "All I heard was that you have some juice—as far as protection goes. That's all." He laughs to lighten the mood, but the shit sounds like a rusted muffler backfiring. "I mean, bruhs don't fuck with you for whatever reason—and I guess I wanted a little of that to rub off on me." He shrugs. "You can't blame a brother, right? I don't know anybody up in this joint. I'm trying to get in where I fit in, you feel me?"

I relax and laugh again in his face. "You really are a rookie at this, aren't you?"

He doesn't know how to take the question.

I wave him off. "Look, man. You're going to have to fight your own battles and find your own situation around here. That's the only way you're going to get and receive respect."

He nods, but I know that he's disappointed in my answer, but truth is often best served cold.

Life has been strange ever since my ass first strolled through these bars. I'm not too clear how the fuck I ended up here. The story my man Isaiah told didn't and still don't make much sense. The voice in the back of my head says to me that Isaiah struck some kind of deal, but the loyal part of me fights the accusation. I long for the opportunity to ask him face-to-face again, but the state tried us separately and, after a fallout, we're serving in separate prisons. Letter writing and phone calls are not an option. In the meantime, my imagination runs wild.

"So is it true?" RaShawn asks out of the blue.

"Is what true?"

RaShawn hems and haws. "You know. That you and your old partner are caked up on the outside."

These niggas really have been bumping their gums around this newbie. When I don't answer, this muthafucka takes it as a sign to keep interrogating.

"I heard that it's millions."

I cut him a sharp warning look, but he's too stupid to take it for what it is.

"Nah. I mean. It makes sense," RaShawn says. "You're not part of any gang or crew up in here, yet, at the same time, nobody sweats you, either. You gotta be paying for protection, right?"

"Stop talking."

"What? I'm just saying—"

In a flash, I'm across the cell, lifting and slamming this mouthy muthafucka against the concrete wall. "Shut your fucking mouth, you piece of shit. What the fuck is wrong with you?"

After shaking the stars from his eyes, RaShawn tries to twist out of my clutches. "Yo, bruh! What's the problem? We're just having a fucking conversation."

"Nah, nigga. A conversation requires two people. You're talking all over yourself, asking shit that ain't got shit to do with you." I cock my head and take a fresh look at this brother. "What are you, a cop? A snitch? What?"

"Whoa. Whoa." RaShawn's eyes bug out while he looks around the dark cell like a super-convict is coming to rescue his ass. "Lower your voice," he begs. "Are you trying to get me killed in this bitch?"

"Muthafucka, you're doing that shit on your own."

The top three most dangerous people to be in prison are: pedophiles, ex-cops, and snitches. Prison snitches have fucked up plenty of brothers in this bitch. They snoop out weak niggas in a confessing mood and then snitch every damn thing that was said in order to get their own long-ass sentences reduced.

"I ain't no snitch," he hisses, glaring.

I keep him pinned up until I'm satisfied that he's telling the truth. When I release him, I give him parting advice. "Shut your gossiping ass up and stay out of my business."

As I move to climb back into bed, RaShawn drops a bomb.

"Does that mean that you don't want to hear about your ex-partner getting early release?"

I whip around. "Say what?"

RaShawn's fucked-up grill flashes. "Probably not. Seeing how I'm just some gossiping prison yard nigga, huh?" He eases back into his bunk.

My heart starts skipping beats up inside my chest. "What the fuck are you talking about, Ra? Isaiah got ten years. Same as me."

"Apparently not." He shrugs and closes his eyes, pretending to go back to sleep.

I snatch him back out of the bed. "Don't fuck with me. How in the hell is his ass getting out?"

Ra gloats in my face. "Nobody knows, bruh. Some say for good behavior—some say that he struck a deal. Who knows? All I know is that he's been the one bragging about some money y'all got caked up."

I toss Ra down onto the floor while my mind races. *The money. He's going to go after my money.*

3

Harlem

My twenty-five million dollars are at stake.

On the prison yard, I take out my frustrations on the weights. I always think better when my heart rate is up. But my solitude is broken when a team of Gangster Disciples rolls up on me.

"Yo, nigga," Goon, their prison chief, calls out. "Whatchu benching now? Two hundred? Three hundred?" He places a foot on the bench above my head and leans over, smiling.

Trouble. I attempt to return the weight bar back on the stand, but his main enforcer, Crusher, grabs hold of the bar and forces it back down near my throat.

"Nah. Nah. You don't have to stop whatchu doin', man." Goon smiles. "I know how important it is for muthafuckas to stick with a regimen out here."

I grunt at the pressure applied to my larynx and fight like hell to get the bar back up. It's like a single fly pushing against an elephant. Crusher's muscles have muscles. The bar isn't going no damn where unless he wants it to.

Goon's smile spreads wider. "Listen here, money. We aren't going to fuck with you too long out here. We've had a good arrangement going for the past five years, right? The Gangster Disciples makes sure that your heart keeps pumping in exchange for a big slice of that bread you got waiting for you on the outside when you get out, right?"

More grunting. I can't breathe.

"Just nod your head if you agree," Goon says.

I nod.

"Good. Good. Because that's what I thought. But, uh, there's been some talk circulating around this joint that's got me a little concerned. Instead of me participating and speculating in prison bitches' idle gossip, I've always said that it's best to just go to the source, nawhatImean?"

Another grunt.

"Cool. Now word is that the nigga that you pulled most of those bank jobs and whatnots with is beating you out from behind these iron bars. You hear about that?"

When I don't respond, he signals to Crusher to let me steal a gulp of air. The bar is lifted a full second, allowing my lungs to fill to capacity—but then the pressure is reapplied to my neck.

"Was that a yes or a no?"

I nod.

"All right. So what I need to know from you is: how does this shit affect my money?"

The bar comes up two inches.

Gasping and coughing, I struggle to get a hold of myself.

"A'ight, money. I haven't got all muthafuckin' day," Goon says tightly.

"It's a problem," I tell him honestly. There's no point in my lying and saying shit is all good. Niggas 'round here know Isaiah and I had an epic fallout years ago that resulted in him being transferred to another prison. I blamed him and he came at me sideways, blaming my relationship with Johnnie as the reason for our asses getting pinched—which was ridiculous because no one knew about us. I may have overreacted and tried to break his face. The shit landed me in solitary for a couple of months and we never spoke again.

Goon sighs. "Damn, nigga. I wish your ass didn't say that shit. I kind of like your cool ass." He stands up as the bar descends. "Broke-ass muthafuckas always got to fuck shit up."

"A problem always has a solution," I spit out quickly.

The bar stops.

"I'm listening," Goon says.

"I just got to beat him to the money."

"Oh? Is that all?" He looks over at Crusher and they share a laugh. "Tell you what: why don't you tell me and my boy here where you stashed the money and I'll send some of my folks on the outside to go and pick it up for you?"

That shit is not happening. I glare up at him.

"No?" He shrugs. "Sounds like a fair offer to me. Seeing how you're in danger of reneging on a steep debt. After all, I am not running a fucking charity up in this bitch. Niggas pay their tabs— one way or another."

"Kill me and you'll never get your money." Our gazes lock and I can literally see the wheels turning through his eyes.

"How?"

The bar goes up.

"Like I said. I have to beat him to the money."

Our gazes crash for a long silent moment. "To make sure I understand what you're suggesting: you want help in organizing a jail break?"

"Yeah. I busted my ass into a lot of muthafuckin' places in my time. I'm sure that I can bust my way out of here."

We engage in another staring contest. "All right. Bet."

He signals to Crusher again and the bar finally returns to the rack.

I spring up like a jack-in-the-box, coughing and rubbing my neck. It takes everything I have not to start swinging on big homie, but that would be suicide given the power and reach on the brother.

Crusher shrugs, making it painfully clear that the shit wasn't personal. Just business.

"A'ight, money," Goon says, looking up since I have two inches on him. "What's your play?"

"Work detail," I spit out. "It's the most vulnerable time. There's only two guards with my crew when we go out on trash detail."

"Stage a rebellion and overpower the guards?" Goon fills in, looking and sounding bored and unimpressed.

"Yeah. Why not?"

"Then what? Kill the guards, steal their keys to unchain your-self and then run off into the sunset?"

I clamp my mouth shut because it sounds a little shaky when he says it.

"No car waiting, just a group of big-ass niggas in orange prison uniforms out for a jog, huh? Trust me. The US Marshals will have no problem scooping y'all up before the five o'clock news."

He's right. I have to figure out another way out of this place, but everything else takes time.

"You know what?" Goon says, reading my distress. "I *am* going to help you out."

"What?"

"But your tab just doubled," he adds seriously. "Two million. I'll get you the name of my partner on the outside that you need to deliver the money to. You got three days after you out of here or my folks are going to pay your daughter and your grandma a little visit."

I take a reflexive step forward at the unveiled threat to my family. Crusher meets my challenge with a step forward himself.

Goon laughs. "Keep your head, money. We're talking business. I need guarantees now. Your credit has just taken a huge hit. You understand that."

I do but I don't want to admit it. "I need more time."

Goon sighs.

"The money is not in New York."

"Damn, bruh. You're really testing my patience." When I don't respond, he admits another sigh. "How much more time?"

"Maybe seven days. And that's probably stretching it since I'll have to remain below the radar."

He twirls his toothpick. "All right. I'll do you one better. You got ten days. And don't think that you're going to sneak your people out of reach. I'll have my folks watching them like the mutha-fuckin' NSA starting five minutes from now. You got that?"

"Got it." Like OG cats, we shake on it. "So . . . what's the plan?"

4
Harlem

"LIGHTS OUT!" a guard shouts at exactly eleven o'clock. A second later, the concrete plantation's lights dim. However, the place still hums with activity.

RaShawn paces like a caged animal but I hardly have time to be concerned about him. I'm still in the dark about how Goon and his boys are going to bust me out of here. The clock is ticking. Isaiah is going to be released tomorrow, if the rumors are true.

Twenty minutes after lights out, I heave a frustrated breath and turn away from the iron bars. When I do, RaShawn surprises me with a mean right hook that snaps my head back.

What the fuck? I recover quickly and unleash a series of punches that fucks Ra all the way up.

Brothers from the other cages hoot and holler, egging on the fight. An alarm sounds and the lights come back up. By the time our cell number is called and our bars are opened, I've reduced Ra to a bloody pulp. I'm still swinging and trying to get at this nigga despite the guards prying us apart.

Next thing I know, they are beating me over the head and dragging me to solitary confinement. At the sight of me covered in Ra's blood and still fighting the guards, the cheers go up. I even get a standing ovation.

After I'm forced through several electronic doors, one of the guards hisses Goon's name. That shit cuts through my angry fog with a quickness. I'm not taken to solitary but toward the medical wing. When the guards can tell that they've gotten my attention, a series of instructions are whispered to me.

At the next door, I make a grab for one of the guard's batons and start whacking away. Making it look good, the second guard goes for his weapon, but I knock him out with a hard uppercut with the baton. Both dudes down, I snatch the set of keys from one of their hips and then race through the open door, hook a right like instructed and follow the short maze to a personnel door that leads to where most guards take their smoking breaks.

I push all fear of the dudes in the watchtowers and random search lights aside and make a mad dash to the farthest left side of the first fence. Once there, I feel around on the grass and find a pair of wire cutters, stolen from the workshop by a member of the Gangster Disciples. I get through the fence within minutes and then race toward the next fence. This one is barbed. My only option is to climb—quickly and carefully. Ten minutes later, my own blood is added to the mix on my torn prison uniform. My hands alone feel like Swiss cheese. A mile jog down the road, I spot a car. I made it. I'm fucking free.

5

Sam

"We have a runner," I announce to my team of five. After a long groan, everyone's heads swivel toward the big clock on the wall to read that it's edging toward midnight.

"I know. I know. You all want to go home. Trust me, I'd like nothing better to go home, get out this wired bra, and toss back a couple of brewskies, but we're the next team up."

"How can that be?" my left-hand man, Greg, asks. "We just captured Juan Murais and dragged his ass back to Jersey not three hours ago."

I can only shrug. "Look. The call just came in. The prison has completed their sweep and they are certain that one"—I look down at my notepad—"Harlem Richard Banks is missing."

"Why do I know that name?" Max asks, frowning.

"Because you know every damn body," I say, only half joking. The rest of the team laughs, nodding in agreement. "Quick notes," I continue, approaching the corkboard. "The talented Mr. Banks is a jack of all trades, apparently. Over the years, he has beeped on the FBI's radar at one time or another. The only case anyone has ever been able to make stick was an arms charge five years ago. Him and his partner, Isaiah Kane, were sentenced to ten years but clearly that was five years too long for Mr. Banks."

Everyone starts clicking and clacking on computers to pull up Banks's record.

"At the moment, he has about a two-hour head start. Renee, Nick, and Frank, I need for you guys to head over to the prison for their official report and conduct the interviews. Pull the visitors' logs while you're at it."

"We're on it, boss," Frank says, jumping up. Despite the smile on his face, I know that it's the rings around his eyes that reflect how he truly feels about us taking yet another case in the middle of the night.

"The rest of us," I say, "will get on whether our fugitive will make the usual mistakes by contacting family or friends."

"If this cat is half as slippery as you suggest, I think that it's a safe bet that he's in the wind. He's probably halfway to Mexico as we speak," Greg says.

I chuckle and grab my coffee cup that I left cooling on a desk earlier. "Oh ye of little faith." I take a sip and then spit it back out. "Ugh. It's cold."

"You know, just because you have a forty-six and oh record doesn't mean that you're invincible," Greg continues.

"How come I always get the sense that you're rooting for me to fail?"

Greg flashes me a loopy grin. "Nah. I'm waiting for you to prove that you're *human*."

"Awww. You say the nicest things." I snatch up my US Mar-

shals jacket. "I changed my mind. We're all going out to the site."
I toss him the car keys. "Let's go. You drive."

Sighing, Greg stands. "Yes, ma'am, Miss Daisy."

We arrive at the federal prison thirty minutes later. Sheriff Lee
Walton is the first to shake my hand and update me on the checkpoints his officers have up every fifteen miles and how his department are combing every road, backstreet and alley. But with
budget cuts being what they are . . .

"Good. Good job." I flash him a smile. However, I can tell that
he's too busy assessing my five-foot-two, one-hundred-pound
body and probably wondering how in the hell I'm an assistant
deputy chief with the US Marshals. But I've always believed, like
Bruce Lee, that might can be light.

The prison's warden is the next to shake my hand. A big robust
man, he's upset about how this jailbreak happened. When he gears
up to rant about all of his security measures and how something
like this has never happened, I cut him off. "I'm sure all your men
performed admirably," I assure him. "I'm only interested in cap-
turing the fugitive."

"Uh, yes, ma'am. I—I just finished talking to a few of your
guys. They're going over Banks's records here—but I have to tell
you, before tonight, the guy has stayed below the radar."

Greg and I share another look at our earlier phrasing.

"In five years, he has had just one write-up: a fight, between
him and another inmate. But that was years ago. He'd since settled
in and has been as quiet as a church mouse. Then tonight: *BAM!*
He unleashes holy hell on his cellmate. The man is trying to
breathe through a fucking tube as we speak. Something must've
happened to make him snap."

I nod. "The average foot speed for a healthy adult is four miles per hour. We're now rolling on approximately three hours behind. That's twelve miles."

"Unless he had a car waiting for him," the warden suggests.

"Clearly. In that case he can be as far as two or three states away." I cock my head at the helpful warden. "You have any reason to believe this was a planned jailbreak instead of a spontaneous opportunity that presented itself?"

"To be honest with you, ma'am, I don't know what to think."

"It looks like we're in for a long night." Greg sighs.

"Is there any other kind?" I ask before walking away. It's not that I'm unsympathetic to Greg. He can be cranky when he's tired. I, on the other hand, enjoy the adrenaline a fresh hunt gives me. A worthy prey can be mentally stimulating. I'm hoping that Harlem Banks is such a prey.

6

Harlem

"Baby, wake up."

My six-year-old baby, Tyler, peels open her eyes and then a smile spreads across her face. "Daddy? Is it really you?"

"Shh." I place a finger against my lips to let her know that she needs to keep her voice down so that we don't wake her grandmother. That's the last thing that I want. "Yes. It's really me," I tell her, unable to resist stroking her chubby cheeks. "How is my pretty girl feeling?"

"I'm good," she says bravely.

A knot lodges and tightens in my throat. She's so small and so perfect. It's not fair that her little heart doesn't work right.

"Are you going to stay forever?" Hope shines in her eyes.

For the first time in a long while, tears burn the backs of my eyes. "I wish that I could, baby girl."

"Ooh." Tyler's bottom lip stretches down and trembles.

"Daddy has to go and get some money so that you can have that surgery to fix your heart. You understand that, don't you?"

She sighs, probably from the thought of more surgery. "Well, after you get some money, *then* can you come live with me and Granny?"

I flash a smile. "We'll see." Those big brown eyes see right through me, but she smiles anyway. Leaning down, I brush another kiss against her forehead. As much as I love Johnnie and regret messing things up with her, Tyler is my heart. Always has been since the doctors placed her in my arms. No one ever told me how a baby girl could wrap you around her little finger. It's not too surprising that Tyler has developed heart problems. Her mother, Keisha, wasn't able to stay away from the glass pipe the entire nine months she carried Tyler. After Keisha delivered her, she went back to her crack until she was found dead in a Brooklyn back alley a few months ago.

I kiss her again and wish that I could've brought her *something*. Tyler throws her arms around my neck and kisses me back. "I love you, Daddy."

"I love you, too, baby girl." We squeeze each other tight. She still smells brand new with baby powder clinging to her skin. "All right now. You gotta go back to sleep."

"Aww. Do I have to? You just got here," she asks, yawning and rubbing her eyes.

"Yeah. I'm sorry, baby. But you'll see me again."

"When?" After another yawn, her eyes droop low.

"Soon," I lie, but I hope I'm telling the truth, if that makes a difference.

"Okay."

"Good night, baby." One last kiss and I stand up from the bed and creep out of the bedroom. The second I close the door, the light in the living room clicks on.

Standing on the other side of the room with a twelve-gauge shotgun is Nana Gloria, but at least the damn thing isn't pointed at my head.

"What are you doing here?" she asks warily. *"How* are you here?"

"I needed a place to shower and clean up. Plus to pick up this." I gesture to my bag that holds about everything I'm going to need for my coming road trip. "As for the how, maybe the less you know, the better."

She sighs just like Tyler while her entire body droops. "Harlem, baby. What are you doing? They're going to catch you and then you'll never get out of that damn prison."

"I gotta get you that money, Nana."

Some of the disappointment erases, but she remains cautious. "How? You said that people were watching."

"They are, but I'm hoping I'm a little quicker than they are." We search each other's gazes. I can tell that she *wants* to believe me. "I am going to get you that money."

Her eyes wet up while an internal conflict rages on inside of her. "We really could use that money," she says.

"I know."

After another beat, she gives a nod. A good sign that she's not going to turn me in herself. It's fucked up, but she's done it before. I was nine and had stolen some candy from the corner store. When she came into my room without knocking, she caught me and Isaiah overdosing on Red Hots and Milk Duds. To our shock, she called the police. The boys in blue came and slapped on the handcuffs and then drove us downtown.

I was scared as shit, but both Isaiah and I were determined not to show it.

The store's owner, being a member of Nana's church, didn't press charges, so our punishment ended up being a few long lectures from the police, the store owner, Nana's pastor and, worst of all, Nana Gloria.

But none of that shit deterred us from a life of crime—to Nana's great disappointment.

"Have you eaten?" she asks.

"Yeah." The silence grows awkward. "I gotta go."

She nods. Her eyes wet.

Despite the mean looking gun, I cross the room and sweep her into a big embrace.

She melts in my arms. "Oh, Harlem. Please be careful."

"I will." I hold her tighter. Despite her feeling like home, I release her and head out the door.

7

Johnnie

The wedding rehearsal is running waaay late. I'm starting to worry about my not being thrilled about the big day tomorrow. The rest of the wedding party clearly is, especially my parents and my fiancé, Reese Singleton. However, I keep smiling and nodding, but so far, no dice. My best friend, Janine, is catching on. More than once she's pulled me aside to ask whether everything is all right. Each time I've wanted to tell her that I couldn't breathe, or maybe someone should rush me to the emergency room, but I don't dare.

Instead, I plaster on a stupid smile and watch my family and friends make one toast after the other. Each of them trills on about how much Reese, the city's rising political star, and I make the perfect couple. We're attractive, driven, and successful in our own rights. Surely we're going to be the next Barack and Michelle.

So why don't I feel it—or believe it?

On paper, every box is checked. Most women in New York would slit my throat to be able to walk down the aisle toward Reese. Me? I'm still thinking about a damn criminal locked down in a federal penitentiary. He's a sexy criminal, but a criminal all the same.

I shouldn't have pulled those strings for that conjugal visit last month. Now he's in my system again. After I'd worked so hard to get him out. I'm lucky that all I got was a broken heart when the truth came out about him. If I had married him, or gone public, it would have entangled my parents' good name and it would have been a disaster of epic proportions. It's important that I keep reminding myself of that, but throughout the course of this long-ass dinner, I can't stop thinking about how Harlem's hands felt all over my body last month. How wonderful his mouth felt delving into my pussy. The memory is so strong that I close my eyes and do a small roll of my hips as if I was sitting there naked in his lap at this very moment.

Reese leans over to ask, "Tired, babe?"

Startled, I snatch my eyes open and then flutter a guilty smile his way. "Nah. I'm good."

"Great." He plants a sloppy kiss on the side of my face, close to my damn eyeball. *He's drunk—again.*

"Another toast," my father, Governor Charles Robinson, shouts, lifting his glass again. He's just as drunk as Reese. I can't tell whether my mother is equally annoyed or just grinning and bearing it like I am.

I'm ready to go. After all, it's well past one in the morning. Thank God the wedding isn't until tomorrow afternoon. Judging by the faces surrounding me, there are going to be quite a few people nursing hangovers in a few hours.

Dad's toast turns into a rambling mess, but Reese saves him by standing and thanking him nonetheless.

"It's going to be a pleasure to call you son," Dad says, swinging his arms around Reese's neck.

"And I'm going to be thrilled to call you dad."

I halfway expect them to start making out the way they're carrying on. *Maybe he should be the one to marry Reese tomorrow.*

"You're frowning again," Janine whispers. "Are you sure that you're all right?"

I don't have it in me to lie again. "Maybe I *am* a little tired."

She looks over at Reese and sees that he and my dad are still chuckling it up. "Did you drive?" Janine asks me.

"No. I rode here with Reese."

"Well, if you want, I can take you home," she suggests. "A bride *must* get her beauty sleep."

Bride. My heart drops like a stone.

"Yeah. Let's get you home. You don't look too good."

I grab my purse and make my excuses as we try to make our way out of the restaurant.

Reese puts in a weak attempt to say that he can take me home, but then thanks Janine for offering to do it herself. "Guess that means that the next time I see you it'll be in front of the preacher," he jokes.

"Guess so." My smile cracks.

"Our last night as two hot single people." A thought occurs to him. "Hey, maybe I should drive you home?" When he wiggles his groomed brows at me, I'm nauseous.

"No. None of that until *after* the ceremony and I'm Mrs. Reese Michael Singleton." I glue on another smile.

"Can't blame a brother for trying." He winks.

Was he always this cheesy? "Enjoy your last night of freedom," I tell him and brush a chaste kiss against his cheek. I don't realize how much I needed fresh air until we're outside waiting for the valet.

But once I'm tucked into Janine's black Mercedes, she goes on and on about how excited I must be and how lucky I am, but also carries on about the black woman's burden: finding a good man.

Oh God. I don't think that I can do this.

The forty-minute drive to my house in Greenwich, Connecticut, *feels* like forever, mainly because Janine never stops talking.

"Thanks for the ride." I unbuckle my seatbelt and open the car door almost at the same time.

"Want me to come in? We can have our last girls' pajama party before you're a married woman."

"No, girl. I really do need to hit the sack. It's been a long day."

"I feel ya. See you tomorrow."

After exchanging cheek-kisses, I climb out of the car and rush to my front door in front of the bright spotlight from her car's high beams. Once I get the door unlocked, I wave back to her and enter the house.

Inside, I collapse back against the door and again wonder what in the hell I got myself into. "It's just wedding jitters," I whisper into the dark.

A deep voice rings out from the darkness. "Or you're about to marry the wrong dude."

"What? Who's there?" I demand, panicked.

A light clicks on and my breath seizes in my chest. "Hello, Johnnie."

I'm seeing things. I have to be. There's no way Harlem Banks is sitting in my living room, fresh shaven and looking fine as hell in all black.

Then he stands and swallows up the entire space of the room. At least it seems that way. "I know that I shouldn't be here, but I had to see you again."

"They released you?" I ask, stunned that I'm able to get the words out.

A slick smile slides across his face. "Not exactly."

Alarm bells sound off in my head. "You escaped?"

Harlem doesn't have to respond, the answer is written all over his face.

I race to the house phone on the other side of the room. Harlem has no problems blocking me off in a few strides.

"Ahh. Ahh. Ahh. I can't let you do that."

I open my purse, but before I can dig out my cell phone, Harlem snatches the whole thing from my arm. "Give me that back!"

"Sorry, but I can't do that either." He rummages through it, takes out my phone and then removes the battery.

"Hey!"

"I'm sure that you understand. Precaution."

The smirk on his face gets under my skin. "Fine. What in the hell do you want?"

His grin softens as he stares at me. "The same thing that you wanted." He caresses the side of my face. "To say a proper good-bye."

Instead of flinching or moving away, my knees buckle at the feel of his touch. That's all the permission he needs to swoop down and steal a soul-stirring kiss.

The next thing I know my clothes disappear and I'm being pressed down into my big bed. Harlem's head dips low as he fills his mouth with one of my full breasts. As he sucks and gently scrapes his teeth against the sensitive flesh, I shiver. With trembling hands I caress and then push his head even lower.

I don't care that I can hardly breathe. I need this man inside of me as fast as possible. However, Harlem makes it clear that he's in no hurry. The idea of him taking his time to take and savor every inch of me is enough to give me my first orgasm. I hold my breath as he plants kisses down the center of my body. By the time he reaches my thighs, I'm lightheaded and have to force myself to suck in oxygen.

The way the moonlight peeks through the window, it highlights the V of black curls between my legs. "You're so fucking beautiful," he gasps. With a groan, he drops his head and plunges his tongue deep inside of me.

I cry out toward the ceiling while fisting the silk sheets. Around and around his tongue twirls, lapping me up. Lifting my legs, I hook them over his shoulders. But I can't keep them still. They keep fluttering on the side of his head like a butterfly. When that unmistakable pressure builds, my toes curl and my back arches.

There's no time to announce that I'm about to come, the big O hits fast and hard. Again, I'm breathless. Without missing a beat, Harlem springs up onto his knees and then spreads my legs even wider. He enters with one smooth stroke and fills me up completely. The rest of the session is like an out-of-body experience. He wrangles emotions out of me that I've long suppressed. At the same time, I can't get enough of him: tasting him, fucking him—loving him. Some time during the night, the sweetness of our bodies slapping together causes tears to roll down my cheeks. Seconds after my fifth orgasm of the night, I drift off to sleep—well satisfied.

8

Johnnie

Four a.m.

I wake aware that there's a smile on my face—but when the reality as to why seeps into my brain, the smile fades and my eyes snap open. *What in the hell did I just do?*

It's officially my damn wedding day—but damn, the dick was good.

Smiling again, I stretch out, arching my back almost as far as it will go and purring like a cat. However, when my hand reaches across the bed to an empty space, I jump up.

Harlem is gone.

A car door shuts outside of my bedroom window and I pop out the bed like a toasted Pop-Tart. Panic as well as suspicion has me snatching up panties and a bra as I race over to the window. Sure enough, Harlem is behind the wheel of my Audi and starting it up.

"No. No. No." Panties on, I jump into the pair of sweatpants I left hanging on the arm of the treadmill. I have the matching sweatshirt on by the time I'm in the living room and hobbling into a pair of sneakers, kept by the front door as I race out of it. "Come back here, you two-bit thief!"

Harlem is creeping back out of the driveway until he spots me racing toward him. Then he jams onto the accelerator, swinging wide into the yard to try and turn around. But that move gives me time to stretch my high school track star legs as far as they can go so that I reach the passenger-side door. He's turning when I hop inside and pummel him on his head.

"You asshole!" *Whack! Whack!* "How fucking dare you steal my car!" *Whack! Whack!*

Still driving, Harlem ducks and blocks my blows. For a while, anyway, the second one of my punches drives across his jaw, and I'm shoved back so hard that I nearly tumble out of the car backward, since the door is still open.

At my horrified scream, Harlem grabs the front of my sweatshirt and finally slams on the brakes to save me. It takes a few seconds for the shock to fade and the dust to settle. After that, I launch at him again.

"Son of a bitch!" *Whack! Whack!*

"All right. Enough, Johnnie. Calm down," he barks.

"Calm down?" I bellow. "How in the fuck do you expect me to calm down? You're stealing my car!"

He shrugs like it's a mild inconvenience. "I'm sorry about that. I really am—but if all goes well, you'll get it back."

"If it all goes well? Have you lost your fucking mind? You're not going anywhere with my car. Get out!"

Another shrug. "Sorry, but I am. Now you can either get out or I'm going to have to drag you out."

I do a double take. "I like your nerve." I cross my arms and glare up at him. "I'm not going any damn where." When he makes a move toward me, I grab and strap in with the seatbelt. We fight as he tries to unlock it.

His patience clearly thin, he snaps, "Fuck it! Then you can just come with me." He slams on the accelerator. This time the passenger-side door slams shut from the force.

A new panic surges through me. "What the fuck do you think that you're doing?"

"Exactly what you think I'm doing. I'm *borrowing* your car while I run from the law. I'm sure that you understand."

"No. You can't do that and no, I don't understand any of this." My barking goes in one ear and out the other because he peels off into the night like a bat out of hell. I have to say or do something, but what? I'm in a fucking car with an escaped convict. "I'm being kidnapped," I say as I realize.

"What?" Harlem spears me with a look.

"You're kidnapping me," I repeat.

"How the fuck do you figure that? You're the one that refused to get out of the car."

"Again, *my* car!"

"So what? You can afford another one," he charges back.

"How in the hell do you know what the fuck I can afford? You're not my accountant."

"The fact that you even have an accountant tells me all that I need to know."

"Humph! Tells what you know. A lot of *tax-paying* people have accountants. It doesn't mean anything."

"All right then. *Can* you afford another car?" he asks sharply.

I chew on whether I should lie, but what's the point in that? "Whether or not I can or can't is beside the point."

He laughs and rolls his eyes. "That's what I thought."

"Again. Not the point."

"I'm sorry. I forgot. What *is* the point?"

"That you're a fucking kidnapper!"

Harlem's face twists at me sounding like a screaming lunatic, but remains unmoved by my argument. "Well, under the circumstances, what's one more federal charge?"

You could tell him to stop so you can get out of the car. Then you can go back home and proceed to marry Reese Singleton. My heart drops. *Mrs. Reese Michael Singleton.*

This is the part where I take leave of my senses and shut the hell up.

9

Sam

Six a.m.

BOOM!

I jump straight up from my desk to see the district deputy chief, Karl Bell, grinning down at me. "What can I do for you, boss?" I rotate and massage the crick out of my neck.

He shakes his head. "Don't you sleep at your place anymore?"

"What are you talking about? This *is* my place," I joke. While he throws back his well-rested head and laughs, I steal a look up at the clock. Twenty minutes of sleep isn't so bad.

"I heard that you had another slippery one last night. We got any leads?"

"Nothing popped up on the ground sweep or the checkpoints. So I doubt he got away on foot."

"A planned escape then? Not a golden opportunity thing?"

"Has to be. The fence was cut with wire cutters taken from the workshop, but the strange thing is that Harlem's work detail doesn't have him working in the workshop. He's assigned to trash detail."

"So he had help?"

"Yep. But finding out *who* helped him is going to be like searching for a needle in a haystack."

"It always is. We'll leave that investigation up to the warden." He gestures down at the files I'd been drooling on. "So what do we know about this fugitive? Anything interesting? I have a nine o'clock press conference with the sheriff's department. Do I need to tell the public to panic or not?"

"Not with my team on the case," I brag.

The chief takes it for the joke that it's meant to be. "Believe me, I'm not worried. You always get your man."

"Damn right, sir." I climb to my feet just as Greg, Nick, and Frank rush into the office. "Combed through the visitor's logs. Seems the only person that ever visited Mr. Banks is his grandmother, Gloria Banks. We have her address if you're ready to ride out," Greg says. His eye bags are starting to look like luggage.

"Sure. Just give me a second to make a run to the ladies' room." I turn my attention back to the boss man. "I'll keep you abreast to anything we find."

"I'm sure you will." He winks. "Go get him." With that he turns and walks out of my office.

I follow close behind, but when I near the bathroom, I remind my team, "Give me one minute."

"You got it, chief."

I rush inside and make a beeline to the first stall. I smack myself awake while I empty about five hours of stale coffee. At the sink, I wash my hands, use the hand soap to hit under my arms, and even splash some water onto my face. The hair—well. The best I can do is slick down the baby hairs around the edges of my ponytail and let it ride. I *have* to keep this week's hair appointment or do the big chop to join the natural movement. Aware that I took two minutes instead of one, I apologize when I exit.

Traffic is a bitch, but we make it to Gloria Banks's residence within an hour. Frank pounds on the door like his fist is a battering ram. Despite that, Gloria Banks takes her sweet time answering it.

"Can I help you?" She asks calmly as if the US Marshals being at the door was a normal occurrence.

"Gloria Banks?" I ask, meeting her gaze as we both stand at the same height.

"Yes."

"Hello, ma'am. I'm assistant deputy chief Samantha Reynolds with the US Marshals. May we come in and speak with you about your grandson, Harlem Banks?"

The question hangs in the air between us as she takes my measure. I can read that she wants to slam this door in my face.

"What about him?" she asks, not budging from the door.

I cut a quick look to Greg and his expression mirrors the annoyance that I'm feeling.

"Ma'am, at approximately ten-thirty last night, your grandson escaped from a federal prison." I wait for a response or a reaction. There isn't one. "Did you already know that?"

"Why would I know that?"

Answering a question with another question sets off another set of bells inside my head. "Ma'am, you need to know that if you're in any way aiding or abetting your grandson that you can and will be subjected to federal charges yourself."

"Nana?" a soft voice floats from behind the older woman.

"Tyler, go back and finish eating your cereal," she calls back. When Gloria returns her attention to us, she remains planted in front of the door.

"I can have a warrant here before your great-granddaughter finishes that bowl of cereal—and I won't be in such an amenable mood," I warn her.

Gloria's gaze scatters away from mine as she finally steps back and invites us inside. "C'mon in."

"Thank you." I step across the threshold first and take a wide sweeping gaze around the immaculate brownstone. "Nice place you have here, ma'am." I can't help but pick up the strong scent of bleach. *She's been cleaning.*

The rest of my team enters, nodding and looking around. But my gaze zooms to the adorable little girl, sitting at the breakfast table. Her big brown eyes give her a baby-doll appearance. I wave, but her small body shrinks as if terrified by the looks of us.

"Okay. You're inside. Now what?" Gloria asks, stepping into my line of vision of her great-granddaughter.

"Have you been in contact with Harlem?" I ask pointedly.

There's a beat of hesitation before she says, "No."

"I have to tell you that wasn't very convincing," I say. "Do I need to remind you of the consequences in hindering his capture?"

"He's not here," she snaps.

"Then you won't mind if we take a look around?" Greg asks.

She hesitates again.

"Now or an hour from now," I tell her. "The search *will* happen."

"Then why bother asking?" she sasses.

My team all share looks before we answer at the same time, "Good manners."

Ms. Banks isn't amused by our sense of humor, but this isn't about us making friends. The team splits up to conduct a thorough sweep of the place.

Gloria, with her jaw clenched, glares at us while we invade her home. Fortunately, it doesn't take long for us to comb through the spotless house. However, I'm surprised to find a twelve-gauge shotgun in a gun cabinet. She doesn't strike me as the type.

"Satisfied?" she asks.

"Ma'am, we're not the enemy. Your grandson is a convicted criminal. He's just making it worse for himself the longer he stays out."

"Are you trying to put my daddy back in jail?"

"Tyler," Gloria snaps. "What did I tell you about talking when grown folks are talking?"

Back?

"Yes, ma'am." She hangs her head and then shovels in another mouthful of Cheerios into her mouth.

I shake my head at Gloria. She must know that she's been caught in a lie. I walk over to the dining room table and pull out a chair next to Tyler.

"Hey. I'm Samantha. Your name is Tyler, right?"

The girl's eyes grow larger instead of answering.

I suck in a deep breath and pray for patience. "Tyler, I need to ask you a very important question and I need you to be honest with me, okay? It's very important. You understand?"

She blinks her long lashes at me and then cuts a look at her great-grandmother.

"I need you to look at me, sweetie," I coach. "You understand?" I ask again.

"Yes, ma'am," she says shakily.

"Did your father come and see you last night—or this morning?"

A long, pregnant pause follows my question. I find myself holding my breath waiting for her answer.

Finally, she shakes her head.

I exhale with disappointment. "Are you telling me the truth?"

"She answered your question," Gloria says. "Now will you people please leave? Harlem hasn't been here and we don't know where he is."

When Tyler's large eyes fill with tears, I back off and thank the little girl for lying to my face. I stand and signal to the team to head out.

A grateful Gloria follows us to the door, but before I step out, I turn toward her a final time. *"If* Harlem contacts you," I begin, reaching into my jacket and retrieving my card, "make sure that you give us a call."

With her jaw stiff with anger, Gloria takes the card, but makes no such promise.

"You're not helping him, you know? We *will* catch him."

"Then I'll let you get to it."

Sighing, I walk out of the door. I hate when people try to make my job harder.

"Get me a warrant for a wiretap and put some eyes on these two in case Banks comes back."

"You got it, boss."

10
Harlem

"What the hell is this?" I ask, spotting the long snake of traffic up ahead.

Johnnie sits up in her seat with a sudden smirk. "Could be a police checkpoint."

That's exactly what I'm thinking. Paranoia seizes me in its grip. I check around to see how to get off this road, but it looks like it may be too late. The cars packed in tight behind one another. I could pull off the road, but then what?

Heat infuses my body. The only thing I can do that won't draw attention to the vehicle—or myself—is to go straight through.

"Why don't you just turn yourself in?" Johnnie asks. "You can't truly believe that you're going to get to where it is that you trying to go. You gotta know that, right?"

"Then you have nothing to worry about," I tell her, reaching into the backseat for the bag I'd tossed back there. "If you're lucky, they'll have me in handcuffs in time for your wedding."

She clams up and I remember what she'd said when she came home last night. "That is, *if* you still want to marry ol' boy."

"Shut up. Of course I want to marry Reese. I . . . love him."

Johnnie is so obviously lying that I laugh in her face. "You'll never get an Oscar with a performance like that."

"Fuck you."

"You already did that—and quite well, too, if I may add. Doesn't look to me that I'm out of your system yet. But then, I'm biased." I remove one of the IDs and a .45mm handgun from the bag.

"What in the hell is that?" Johnnie thunders like she's never seen a real gun before.

"Calm the fuck down," I tell her. "This is just a little insurance."

"Your idea of an insurance plan is to shoot your way out?" she screams. "You're going to get us killed."

I look around to make sure no one in the other cars is watching her lose her mind.

"I'm getting out of here," she announces as if she's finished playing Bonnie and Clyde for the day and she's ready to go back to her bougie life.

I hit the childproof lock button and lock her inside. "Sorry, princess. It doesn't work like that. You wanted to be a part of this joyride; now deal with the consequences."

"Oh yeah? And what are you going to do when I yell to the cops that you're a wanted fugitive?"

Regretfully, I unclick the safety.

Johnnie's eyes double in size. "You wouldn't dare."

"Sorry, but desperate times call for desperate measures."

Her expression registers her sense of betrayal.

"Oh, don't look like that. It's not like dropping by a prison to fuck my brains out and then telling me that you're marrying another dude type of fucked up."

"Threatening to *kill* me registers *lower* on the betrayal scale? Are you shitting me?"

"Don't be dramatic," I say as we creep forward. Judging her face, I don't know how serious she's taking my threat—but it's im-

portant that she believes me. "If you do anything to blow this, the
first bullet is yours." When she reads me this time, fear ripples in
her eyes.

Closer and closer we approach the blue and white lights. I lower
the gun to my left side, but keep my hand near the trigger for a
quick draw. However, it's not a checkpoint, but a five-car pile up.
The long traffic jam is due to the three lanes being reduced to one
and nosy muthafuckas, like myself, rubbernecking to see what's
going on. The young, pimply police officer in the middle of the
road windmills his arms, telling us to go through without sparing
me a second look.

Once we get past the wreckage, the road expands back out to
three lanes and we're back to coasting at the speed limit in no time.

My fears and paranoia ease and I click the safety back on the
gun. "Well. That turned out better than expected." I glance over at
Johnnie—and she's crying. Not blubbering uncontrollably, but
more of a silent cry with her chin jacked up, her bottom lip quivering and one or two tears rolling down her face. Not good.

Now what do I do? Apologize? Then what will happen if and
when we *do* come across a real checkpoint? I can't bluff twice.

"I hate you," she says, breaking the silence. "I hate the day that
I ever laid eyes on you."

I figure the best thing for me to do is to be quiet while she stays
all up in her feelings for a few minutes—or hours.

"Was there anything about us real?"

I keep my mouth shut.

"Well? I'm asking you a question, Mr. Big Time Criminal.
Clearly, you never told me the truth about anything. Your name.
What you did for a living. Your daughter. And certainly not that
you're capable of *murder*."

When the tears skip down her face again, I go back to feeling
like a pile of shit. So far, nothing has changed on this trip.

11

Sam

"This is interesting," Greg says from the passenger seat of our SUV.

"Hit me."

"It says here that Isaiah Kane is scheduled for early release today."

"What? I thought both him and Harlem were sentenced a mandatory ten years?" I know that I'm tired, but I'm sure that I read that correctly.

Greg spins the laptop toward me so I can read for myself.

"What the hell is that all about?" I ask, surprised.

"Don't know, but it can't be a coincidence," he says.

I shake my head. "You know that I don't believe in coincidence." I hit my lights and then hang an illegal U-turn. "Call down to the justice department's office and see if you can find out what they know about this and whether Mr. Kane has already been released."

"It's just nine a.m. I doubt that he's been processed yet," Greg says confidently. Ten minutes later, we find out that's not true. Seems the people over at the prison are on the ball in releasing Mr. Kane. But luckily he's being released to serve the first six months at a halfway house less than fifteen minutes from where we are. I make it over there in half that. It's perfect timing because the new tenants at the halfway house have just arrived from the prison.

It isn't hard to pick out Isaiah Kane. He still looks exactly like his last mug shot. An even six-foot with dark maple complexion, he has a solid build. He's handsome, but not in a pretty-boy way.

I march straight up to him. "Isaiah Kane?"

His thick eyebrows do a head collision over his confused dark eyes. "Yeah?"

I launch my introduction again, this time including Greg, before asking, "We need to ask you a few questions about your former childhood friend and partner-in-crime, Harlem Banks."

"Well, let me stop you right there," he says. "You're wasting your time. Harlem and I don't fuck with each other anymore."

"Yeah. Separate prisons tends to fuck up friendships," I say sarcastically.

"Whatever. I haven't heard or talked to him in years."

"So you have no idea why he busted out of prison last night?" I ask.

"What?" His entire body language changes. He's more aggressive. "What do you mean?"

"Exactly what I said. The way we see it, it can't be coincidence that he bails the night before you're scheduled for early release. The two have to be connected."

Isaiah pulls his anger back in check. "I don't know what you're talking about. Like I told you. I haven't talked to him in years. I'm sure that y'all can verify that."

"That's being done as we speak. But maybe you can solve a riddle for us: how is that you've secured a five-year early release on a mandatory ten-year sentence?"

He shrugs his thick shoulders. "I've never been the type of guy to look a gift horse in the mouth," he says.

"Oookay. But you used to know Harlem pretty well. Have any idea where he would go? Any special people that he would try to see?"

He shakes his head—there was a slight beat of hesitation.

"Anything would help—and will be much appreciated."

"I couldn't possibly tell you where that nigga's head is at. As far as whom he might visit: check in with his grandmother. Those two were as thick as cornbread the last time I checked. Plus, I'd imagine that she's still raising his daughter."

I nod. "We already paid her a visit."

"And?"

"Still in review. Anyone else?"

"I got nothing."

Greg jumps in. "Are you sure that he won't try and come and see you?"

"Me?" His laugh sounds like a misfired tailpipe.

I follow Greg's line of questioning. "Maybe you two have an old beef that he intends on settling? Maybe we should get you a few agents out here to make sure that he doesn't come for you."

Isaiah's fake amusement fades. "Nah. That's totally not necessary. I don't need any more babysitters than I already got around here."

We hit on something. I stare him down while I try to figure shit out.

When he grins at me, I have a sudden urge for a real shower. "There's something strange about this whole thing," I say, studying him. But he's comfortable behind a straight poker face. "But you know what? My team and I are pretty smart people. We're going to figure out what's going on. And the first thing on my list is finding out how this whole release thing happened. If *all* the details don't check out, trust and believe, you'll be hauled right back to your tiny jail cell where you belong."

Poker face.

"Check you later, slick." I turn and storm away—but when I reach the door, Isaiah calls out.

"There is this one chick homie used to fuck with."

I turn around with my interest piqued. "Yeah?"

"He was crazy about her—even proposed, I think," Isaiah goes on.

"And who's that?"

He shrugs. "I only met her once—and at a club, at that, but I know her name was Johnnie."

I whip out my steno pad to jot down the information. "Does Johnnie have a last name?"

"I'm sure that she does—but I don't remember it. Harlem would never bring her around me. But I believe she is some kind of lawyer and her people are supposedly important."

"Well," Greg quips. "That should narrow it down."

Isaiah looks affronted. "You said that the help would be appreciated."

I sigh and put my pad away. "It is. Thanks."

"Any time."

I head back out the door.

Greg marches behind me. "What are you thinking?"

"I'm thinking that this shit stinks to high heaven."

"Good. So do I."

"Get us two more agents down here to sit on Isaiah, too. He looked pretty freaked out when I suggested it."

"Yeah. I caught that, too," Greg says. "What do you think about this Johnnie? Think he's just trying to throw us off or throw us a bone?"

"Leave no stone unturned," I say. "Let's comb everything we got again and see if we can find a chick named Johnnie."

12

Johnnie

What the fuck have I done? The question loops over and over in my mind until I'm fucking dizzy. The only answer is: temporary insanity. I never believed in such a term until today. It always seemed more like an excuse of convenience than anything based in reality. People do things in a fit of anger or passion and then are crushed with guilt or regret. They don't want to take responsibility for their actions so they plead *temporary insanity.* Shit. Maybe that's exactly what's happening now.

I perform a silent face-palm and then mentally berate my poor decision-making.

This asshole actually threatened me with a gun. That tells me everything that I need to know about this man. I've been trying to get over Harlem for five years and I'm no more than what? A good fuck that he can plant a bullet into once he's done with me?

I hopped into the car with him instead of walking down the aisle with Reese Singleton? Reese may be a bit of a bore, but he checks a lot of boxes for what women *should* want. He's handsome, successful with a great future ahead of him. As far as sex, he can't hit a G-spot with a baseball bat. And there's the potential of him having an alcohol problem, but my mother is right. There's enough of a foundation to carve out a decent and good life.

Harlem, on the other hand, is a dead end. Literally. He's not only criminal, but also an escaped fugitive no doubt with the US Marshals on his ass. *And I jumped in the car with him.*

Temporary insanity.

I peek at him between my fingers and still feel . . . *something.* Just like I did when the judge handed down his sentence and the prison guards hauled him off, while I sat in the back of the courtroom. The same *something* that I've been trying to cut, bury, and ignore for five years. *It's not love. It's not love.* I shake my head because the lie is still not working.

"How long are you going to sit over there and mope?" Harlem asks, breaking our two-hour silence.

I lift my head, but turn my gaze out the passenger-side window instead of answering him.

"Really?" he asks. "The silent treatment?"

Silence.

Harlem sighs. "Look . . . I know that it was fucked up what I did back there, but you gotta see this shit from my side for a minute. I couldn't risk you turning me in back there. At least, not yet. There's something I . . . I got to take care of first and then . . . you know. Whatever."

"Take care of?" I wince at breaking my silence, but then throw up my hand as a brick wall. "No. Don't answer that. I don't want to know and I don't care. You need to pull over somewhere and let me out."

"Can't do that," he tells me again. "You had your chance to bail. If I let you out now, you'll call the cops and I can't afford that. The only thing that's working in my favor is that only one other person even knows where I'm headed."

"What the fuck are you talking about? I don't know where the hell you're going. You wouldn't tell me, remember?"

"Not you." He shakes his head. "Never mind."

I roll my eyes and we fall back into an awkward and strained silence. I glance over at the car's clock. It's nearing noon. I should be at the hotel, sipping on champagne and getting my hair and makeup done with my bridesmaids. Strangely, the thought still causes my stomach to knot. That makes it official, there's something wrong with me.

"I wouldn't have shot you," Harlem finally growls out like it's killing him to admit it.

I want to be indifferent to the confession, but the relief is so overwhelming that I'm barely able to blink back a rush of tears. I do knuckle away the few teardrops that managed to leak.

Harlem must've seen because he adds, "I'm sorry."

"It doesn't matter," I lie.

The dashboard dings and a red light alerts us that we're running low on gasoline.

"Shit," Harlem mumbles, looking around. He's in luck because there's a gas station up ahead.

We coast into the station on fumes. The car shuts off the second Harlem pulls up to an available pump. But he doesn't immediately hop out of the car. Instead, he squares in the driver's seat to stare at me. "Look. I know that you hate me right now. I get that. I can only hope that you can accept my apology for what it is. I know I should have never involved you in this in the first place. But I *had* to see you again because . . . I haven't been able to forget you. I don't know anything about this other man that you're supposed to be marrying, but I know that he hasn't been loving you right. Can't be. Or you would've never arranged that conjugal visit. I don't give a damn what you say. I'm in your system just as badly as you're in mine."

My gaze creeps over to his. And when I look into those deep dark eyes, my entire body responds. I suddenly want his mouth on mine and his hands on my body.

He reaches over and takes my hand. For a few seconds I enjoy the warmth rushing up my arm, but then I feel something hard and plastic being wrapped around them.

"What the—?"

"I'm going to have to apologize again," he says. "But now that you know that I won't shoot you, I can't trust that you'll remain seated in your chair like a good girl."

"What?" I jerk my hands back, but the plastic cuffs cut hard against my wrists. "You can't do this."

"Sorry," he says again. "But I can and I will."

"HELP! HELP!" I shout as he wraps the plastic cuff around the steering wheel.

Harlem sighs. We both know that the car's soundproof windows buffer my screams. Not that it would matter: I don't see anyone else walking around. But clearly he thinks he needs extra insurance and produces a roll of duct tape.

"What the fuck? You got the damn kitchen sink in that bag?"

"Be prepared is my motto," he says before slapping that shit across my mouth.

I try to wrestle my face away, but the shit is useless.

Proud of his handiwork, Harlem smiles and delivers a quick kiss against my forehead. "I'll be back," he says in his best Terminator voice and then pops out of the car to fill up the tank.

Humiliation doesn't describe what I'm going through. But I will get him back for this shit—even if it's the last thing I do.

13

Isaiah

I must get to that money. It's the only damn thing that I can think about since that nosy, bitch-ass deputy chief rolled up in here. I don't know how in the fuck Harlem pulled a damn jailbreak off, but clearly I don't know ol' boy as well as I thought I did. *Think. Think.* I've put waaay too much into this and owe waaay too many people to fall short now. But the first day up in this halfway house joint has too many people up in my face, going over all the house rules. Add to that, the US Marshals have made me the most popular brother up in here for the moment. The attention is the last thing I need right now. It's just going to make shit harder for me to get away from this place.

The brother who runs this place finally stops bumping his gums and tells the new crew that we're free to get settled in. I rush back up to my assigned room and take a quick look out of the window. The foot traffic is a bit light outside, but I'm scanning the curbs for federal agents tryna blend. I spot the unmarked SUV parked two houses down.

"Shit."

"Something going down out there?" a voice floats over to me.

I turn to see a tall, lanky young brother entering the room.

"Nah. Nah. Everything is cool." I dismiss him and take another glance out of the window.

"You sure?" he asks. "Those two agents posted up out there ain't giving you heartburn?"

He wrangles back my full attention. I assess him again, this time taking special note of the number of tats sleeving his arms, the long dreads, and the single fat diamond stud blinking in his right ear. "What you know about it?"

"You shouldn't worry about my damn IQ. You need to be focused on getting Kingston West his damn money. That's why the fuck you're out now, isn't it?"

I square back around, mentally noting to never turn my back on him again. "Who are you?"

Chuckling, he leans back against one of the twin beds. "Just call me your friendly neighborhood reminder."

"Well, Mr. Reminder, since you're aware of my new added surveillance problem, you wouldn't also happen to know of a way of me getting around it, would you?"

He studies me for a few seconds. "I might."

Figures. Everything in the game costs. "What do you want?"

"Whatcha got?"

I shake my head and spread my hands. "Nothing. I'm fresh out the joint—unless you want to take an IOU."

Dreadlocks laughs. "Nah, nigga. I heard your damn IOUs are a bit shaky and takes a little too long to cash in."

My flash of anger roasts me from the inside out. How many brothers out here in the streets know my business? "Then what?"

A strange sparkle flashes in his eyes as he moves from the bed over to the room's door. When he closes the muthafucka and turns back toward me, he's clutching his balls.

It takes me no time to understand his price. My hands ball into fists at my sides. "Nigga, have you lost your fuckin' mind? I should snap your damn neck for even suggesting that gay bullshit."

"Lower your fucking voice," he barks back, unfazed. "You're the muthafucka looking for a goddamn handout. I ain't got to do shit but hang the fuck out and watch either those agents outside catch you trying to break out this bitch or wait for a phone call from Kingston West to shank your ass for non-payment." The entire time he's talking, he's stroking his dick through his loose jean pants.

When it's clear that there's no negotiating from his position, my gaze shifts to the closed door.

"Don't worry," he says. "Ain't nobody coming in here to disturb us."

My entire stomach drops to my knees.

Dreadlocks sits down on the bed and whips out a monstrous-size dick for a man so lanky. "Hey, dude. If this is your first time, I promise that I'll be gentle."

No. No. This shit isn't happening.

"So what's it going to be, nigga? I haven't got all day for you to make up your mind. You want to get your money or not?" As he continues stroking, the muthafucka gets bigger.

Twenty-five million dollars? A knot forms in the center of my throat. I can't even swallow that shit let alone attempt to put that black dick in my mouth.

"Today, nigga," Dreadlocks snaps, impatient.

Somehow I unglue my feet from by the window and walk over to him. Everything in me withers and dies as I sit down next to him.

"That's right, nigga. You can play my bitch for a little while." With his right hand, he reaches up, places it on the back of my head and then guides me down toward his cock.

Completely washed in shame, I close my eyes and open wide.

14

Sam

"Tell me something good," the district chief, Bell, says through our vehicle's speakers. "Since I'm calling you, I take it that we don't have Mr. Harlem Banks in custody?"

"Not yet, sir," I respond. "We're still working down the list of close contacts. There's one possibility that the grandmother is holding out on us. We got the warrant for a wiretap. It should be up right now. Plus, I put two agents out to sit on her."

"So you believe that he's still in the state?" the chief asks.

I glance over at Greg in the passenger seat and he gives me his opinion with a short shrug. "It's fifty-fifty. He could be in the wind, but we're working to find out possible spots that he would hide."

"Humph. It's probably the usual destination: Mexico."

"If so, then we'll find him there, too," I promise.

"All right. Keep me posted."

"Will do." I disconnect the call and sigh.

Greg pulls his attention from his laptop. "Do you *really* think that Banks is still in New York?"

"Could be. After all, he does have a sick daughter still here," I say, referring to the information retrieved about the little girl needing heart surgery. "If he risked going to see her, like I believe he did, then I can't see him being the type of father to completely abandon her."

"You never know. We've seen stranger stuff from these cats out here nowadays. They only think and care about themselves. Right now he's probably enjoying the sweet taste of freedom."

"Yeah. Right now, it would really help if we can find anything on this Johnnie chick."

"Max and Renee are on it. If her name is mentioned anywhere in his files, they'll find it."

On cue, my cell phone rings. According to the dashboard, it's Renee. "Tell me that you got good news," I greet.

"Definitely good *and* interesting news," Renee says breathlessly. "How about the name Johanna Robinson? She's affectionately called Johnnie by family and friends."

The name does have a ring of familiarity about it. "Why do I know that name?"

Greg cuts in, "Not as in Charles Robinson, the governor's daughter?"

"The one and the same," Renee crows.

"We met her at the Governor's Ball earlier this year," Greg reminds me.

Suddenly the image of a tall, voluptuous woman in a golden dress jumped to the front of my mind. She was absolutely stunning and set more than just the man on her arm's tongue wagging when she was introduced around the room. I, on the other hand, coveted her height. "Yeah. Yeah. I remember now. Her mother is some political hotshot too, isn't she?"

"Yeah. She once ran for Senate back in the nineties."

"So what are you telling me?" I ask Renee. "Harlem Banks and

Johnnie Robinson had a thing? In what social fantasy world did that happen?"

"We don't know the how, but get this: earlier this week, Harlem Banks had his first and only conjugal visit. Want to guess the name?"

"Wait. How in the hell did he qualify for a conjugal visit when he's not married?"

"Seems like Ms. Robinson knows what strings to pull to get what she wants."

"Does she also know which strings could help him bust out of prison?" I ask.

"Good question," Renee says. "Max and I will head back over to the prison and have another talk with the warden. You and Greg want to go and talk to Ms. Robinson?"

"Yeah. Give us the address."

Renee rattles it off while Greg jots it down and then enters it into the GPS unit. After I disconnect the call, something else starts bothering me. "Weird."

"What?" Greg asks.

"I could've sworn that night we met Johnnie Robinson that she was recently engaged. I seem to remember a boulder of a diamond on her finger."

Greg rubs his tired eyes. I can't tell if he's warding off sleep or trying to get his memory to kick in gear. "Yeah. To the new *it* boy: Reese Singleton."

"Right!" I remember now. "His picture has been all over the New York social scene, speculating that he's going to run for mayor—or governor. I can't remember which."

"This damn case is getting stranger by the second."

When we pull into the driveway of Johnnie Robinson's residence in Greenwich, Connecticut, things take another turn. Two police cars are already crammed into the drive and there's a small crowd of people outside the door hugging and crying.

"This doesn't look too good." Greg sighs.

"You don't say." I park the SUV and climb out. As we approach the door, I try to assess all the possible scenarios before someone actually breaks the news to me. When the crowd notices us, their open grief shifts into confusion.

"Excuse me, but where is the officer-in-charge?" I ask.

One woman, who could easily pass as Johnnie's sister, jabs a thumb over her shoulder to indicate the house. "Inside. They are still talking to the groom and my parents."

"Thank you." Since the door is already open, I step into the house and easily find the officers and another grieving crowd. The bright yellow *US Marshals* across our jackets catches everyone's attention, including the middle-aged officer who is taking notes.

"Uh. Can I help you folks?"

"Yes. Are you the officer-in-charge?"

He nods slowly like he's wondering whether I'm there for him.

Approaching, I launch into my introductions again and then ask to speak with him privately for a moment. Of course he agrees and we move into the adjoining kitchen for some semi-privacy.

"What's going on here?" I ask.

Again, he seems to be thrown for a loop for a couple of seconds. "Uhm, they're filing a missing person's report."

"Missing?"

"Yes." He clears his throat. "Apparently, Mr. and Mrs. Charles Robinson's oldest daughter has gone missing. She's supposed to be getting married today, but no one can find her." He looks around then leans in to whisper conspiratorially, "Frankly, I think that it's probably just wedding jitters." He beams as if proud of his conclusion, but when we don't join in, he asks us a question.

"Why are you guys here?"

"We're hunting a fugitive who we believe Ms. Robinson knows personally. He escaped from prison last night."

There's a soft gasp from behind me.

I turn around to the Johnnie look-alike, trying to act like the noise didn't come from her and her sloppy ear hustling. I don't have time to waste, so I turn from the cop to walk over to her. "Do *you* know anything about Harlem Banks?"

Her gaze first shoots over to her wide-eyed parents before she shakes her head at me.

Another liar. Drawing in a long, patient breath, I try again. "What is your name?"

"K-Kasey," she stutters out nervously.

When her parents turn and edge toward us, she fidgets with her hands and shifts on her feet. She's scared that she is about to get in trouble.

"Look, Kasey. This is very important. If my suspicions are right, your sister may *not* have left here voluntarily."

This time, the mother gasps.

"My God," the unmistakable Reese Singleton chimes in. "Am I understanding this right? You think my fiancée may have been kidnapped by that runaway fugitive that was on the news this morning?"

From there, a ripple of gasps spreads among the crowd.

"I don't know if he took her or she went voluntarily," I clear up. "But either is a possibility. Isn't it, Kasey?"

"That's ridiculous," Governor Robinson thunders indignantly. "My daughter doesn't associate with known criminals! I don't know where you're getting your information, but it's absolutely wrong."

My eyes never waver from Kasey's. "Am I wrong, Kasey?"

This time the young girl collapses into tears. "I'm not supposed to tell anybody about him," she wails. "I promised."

More gasping ensues while Mrs. Robinson grabs hold of her husband in order not to hit the floor.

Taking hold of Kasey's hands, I give her a sympathetic smile. "It's okay. You're doing the right thing. It'll help us find your sister."

Like her mother, Kasey looks ready to faint.

"Can someone get her some water?" I ask.

A string of volunteers rush to fill the request, nearly running Greg over in the process.

Meanwhile, I lead Kasey over to the dining room table and instruct her to take a seat. Within seconds someone is handing her a glass of water.

Kasey thanks the woman and then downs the entire eight ounces in one gulp.

"Feel better?" I ask.

She nods.

"All right. Now tell us everything that you know about Johnnie and Harlem."

15

Harlem

"I have to go to the bathroom," Johnnie announces just outside of nowhere, Tennessee.

Groaning, I cut a suspicious look at her since it's the first words that she's uttered since we left the gas station in Blacksburg, Virginia.

"What? We've been in this car for like forever. I'm surprised that your bladder isn't the size of a bowling ball too."

"Now that you mention it," I say, suddenly feeling the pressure building inside my bladder. I check out our surroundings, but there are only acres of flat land stretching out before us on these back roads. "I guess we can just pull over somewhere."

Her neck snakes around like my ass cursed her out or something. "I know that you're not suggesting that I pop a squat on the side of the road to take a piss."

I throw back the same attitude. "That's exactly what I'm suggesting, *princess.* If you'd notice there aren't any golden toilets around for you to plant your spoiled ass on at the moment."

"Then find one," she says, indignant. "You got me seriously fucked up if you think I'm wiping my ass with grass or some shit."

"Oh, my God. You are seriously working my nerves."

"Right back at you," she snaps. "I keep asking you to let me out of this bullshit joyride, remember?"

"Well, maybe I should do that right now since there's nothing around for miles. You can hitch a ride right after you take that piss you're bitching about."

"You get out. This is my fucking car."

I open my mouth to go in, but then stop myself and take a deep breath. "We're starting to sound like an old married couple," I gripe.

"Humph!" She folds her arms and continues to stare out of the side window.

The car is silent again during the next twenty-two miles until we come across an old gas station that looks to be at least a half a century old and hasn't seen better days in quite a while.

When I pull up toward the back and a faded bathroom sign, Johnnie starts twisting up her face.

"I don't know about this," she says.

"What? It's not the side of the road." I grin while I retrieve my gun.

Her gaze drops to the weapon and then glances back up at me questioningly.

"Protection," I say. "We are in redneck territory, you know."

Her gaze says that she doesn't believe me, but I'm not about to waste more time trying to convince her, either.

"C'mon. Let's go ahead and get this over with." I pocket the car key and then we both climb out of the car at the same time. We look around and note there's not a soul in sight. We head straight to the bathroom door, but discover that it's locked.

Shit. "We got to go inside and ask for the key," I tell her. At the flash of hope in her eyes, I reflexively place my hand over the gun tucked at my side. Her hope is replaced by anger. She reads the move as another threat and I'm going to let her roll with that. "C'mon." I grab her by the arm and direct her to the front of the gas station.

Opening the front door, a bell jiggles overhead. An old geezer with black-rimmed glasses looks up from a small five-inch television to look us over. Immediately, I can tell that he doesn't like the looks of us.

"You folks lost?"

I tense because he said the word *folks* like rednecks usually say the word *nigger*.

"No. My lady needs to use your restroom. Any way we can get the key?"

"You plan on buying anything?" he asks.

I turn and look at the anemic rows of candy and stale-ass looking potato chips. "Sure. Why not?" I glance at Johnnie. "Want something, sweetheart?" If looks could kill, Boss Hog at the counter there would be white-chalking my ass personally. But to my relief, she doesn't appear that she likes or trusts this man any more than I do.

I pull her toward the first aisle with me and just grab the first couple of bags I come across and then take them up to the counter.

Boss Hog doesn't look impressed, but tosses down the restroom key first before ringing up our items.

Johnnie, lightning fast, snatches the key with a smile. "Thanks." She attempts to break away from me to head toward the door.

"Johnnie," I hiss, snatching her back by her arm. "I'll go with you."

"That's not necessary, *sweetheart*," she hisses back with a wooden smile. She pulls away again, but I'm not having it. We engage in an awkward tug-of-war while Boss Hog rattles off my total.

"That'll be seven dollars and sixty-five cents."

With my free hand, I toss down a ten-dollar bill. "Keep the change."

We start for the door still tugging back and forth.

"Hey," he barks. "Don't you want your chips?"

"Oh. Sorry." I snatch them up while continuing my mini-war with Johnnie.

"You don't want to put them in a bag?"

"Nah. That's all right. We're good." Out the door we go. My annoyance with this chick skyrockets. "Nice try, slick."

"What? I have to go to the bathroom," she insists and adds a little dance as we head toward the back of the building.

I don't buy her act. When we reach the bathroom door again, I hover patiently outside of it while she uses the key to gain access. But when she steps in with me right behind her, she stops and blocks my entrance.

"Uh, where in the hell do you think you're going?" she asks.

"Where does it look like?"

"Oh no the fuck you're not. You're not going to stand over me while I take a piss. Have you lost your damn mind?"

I glance over her head to see that the bathroom is a single room with a lone toilet, a sink, and a mirror. "All right. But hurry up."

Her response is to slam the damn door in my face.

I spin away angrily, wishing that I had something that I could punch. How has a woman that I've spent five years loving and dreaming about be riding my last nerve after spending less than twenty-four hours with her? Granted, we're not doing the normal things that couples do, and yes, I did steal her car, kind of kidnapped her, and then threatened her life with a gun, but still.

All right. That evaluation doesn't sit right with me so I start pacing outside of the door. The voice in the back of my head gnaws at me. I still love Johnnie and I don't want anything to happen to her, regardless of how this whole thing turns out. I also don't want her going back to Connecticut so that she can marry that clown that's waiting for her at the altar—or any other clown, for that matter. *But what the fuck can you do to stop it?* I shake my head as my pacing picks up.

My attention is pulled from the bathroom door when another car pulls up into the old gas station. When I look over to see it's a sheriff's patrol car, I experience something close to a heart attack.

When this good ole boy climbs out from the car, his gaze zeroes in on me like a laser.

I force on a smile and nod as a greeting.

The sheriff doesn't say anything as he heads into the station's front door.

The moment he's inside, I turn back toward the bathroom and hammer the door. "Johnnie, we gotta go," I hiss.

No response.

"Johnnie!" *Bam! Bam!*

What the fuck? I slip the key back into the lock and push inside. The muthafucka is empty. For a few seconds I just stand there blinking, unable to process how the fuck this shit could be—then I notice the rectangular window high above the mirror. Clearly, she could've reached it if she stood on the sink.

Rushing inside, I hop up on the sink. The porcelain bowl wobbles beneath my weight, but I get a good look out the window to see where the muthafucka leads and if I can spot Johnnie. But I hear something behind me and before the door slams shut, I catch sight of Johnnie's long legs bolting from the door and slamming it shut.

She was hiding behind the door the whole time. I jump down off the sink, stumble about a foot before I reached the door. *Locked.* As I fumble to unlock the door, I hear the roar of a car engine. *How in the fuck?* The car key is still in my pocket so I know Johnnie can't possibly be behind the wheel of the car. But when I bolt out of the door, that's exactly where she is. The car speeds back in reverse.

In an ironic replay with the roles reversed, I race toward the passenger-side door as she tries to whip around to head back out of the gas station. I get the door open but then nearly stumble and wipe out when she shifts into drive and floors it. It's just a miracle that I'm able to heft my way into the speeding car.

"Stop the fucking car!"

"No. You get the fuck out," she shouts, swinging her right arm wildly at me in an attempt to knock me back out the car. With the speed accelerating, it's attempted murder in my eyes.

I duck and dodge the blows, but make sure that I go ahead and slam my car door. Next, I dive to wrench hold of the steering wheel. We zip and zag all over the road.

"Let go," Johnnie shouts, snatching the wheel in the opposite direction.

The wail of a police siren draws my attention. I jerk my head toward the back window to see the same sheriff's patrol car now gaining speed on us.

"FUCK!"

16

Sam

After Kasey completes her story about how her older sister Johnnie and Harlem met and fell in love, the entire Robinson family is in shock. Apparently, the younger sister was the only person Johnnie had ever truly confided in. When I add the fact that Johnnie had recently pulled strings to see Harlem last month to possibly plan or aid in his escape, Reese Singleton turns apoplectic.

"This is going to be a scandal," Mrs. Robinson whispers. Her face drains more blood by the second.

"I still say that this is some horseshit," Mr. Robinson barks. "You say this man escaped last night, but our daughter was with us the entire day for the wedding rehearsal and the dinner. And we can all vouch that she didn't leave that dinner until this morning. Her friend Janine drove her home, isn't that right?" He glances over to the woman I presume is Janine.

She nods. "Yeah. Gosh. It had to be like one—one-thirty. I watched her as she went into the house."

"Doesn't rule out that Mr. Banks was waiting for her inside."

The idea clearly horrifies the woman. "Maybe I should've walked her inside myself."

"And then what? You could've just been in danger yourself," I try to console. "Don't beat yourself up. We're going to find her."

I order more of my team to the scene as we instruct everyone except the immediate-family and fiancé to leave. Within minutes of their arrival, every inch of the house is combed over. Evidence points to Johnnie having a visitor last night—especially in the bedroom. But if Johnnie had *planned* to run off with her ex-lover, she forgot the clothes she'd packed for her honeymoon.

An APB goes out for her vehicle. This now swings the pendulum to Harlem Banks definitely being out of the tri-state area, crushing my assumption that he wouldn't leave his sick child behind.

"Still have my money on Mexico," Greg deadpans.

"You may be right." I dig my cell from out of my pants pocket and quickly get the chief on the other line for the latest updates. The local story will be national within the hour. Harlem's name and picture will shoot up the FBI's Most Wanted List. No sooner do I disconnect the call with the chief than the first news van arrives outside of the house.

"Oh God," Mrs. Robinson laments. "What are we going to say?"

I shake my head because I can't tell whether she is more concerned for her daughter or their image.

Reese Singleton, however, is definitely more pissed than concerned. The brewing scandal will tarnish him just as much as the Robinsons, if not more. In politics, a rising star can quickly turn into a dying star in a single news cycle.

For me, our best option is to continue to press Kasey for more information.

"I need you to think. Did your sister ever mention any place that she'd be dying to go—or any talk of her and Harlem wanting to go somewhere?"

The young girl is completely drained and keeps shaking her head. "No. No nothing like that. She was determined to move on. I swear."

"Then why the visit?" I counter.

Kasey's large brown eyes keep filling with tears. "I don't know. Clearly, she kept some secrets from me, too." She glances to her family for help, but their disappointment trumps their sympathy for her at the moment.

My phone rings. It's Max. "Tell me some good news."

"Not today, boss," he says. "We got another runner."

"What?"

"Isaiah Kane. He's missing from the halfway house."

"Shit!" All heads in the house whip in my direction. "Excuse me," I tell them, climbing up from the sofa and seeking out a corner in the house for some privacy. "What happened to the team posted outside?" I ask Max.

"Apparently, they didn't see a damn thing. And neither did anyone else in the damn house. I'm on my way to talk to the community corrections manager. I'll keep you updated."

"All right. Thanks." I disconnect the call with a "fuck," mumbled under my breath.

"That doesn't sound promising," Greg says, cornering me.

"Isaiah Kane is in the wind."

Greg doesn't look the least bit surprised. "I knew that dude wasn't on the up and up."

"Which means that there's a huge part of this puzzle that we're missing. They're all in this together somehow and there's got to be some powerful people helping them out, too. They could be headed for Mexico or halfway around the world for all we know." The idea of these people slipping through my grasp is starting to give me my first ulcer.

Outside, two more news vehicles arrive. One manages to successfully persuade Reese Singleton to the sidelines to get his take on what happened to his runaway bride and the escaped convict. I can't hear what he's saying, but I'm sure that he's broadcasting his ignorance and throwing his deceitful fiancée under the bus. The victim card is probably the best way to save his promising career.

I pull in a deep breath as my exhaustion becomes extremely difficult to ignore. My ringing phone pulls me back to the job at hand. Since it's too much to hope for good news, I answer with a flat, "Yeah."

"We got something!"

The announcement hits me like an injection of adrenaline straight to the heart. "Hit me."

"Johnnie Robinson's vehicle is in the middle of an active police chase right outside Cleveland, Tennessee."

"Yes!" I signal to Greg for us to roll out. "Get me the number for the district US Marshal for that area and you guys get ready for a field trip."

17

Johnnie

My life has flashed before my eyes at least three times during the high-speed police chase out here in the back roads of Tennessee—and that's before Harlem started firing at the cops. Any illusions of my believing Harlem wouldn't cause me any real harm flies out of the window. When I try to slam on the brakes, I'm stunned by how he's able to snatch me completely from the driver's seat and over to the passenger's side while simultaneously climbing over.

In a matter of minutes, we go from having one sheriff's car to a whole team of squad cars chasing us down.

"Please," I shout at Harlem. "Just pull over before you get us both killed."

"Can't do that," he says without a second thought. "I have to get to that money before Isaiah. My daughter's life depends on it."

His words rush past me, but I can't make any sense of them. *What money? Isaiah who? And what's wrong with his daughter?* "What are you talking about?"

A squad car tries to come up his left side.

Harlem doesn't bother taking aim, but fires out his window to get the car to fall back a few paces. Once the cop is behind us again, Harlem moves to the center of the two roads to prevent another bypass attempt.

"Harlem," I yell for his attention. "Answer me. What is this all about?"

He cuts me an angry look. "What the hell does it matter now? You just want me to be back behind bars, right? You want to write me off and go back to that rich brother you're trying to marry."

POW! POW! POW!

I scream as the back window of my car explodes.

"Get down," Harlem shouts, pushing my head all the way down toward the floorboard.

He gets no resistance from me this time because I'm literally scared out of my mind. As much as I want to lay the blame on him, I know this time that I'm the one that set this whole chase in motion.

"Oh. I'm sorry. I'm sorry. I'm sorry." The apology is meant for myself, but Harlem thinks it's for him.

"It's okay. It's not your fault," he says, still weaving all over the road. "I never meant to drag you into this . . . but I really did need to see you again."

I don't bother correcting the misunderstanding because it's still nice to hear and believe that he couldn't stay away. "Please. Tell me what's really going on? What's this all about?"

Harlem pulls the wheel hard to the right. The back of my head bangs against the glove compartment, causing it to snap open. At the same time, the police open fire and I can hear the bullets slamming into my car.

I don't mean to lose it, but I can't stop the tears from leaping over my lashes. This is it. I'm going to die in a damn police chase. Me. Little Ms. Goody Two-shoes, as they called me most of my life. My sole crime was falling in love with the wrong man.

"What we had together—what we felt—was real," Harlem says suddenly. "I really need for you to know that. I had every intention to retire. That's why I gave you the ring. I wanted to bring you into my real world. Introduce you to my people—my daughter."

It was hard to catch that last part because of the wail of all the police sirens. I have no idea what's going on the road and I'm too scared to climb up from the floorboard to take a look for myself.

During the break of his storytelling, I share something with him too. "I saw her."

Harlem sneaks another look at me.

"Your daughter," I clarify. "Your grandmother brought her to court a couple of times. She looks a lot like you."

He smiles. "You think so?"

"Yeah. Definitely." The conversation drops there. I'm still not ready to know anything about the mother or the type of relationship he possibly has with her. The knowledge that she even exists fills me with an unexplainable jealousy.

"She's really sick," he blurts out. "My daughter, Tyler. She has to have heart surgery and I couldn't leave the money accessible to my nana. She's been slowly losing everything while I've been locked down. After she drops that news on me, I hear through the prison grapevine that Isaiah has somehow managed an early release—scheduled for today. I don't have to be Einstein to figure out where he's headed at the first opportunity. With twenty-five million, his ass would be in the wind. I'll never see him or my money again. And then Tyler . . ."

He doesn't have to finish the sentence. I get the big picture. Along with my fear of our current situation, I'm also overcome with guilt and compassion.

"I'm sorry. I . . . I wish that I had known." The implication being that he should've told me. I have no real answer to when exactly that should've happened. I'm sure that if he had told me in the beginning, I would have shut him down and not have given him the time of day. And had he told me *later* in the relationship, would I have had the strength to end it and walk away? Somehow, I seriously doubt it. Right or wrong, I'm still connected to this man by something more powerful than logic: love.

Wait. Did he say twenty-five million?

"Oh shit," Harlem swears.

I look up to see terror flash across his face. Before I can get the words out of my mouth to ask what's going on, we hit something—hard, and then, if I'm not mistaken, we're airborne. After that, we clearly smash into a body of water because it quickly fills up the car.

18

Sam

News of Harlem Banks's swan dive off a Tennessee bridge reaches my team while we're still in the air. The idea of these two's Bonnie and Clyde stint being over in less than twenty-four hours fills the team with an undeniable hope. The hope that we can go home and get a decent night's sleep. I'm immune to hope. I never can get myself to trust it.

It's sunset by the time the team makes their way to the crash site. Along with the local police, FBI, and the district US Marshal's office there's a swarm of news vans and helicopters covering the air.

"And you must be Assistant Deputy Chief Marshal Samantha Reynolds," a white-haired southern boy says, thrusting out his thick, liver-spotted hand toward me.

"I am," I respond, throwing on my professional smile.

"Yeah. I'm Chief Deputy George Carter. Your boss called and told me all about you." His pale blue eyes rake over me. He's not impressed, but he continues to pump my arm as if he's jacking up a car.

A line of officers holds the news crews back but their cameras swing in our direction.

"So what news do you have for me, chief?"

"Only that your fugitive is currently at the bottom of this here river, which was witnessed by over half the local sheriff department's men. The crazy fool clipped an eighteen-wheeler and then spun out over the bank. They weren't equipped to attempt a rescue so all they could do is secure the area while the car took approximately eighteen minutes to sink out of their line of vision.

Not good enough.

"Any bodies float to the top?"

"No, ma'am. But trust me. Those two nig—uh, I mean *fugitives* didn't get out of that car."

My smile doesn't budge during his tongue slip. "Well, I'm sure you know how this goes. Trust but verify."

"Yes, ma'am." He laughs, posing for the cameras to get his best profile. "Anyway, we're working on getting a crew here to pull the car back out, but as you know, this is a small town that's not exactly equipped for that sort of thing. The closest department who can help is coming out of Knoxville. Lugging all that is going to take a few hours so we're going to keep the area secure until they get here."

I nod along with the update, not liking the idea of us just sitting on our hands while we wait. But at least the department got us booked at a nearby motel. I glance over my shoulder at my crew, who are talking to a team of local agents and noting how they all look like extras for the show *The Walking Dead.*

"Listen, guys," I address them after talking to Carter. "We got a couple of hours to take a nap and a shower. So let's just say we'll meet back up outside our posh three-star motel at about . . . nine o'clock p.m. before coming back here?"

They nod, looking ready to collapse with relief.

That's exactly what I do the second I'm in my room. Hell, I don't even remember being concerned about whether the sheets are clean before I coast into La La Land. What I do know is that it's a short trip before the alarm on my cell phone is going off. "How in the hell can it be eight forty-five?" I stare at the time in disbelief for a full minute before I swing my legs out of the bed. After a seven-minute shower, I feel fresh as a daisy before breezing back out of the room. When I meet back up with the team, they are looking a bit better, too. The steam trunks that were around Greg's eyes have been reduced to regular bags again.

The weather has taken a nasty turn in the few hours we were gone. Rain and river currents make the recovery effort difficult for the authorities. According to Major Brian Collins with the county sheriff's office, the river's current has more than doubled. Add the drizzling rain and gusting winds and then suddenly there is talk about whether to delay the recovery until the morning.

I toss in my two cents, even though at this point the final decision lies with the district deputy chief. "I'd prefer if we could just push through. If my fugitive is somewhere on foot, I need to know that sooner rather than later."

"I hear what you're saying," Carter says. "But I'm not trying to lose any men out here either."

"What about the side sonars and water cameras? Can we at least find out whether there are bodies inside the car?" I ask.

"Won't rule out whether their bodies were swept farther down the river," he counters.

I wonder why he's fighting me so hard on this, but then it occurs to me that he wants the credit for him and his guys for ending Banks's brazen getaway. At the end of the day, all things end in politics. Drawing a deep breath, I fall back on my professional smile again. "The search isn't called off until I have two bodies. Dead or alive."

19

Harlem

Now that darkness has fallen, I can breathe easier as I trudge through these thick trees. Even as I put one foot in front of the other, I have no damn idea where I'm even going. I'm not even sure that it matters.

"I . . . I'm soooo cold," Johnnie whimpers as I cradle her in my arms.

"I know, princess. So am I." I swallow hard and get moving against the rain and gusting wind. There is a good chance that our asses could simply freeze to death out here and it could be weeks or months before anyone finds our frozen corpses.

"I'm sorry," Johnnie keeps crying, trying her best to hold onto me.

"Please stop apologizing," I tell her. "Put all the blame on me." As usual. It's been a long time since anything I've planned has gone right. I don't know what in the hell possessed me to believe that this jailbreak would be any different. My best friend betrayed me. Not once, but clearly several times. I've disappointed my grandmother and it looks like I'm going to fail my daughter.

The voice in the back of my head keeps telling me to be grateful for the miracle of getting out of that damn river. We have no idea how far the cold current carried us. If I had my guess, it was more than a couple of miles. One thing for sure, we were both human popsicles by the time we were able to drag ourselves out of there.

Johnnie broke down when I told her that we had to keep moving. But we didn't have a choice. She managed about a mile by herself and when it was clear that she couldn't go any further, of course I wasn't going to just leave her out there in the middle of nowhere. Since I'm a big guy, I scooped her up and carried her.

The rain is one thing, but the wind is a killer. The way these thick tree branches keep whipping across my face and arms, I'm going to look like I've been in a fight with Freddy Kruger if we ever get out of here.

About another mile, I'm sure Johnnie has fallen asleep. That or she drifted into a coma. I can't stop to tell which at the moment. A few more steps and then suddenly I'm standing in the backyard of a brick ranch house. There's not a single light on, but that doesn't mean that the owners aren't simply fast asleep inside.

"Johnnie," I whisper, bouncing her in my arms to try and wake her. Thankfully, she stirs. "Huh?"

"Look." I nod toward the house.

She turns her head and then sighs. It's possibly our second miracle.

"I'm going to go and check it out," I tell her and then set her on her feet.

"Be careful," she whispers, slinking over to a nearby tree and waiting for what I find out.

Quickly, I comb the entire perimeter and then peek through all of the windows. "It doesn't look as though anyone is here," I say, returning to the backyard. "Can you walk?"

She nods and then follows me to the back door. In no time, I'm able to break us in. The heat in the house is a welcome relief. Nei-

ther of us wastes time stripping out of our wet clothes and throwing
them into the wash. We also don't blink an eye in hopping into a hot
shower together to wash the goop from the river off our bodies.

After toweling off, Johnnie strips blankets off the beds and I
risk starting a fire in the fireplace.

"What are we going to do if these people return home?" she
asks as we cuddle up in front of the flames.

"To tell you the truth, I have no fucking idea," I answer honestly. At the moment, I can't remember another time when I've
been this exhausted. I can't even process our naked bodies being
pressed together. We're more concerned about getting warm. The
cold seems to be in our bones. ✔

Johnnie has it the worst.

I do what I can by holding her close and rubbing her back and
arms until we fall asleep. According to the clock over the fireplace,
I get a solid five hours. Still tucked beneath my chin and sleeping
like a log is Johnnie. Easing my head back, I take a good look at her
sleeping face and marvel at just how flawless she really is even
without a stitch of makeup.

When I brush a kiss against her forehead, she stirs and moans
softly. Smiling, I brush the second kiss against her upturned nose
and get the same response. So, of course, the third kiss is planted
squarely on her full lips. This time, I'm the one that moans.

Johnnie slides her long arms up and around my neck.

I take it as an open invitation. With no resistance or protest, I
roll her over onto her back and knee open her legs. Breaking our
kiss, I move my lips under her chin and down her graceful neck. In
the back of my head, I know that she can stop me at any time, but
I'm praying that she doesn't.

The odds improve in my favor when I plop a hard nipple into
my mouth and she arches her back to give me even better access. I

don't know if she's forgiven me or she's allowing herself to be swept up into the moment. Selfishly, I'll accept either one.

As I dive between her luscious mounds of pecan-brown skin, Johnnie releases a light, feathery moan. When I slide into position, her legs fall east to west. This lets me know that she's fully awake and is aware of what's about to go down. Once I glide into her warm, wet pussy, those same legs then wrap around my hips. We go at it slow and deep—and long. I don't know why it is, but I'm addicted to the smell of her skin, the way she tastes, and definitely to the way she feels.

We go at it from every position and before I know it, we're both slick with sweat and our knees ache with rug burns. When we're done, we cuddle back up and pepper kisses on each other until she falls back asleep. The next time I open my eyes, a soft light is coming from the living room's back door.

We can't stay here. When I try to pop up, I belatedly remember that Johnnie is still sleeping right up under me. I pause for a few quiet seconds to drink in her beauty and wonder why is it that I still see a future with her. That shit is impossible now. After I get Nana Gloria the money for Tyler's surgery, I'll have to disappear forever or go back to jail. After all of this, they'll never let me out of there.

The money. Snapping out of my little daydream, I try to ease my arm out from around Johnnie without waking her up. The moment I manage to get it halfway out, her eyes flutter open.

I freeze and then force on a smile like I'd been caught with my hands in the cookie jar.

"Morning," she coos.

"Morning." When it looks like she's not in any hurry to get up, I'm forced to remind her, "Uh, I need to get going."

Her smile drops with disappointment as she sits up.

Still, I don't think that my speaking in singular terms registers with her. We rush to toss our clothes into the dryer and then rush to take yet another shower after last night's lovemaking session. While I scramble through the house for things that would be use- ful on the last leg of my road trip, Johnnie rummages through these people's kitchen to fix us a quick breakfast. Overall, I find about thirty bucks in cash and some cheap jewelry in the main bedroom. I take the cash and leave the jewelry.

When I go to join Johnnie and tell her about my decision to leave her, she is standing in the living room in front of an old tele- vision, looking like she's lost color. "What's wrong?"

"They think that I helped you escape," she says and then sits down before falling down.

"What?"

"The people on the news." She pointed at the screen. "They're talking about my visiting you last month and then my disappear- ing with you. They think I'm in on it."

I turn my gaze toward the screen. I recognize Boss Hog from the convenience store yesterday.

"I knew there was something suspicious about those two the mo- ment they walked in here. They were all lovey-dovey when they came in. There's no doubt in my mind that those two were together."

Johnnie groans. "I can't believe this."

The next people the newscasters are trying to talk with are Mr. and Mrs. Charles Robinson. The New York governor looks grim as he stares into the cameras.

"The only statement our family will like to make at this time is: Johanna, if you're able, please come home. We know that you're in- nocent of these ridiculous charges. As for the monster who has snatched you, I promise that if he's harmed a single strand of hair on your head, we will slap the entire federal book at him!"

A reporter jumps in:

"*Mr. Robinson, what do you say about the possibility of the two fugitives being at the bottom of a river?*"

"*I say, we don't believe it. We won't believe it until we physically see our daughter's body.*"

"Humph. So much for my chances of ever meeting the parents," I joke.

Johnnie cuts off the television. "Please say that you don't think any of this is funny."

"No. I guess not." I sigh because this is the perfect time to tell her. "I think that it's time we part ways."

Her attitude melts away. "What?"

I gesture to the blank television screen. "Look. It's the only way that we're going to clear up this confusion. I never planned on bringing you along with me, at the same time I didn't want to let you go—but this shit is too serious. This is the type of shit that ruins lives. Trust me. I know. You still have a chance to get out of this."

"No. I mean." She glances around. "You just can't leave me here. I . . . I . . ."

We both know that there's no reason for her to continue on with me except, "I don't *want* to stay."

Stunned, I can only manage to stare at her.

She sighs as if it's a huge confession for her. "I understand the danger. I do. I just . . . don't care anymore."

"You can't know what you're saying—what you're suggesting that you'd give up. Your life. Your career. Your family. I can't ask you to do all of that to live on the run with me."

"You don't have to ask," she says, standing. "I'm telling you. I don't want to go back to being just another overpriced lawyer on Wall Street, or a barter chip that links my family to the next generation of political leaders. I don't want to be a trophy wife to the future governor of the state. I just want . . . to be with you—for however long that is."

Once that I read that she's serious, I'm rushing forward and drawing her into my arms. When our lips seal together, I know that I'll never let her go as long as she wants to remain at my side. It may be just for another day for all we know, but if we play the few cards we have left right, maybe it can be forever.

20

Sam

"They're not in the car," Major Collins announces to our team as well as the other agencies.

Camera ready, deputy chief can't mask his shock. "How in the hell?"

"Clearly the current carried them out," I state the obvious and then turn back to my crew. "All right. You know what to do. We're going due south in the direction of the current. This news does not rule out the possibility that our fugitives are deceased but if there's a chance that they climbed out, we need to know where."

"Well. Hold on now, little lady," Carter snaps. "This is still my district and my team trumps yours."

My head snaps back in his direction. Behind me, Greg groans. "I'm sorry. What was that?" My fierce look is enough for him to backtrack—sort of.

"I don't mean any disrespect. I'm just saying how it is. If your *boy* is out here, I aim to catch him. No New York city slickers know these parts like my guys do. You're more than welcome to join in, but I'll be the one issuing the orders."

"All due respect, chief, but this is hardly time for us to engage in a pissing contest."

"Hold on now. That's not what's happening, I'm just telling you what is what." He cuts another look toward the bank of cameras. This is definitely his moment to shine and he's hell bent to take advantage of it.

Frankly, there's not a damn thing I can do about it. This mid-south cowboy outranks me and as long as we're in his territory, he's well within his right to seize the investigation from me. In my fourteen years in the department, I've never seen it done. All departments offer their assistance when a fugitive crosses into their districts, but usually the case remains with the initial department conducting the search.

"Do we have a problem?" he asks, grinning.

Forced to eat a healthy chuck of humble pie in front of my team, I force on my same tired-ass smile. "No problem at all." Marching away, I have no intention of taking orders from this country peacock. He's the main reason we weren't searching last night. The proud man was so convinced Banks and Robinson were still in that car.

"Join in with the search," I tell my five-man crew. "But if you see anything first, you come to me." I make sure to make eye contact with each of them. "Do I make myself clear?"

"Got it," they confirm in unison.

As they branch off to blend in with the sheriff's department, the FBI, and the local US Marshals, I scoop out my cell and place a call to my own boss. I give him a brief update and he's equally struck by the Tennessee's district deputy chief's call, but makes the formal call for our team not rocking the boat.

Less than an hour later, while Carter is giving his umpteenth interview to the press, muddy footprints are discovered about a mile from the bridge. A clear track is visible seen leading toward a forest.

"A mile," I mumble under my breath. A lousy mile. They now have hours on us. The hope is that they're still on foot. Plus, after being in that freezing water, and last night's weather will also play in our favor. I'll get my man and Deputy Chief Carter can get his glory.

21

Johnnie

I can't turn back now. That shit is clear. The thing is I keep waiting for this huge wave of regret to wash over me, but so far, all I feel is relief. Relief that I've finally admitted the truth to Harlem—and to myself. If somehow I do survive this shit, I'll probably be thrown into an insane asylum instead of jail.

Still, it's the risk that I'm willing to take because, at the end of the day, I've felt more alive with Harlem in the last twenty-four hours than I've felt in the entire five years that he'd been locked down in prison. I love him. I forgive him. I want to be with him for however long fate allows.

Rumbling down the back roads in this loud, rusty half-century-old pickup truck, I'm huddled up under Harlem on a long single seat, at peace. The gray clouds have parted and there's hardly a soul on the road. I don't have any idea exactly where we are going and what we're supposed to do once we get there. I don't think that Harlem knows either, because he's so quiet.

An hour later, the quiet worries me. Could he be having second thoughts? Is he concerned that I will slow him down? Somehow I have to assure him that won't happen. Now that I'm in this, I'm in it for the long haul. Or he's thinking about that man's face from the news. The other escaped prisoner. *Isaiah Kane*. If memory serves me correct, he's the man Harlem was busted with on the arms dealing charge. They were tried separately so I didn't pay too much attention to the other trial. But I'm pretty sure I'm right about that detail. Did they plan all of this together? If so, why was Harlem so upset?

I want to ask the big questions, but at the same time, I want him to willingly tell me what's going on. I want him to trust me.

By noon we've coasted out of Tennessee and shot through Alabama.

"We're almost there," Harlem says, breaking the silence.

"Okay." I curl my head up at him. "Where is that?" We both know that I'm really asking him to officially put his trust in me. That's a giant leap for our relationship. I love him *despite* that there is a huge part of his life that I've never seen or been a part of.

"We're going to pick up some money that I have stashed away for retirement," he confesses. "Money that I'd stacked from a few heists some years back."

My heart leaps at the word *heist*, but I remain calm on the outside.

"I messed up. I planned for retirement, but never for getting caught. I didn't set a nest egg aside that would easily be accessible to my grandmother and my little girl. All this time I've been locked down, she's been slowly losing everything, trying to take care of Tyler and her healthcare needs."

Surprised, I pull back. "You said that she needed surgery?"

Harlem's profile hardens as he tries to man up and control his emotions. "She has a heart condition. With these damn hospitals, money talks and bullshit walks."

"So this doesn't have anything to do with Isaiah Kane? You're just trying to get money to your little girl?"

Within a snap, Harlem's sadness is replaced with anger. "Actually, this has everything to do with Isaiah."

Now I'm really confused.

"He's going after *my* money."

I open my mouth to ask another question when understanding suddenly slams into me. "Oh."

Harlem continues. "Someone pulls some strings to get him scheduled for an early release. When word spread through the prison grapevine, I knew exactly what was next in his plans. He owes a lot of money to a lot of people—a lot of dangerous people."

"But aren't you two friends?"

"We *used* to be friends. But I'm certain that he's willing to throw me and mine under the bus in order for him to keep breathing. He spent and gambled away all of his money and now he believes that he is entitled to my piece of the pie as well."

"Wow. I guess it's not true what they say. There's no honor among thieves."

His laugh surprises both of us. When the laughter fades, he says, "It is what it is." He looks over at me. "Are you sure you're still down for all this?"

"Positive."

22

Sam

"Damn it! We missed them." It takes everything I have not to lash out at everyone, especially the current idiot-in-charge Carter. He still seems to be operating under the illusion that he and his team are still in the game. The fugitives' muddy footprints led a straight path to an isolated residence embedded in the woods. There's little doubt that they broke and entered the house, but we have no idea how long they stayed.

It doesn't look like they disturbed much or they were good at cleaning up behind themselves. It doesn't take much to find the name of the homeowners. Tracking them down is a much harder trick. They could be anywhere, up to and including on vacation. Until then, we have no idea what was taken.

"We need to put an APB out on all the vehicles registered to the homeowner," I tell an annoyed Carter.

"What if the owners are driving their vehicles? We'll scare them half to death when the dragnet picks them up."

"And maybe we'll pick up our fugitives—or maybe we'll pick up both. Are we sure that Banks and Robinson aren't holding them prisoner?" The look on his face reads that the possibility hadn't occurred to him. Probably for the millionth time that day, I wonder how in the hell this man obtained his position in the agency.

I don't know whether Banks would have taken hostages, but I've been trained to never rule out any and all possibilities.

Grudgingly, Carter orders the APBs while my small team huddles off together.

"What do you think?" Max asks.

"I think Banks and his girl are long gone, probably even out of the state."

Greg nods. "I still hedge my bets that they're headed to Mexico."

I nod. "Still a possibility. But Mexico has a big damn border."

"Maybe he's aware of the government's drastic budget cuts and knows a lot of the smaller towns can't afford expensive roadblocks and dragnets."

"Anything is possible." Even if Banks is headed to Mexico, our investigation won't stop there. What a lot of crooks don't know is that it never does. The US Marshals have international field offices in Mexico, Jamaica, Colombia, and the Dominican Republic. While it's ideal to recapture a fugitive within a forty-eight-hour sweet spot, the agency has had cases that have lasted decades. The point being that, eventually, we always get our man. Harlem Banks will be no exception.

"Get me the team that's working the Isaiah Kane case," I tell Renee while possibilities toss around in my head.

Greg smiles. "I was just thinking about him, too."

"Their runs are related," I say. "At the same time, there's definitely no love lost between the men."

"So maybe it's a race?" Frank contributes. "They're trying to get to something first."

I nod; this line of thought feels like the right track. "Maybe we need to take another look at both of their files. What are the cases that put the men on the other agency's radar?"

Renee jumps back into the mix. "The FBI is adamant that both men were members of an international cyber crime ring. Apparently, they were cyber hacking banks before it was cool."

"Gone are the days of smash and grab, huh?"

"Apparently. You know the FBI recently had a case where a cyber hacking ring had looted forty-five million in a hit that spanned twenty-six countries. There were over thirty-thousand-something transactions done within a matter of ten hours. Let that sink in. No mask. No weapons. Clean."

"And all federally insured," I say.

"Nothing like robbing the government." I suck in a deep, cleansing breath. "So where does that leave us?"

Greg is on a roll. "That leaves us with two thieves that were busted for weapons, but I don't remember anything about any money being recovered. If these guys are such successful thieves—where's the money?"

The puzzle pieces finally click together in my head. Harlem has a sick daughter and cash-strapped grandmother. "They stashed the money."

Frank smiles. "The last one there is a rotten egg."

23

Harlem

For the past five miles my eyes have been more on the truck's gas gauge than the winding road in front of me. Our last fill-up was in Jackson, Mississippi. We're practically running on fumes with nothing but cotton balls in our pockets. That's not completely true. There's the gun I lifted from that house. An old-fashioned gas station robbery is not out of the realm of possibility, but I'm nervous about how that's going to go down with my newly transformed good-girl-gone-bad-sister sitting at my side.

I'm worried that she has romanticized what life on the run is really going to be like. If and when I'm able to get money to Nana Gloria for Tyler's surgery, I will have to walk out of their lives forever. The thought of that shit is tearing me up. Can Johnnie really do the same? She has a larger and closer family than I do and throwing all that away is going to come back and bite her—us. Even though I know that she may be making the biggest mistake of her life, I don't want to let her go, either.

"There's a gas station," Johnnie says, pointing. She must've been watching the gas hand, too.

It's show time. We coast into the station and when I shift the

truck into park, the engine cuts off. We're out of gas. Sighing, I
glance over at Johnnie. "You know what we gotta do, don't you?" I
reach over into the car door and pull out the handgun.

Her brows dip together. "We're out of money?"

Nodding, I take a quick look around. There's only one other car
pulled up at another pump. "I'm going to need you to stay calm
while I go inside and get the clerk to turn on the pump. You pump
the gas and keep the car running. You think you can handle that?"

She hesitates.

"It's either that or we walk the rest of the way."

Johnnie's gaze lowers to the gun. "Are you going to hurt anybody?"

"Not if I can help it," I answer. She's got to know that this is
also a test on whether she's really made for this life.

She looks around the gas station, too.

"Johnnie? Can you do this?"

Without looking at me, she offers up another solution. "What
if we just change cars?"

"What?"

Johnnie gestures toward the car at the other pump.

I follow her line of vision and noticed for the first time that the
owner has the pump going into the gas tank, the driver side door is
open, and he's busily cleaning the front windows.

"It's probably a lot easier to overpower him than to hold up the
clerk," she says as if she's wondering aloud.

She's right. I glance back down at her. "I'm impressed."

"Don't be, yet. We haven't pulled it off." Quickly, Johnnie
slides across the leather seat and hops out of the truck before I get
my door open.

By the time I hop out, the guy has stopped washing the windows and is removing the pump from the gas tank.

Johnnie distracts him.

"Excuse me, sir. Do you know what time it is?"

The guy takes one look at Johnnie and starts smiling. "Uh, sure." He hangs up the pump and glances at his watch. Before he can tell her the time, I've made my way around the other side to press the gun into his back.

"Okay. Let me tell you how this is going to go down."

Johnnie hops into the car's front seat and turns over the engine.

"Hey. That's my car," the guy whines.

"Yeah. And if you want to keep breathing, you'll shut the hell up." I press the gun harder into his back. "Understand? Don't make a sound until we pull off."

The man nods.

"Good. Don't make me shoot you." I step back, but keep the gun leveled at him.

The dude glances back at me over his shoulder.

"What the fuck are you looking at?" I bark.

Seeing that the gun is real, he quickly snaps his head back around. "Nothing, man. Nothing. Please, don't shoot."

The gun stays trained on him until I hop inside the passenger door. I'm barely inside before Johnnie jams on the accelerator.

"Ohmigod. I just stole a car," she announces, astounded.

"Yeah. I know. I was there." I laugh.

"Holy shit." Johnnie cracks up laughing. "I can't believe it. Nobody is ever going to believe it."

"Well. They will if those security cameras were working back there."

"There were cameras?"

"It's the twenty-first century. There are cameras everywhere."

Her laughter fades after that, but her eyes remain wide and her hands seem to tighten on the steering wheel.

"Are you all right?" I ask.

"Uhm, hmm," she says, her voice pitched a bit high.

I watch her for a few minutes while she absorbs her new reality. When she catches me, she flashes a smile. "I'm fine."

I remain dubious.

"Really," Johnnie insists. "My criminal cherry has been officially popped."

That broke the ice. "That's one way of putting it."

"Now. Since I'm the one behind the wheel, where to, Clyde?"

"Texas, Bonnie. Where else?"

24
Sam

"Play it again," I instruct Greg for the third time. It's not that I've never witnessed a car-jacking before, it's just that I'm having a hard time squaring the woman I see participating in this car-jacking with the woman I met at the Governor's Ball earlier this year.

"Doesn't look like she's being coerced to me," Frank says, sighing. "Should be interesting to see how her family spins this one."

"I'm not interested in the spin. I'm more interested in where they're headed."

Renee pops up her laptop next to Greg's on top of the hood of the SUV. "We know that Harlem was born and raised in New York, but I did a background check and cross-reference to see if there are any other connections in that area. Harlem's grandfather was from Laredo, Texas."

Another piece of the puzzle clicks in my head. "Yeah?"

"Where is Grandpa Banks now?"

"Six feet under—in Laredo."

I mull that information over. "Pull various routes from New York to Laredo and see if Mr. Banks's travels so far have us heading in the same direction."

Renee's fingers fly across her keyboard. When a smile creases her face, I have my answer. "Bingo."

"All right, gang. It looks like we're headed to the Lone Star State." The team starts packing up their gear. "Renee, find whatever family Harlem still has in Laredo. Brothers, sisters—cousins. He's on his way to see someone down there."

"You got it, boss."

Exhaling a deep breath, I begin to feel that we're finally getting somewhere with this situation instead of simply reacting. Chances are Harlem and Johnnie have reached Laredo. Depending on how much money we're talking about, once Harlem or Isaiah get their hands on it, I have a feeling that this case may take decades to wrangle them back to prison.

"Greg, make sure you place a call to the local sheriff's department in Laredo and bring them up to speed."

Greg gestures to the phone he has tucked under his ear. "I'm already on it."

A jolt of adrenaline kicks in. We're close. I can feel it. Twenty minutes later, my team is back in the air. "Anything?" I ask Renee.

"Not yet. But I've called the New York office to have a couple of agents pay another visit to Gloria Banks. She's going to be the quickest route in getting the list of names we'll need."

"Humph. She wasn't too helpful the last time," I gripe. Not that I don't understand her position. She's probably relying on Harlem to get his hands on that life-saving money for her great-granddaughter.

When we touch down in Laredo, I'm shaking another district deputy chief's hand. At least this one, Aiden O'Donnell, isn't on an ego trip. It helps that my crew has worked with his department in the past. Renee keeps hitting a brick wall for possible family members living in Laredo, Texas, and the agents back in New York call us back with the unhelpful news that Gloria Banks doesn't know or is pretending not to know anything about her deceased husband's family.

"Two steps forward and then ten steps back," I huff and disconnect the call.

Greg shrugs and adds a suggestion. "We can always kick it old school and just go through the white pages."

"Do they even compile those anymore?" I ask, grunting.

He tosses up his hands. "I'm open to another idea."

"Fine. Whatever. How many Bankses can there possibly be in a town of a quarter million?"

25

Harlem

Webb County Cemetery

"Are you sure that this is it?" Johnnie asks, peering around. It's sunset and the amber sky gives the surrounding gray tombstones an eerie cast.

"This is it," I tell her. "Just follow the winding roads toward the back—where the crypts are."

"Crypts?" She eases off the accelerator. "Is this some sort of joke?"

"It's no joke," I say, smiling. "For obvious reason, I don't trust banks."

"So you what—buried your money at a cemetery?" she asks incredulously.

"It seemed like a safe place at the time."

Johnnie stares at me as if I'd just sprouted a second head. "There's something wrong with you."

"That's probably why you love me." I wink.

"True." She shakes her head. "God help me."

Shortly after I point out where we should park, I tell her that we're going to have to go the rest of the way on foot. I hope that the two of us will be able to lug the huge steamer trunk, weighing nearly five hundred pounds, back to the car ourselves. The money was stacked over time. I've never had to haul all the money at one time. But I guess I'm about to find out. The sun disappears out of the sky halfway toward our destination while the moon plays hide-and-seek among the thicket of trees.

"Are you sure you know where you're going?" Johnnie asks before tripping over the uneven ground.

My reflexes kick in and I catch her before she wipes out. "Whoa. Careful."

Once she's in my arms, she doesn't let go. "This shit ain't cool," she pants. "I can hardly see a damn thing. How much farther?"

Seeing her fear, I can't help but tease her. "What? Are you scared?"

"Dead people aren't exactly my favorite people to hang around," she tells me.

"Don't tell me that you believe in ghosts."

"Not until about five minutes ago," Johnnie whispers, still looking around like she expects someone to leap out at us at any moment.

Unable to contain my amusement, I chuckle and make sure that I keep her tucked at my side. "C'mon. We don't have that much farther to go." And we don't. Around the next bend is my grandfather's resting place. James Harlem Banks Senior's stone crypt is visibly different than the others on this stretch of land, simply because it was built within the last decade. Crypts have long gone out of fashion; hence the other ones in this section of the cemetery were built at the time of the Civil War.

"This is freaking me out," Johnnie whispers.

"Don't worry. We will be out of here in a few minutes." I pat myself down for the key to the iron lock, but while I'm searching Johnnie simply steps forward and pushes on the gate. Good thing that I put the key in my pocket instead of the bag that is currently at the bottom of a river.

"It's already open," she says, puzzled.

My blood seems to freeze in place. "What?"

She pushes the gate again. This time the rusting hinges squeaks in protest.

Isaiah. "No. No. No." I bolt past her and then up the two steps to the heavy iron door. It, too, is already open. Inside are two stone tombs. One is where my grandfather is resting in peace and the other is reserved for my grandmother, which currently should be holding my nest egg. One look at Nana's future resting place and I already know before shifting the stone top aside what the deal is.

"It's gone."

26

Isaiah

I'm on fucking cloud nine rapping Wu-Tang Clan's "C.R.E.A.M." at the top of my voice, "Dolla, dolla, bill y'all." I glance over my shoulder into the backseat to make sure that the monstrous steamer trunk loaded with cash is still back there. It's a new habit I've developed every time I roll up to a traffic light. "Fucking Harlem. I *love* that muthafucka!"

Of course, I wish I could be a fly on Grandpa Banks's crypt wall when Harlem arrives there and sees that all his money is gone. That muthafucka always thought his ass was smarter than me. I bet I just showed his ass. "Ha! How do you like me now?" Chair dancing, I can't stop thinking about all the shit I'm going to buy and the bitches I'm going to fuck once I find a spot on a private island somewhere. This time I'm not going to make all the mistakes I made with my own money. I'm going to just pinch off a little at a time—make the shit last.

Smiling and rapping, I push all guilt to the damn side. This money is going to save my life and get me a new start. I'm thinking beyond just crossing the border to Mexico. This kind of money can get me any damn place I want: Colombia, Fiji, or Ibiza.

I could even double the money! I latch onto the idea. Paying off Kingston West is going to probably take half the stash. What I need to do with the other half is try to flip it. I need to buy into a good game. A list of contacts scrolls through my mind as the devil on my right shoulder warns me about the dangers of my losing money while the other devil on my left encourages me by pointing out that I'm on a streak of good fortune.

No way I'm going to find an underground game here in Laredo. I got to get to my boy Gold Dawg. I know his ass still has the hottest games—and since I got to go see Kingston West in Atlanta anyway . . .

I've completely warmed up to the idea by the time I make it back to a private landing strip a few towns over in Del Mar. It feels good handing the pilot the stack of cash promised to him. It also improves his sour disposition when his small crew has to lug the trunk onto the plane.

"Where to now?" he asks, grinning.

"Atlanta," I boast. "There's a game somewhere calling my name."

"You got it."

I keep a close eye on him as he helps load up my newly found wealth and once we're in the air, I punch in Gold Dawg's number from memory. However, I'm not surprised when an automated voice informs me that the number is no longer in service. I punch in other numbers for other cats who would know how to get in contact with the underground poker host, but the problem with having criminals as friends is that no one has the same cell number for long.

Four hours later, when we touch down in an even smaller landing strip two hours west of Atlanta, I'm no closer to a buy-in to a poker game than when I started. The devil on the right says that it's for the best while the devil on the left rails on about how it's imperative that I get to a game while I'm on a good luck streak. Like a mad man on a mission, I call every number in my mental Rolodex—some twice.

By the time I'm escorted into a five-star hotel, which I've paid for with cash, I'm practically losing my mind. I *have* to find a game.

"Is there anything else that I can do for you?" the bellhop asks, panting after rolling the trunk up on the trolley.

"No. I'm good."

When the guy remains planted in the center of the room, I remember the tip. "Oh. Sorry about that." I scoop out a knot of cash and peel off a Franklin.

"Thank you, sir. If there's *anything* else, please don't hesitate to call me personally."

All right, muthafucka. I heard you the first time. Now go. "Thank you." I start to turn and give the boy my back when I finally catch the glint in his eyes. This young blood works in one of the most prestigious hotels in Atlanta and has serviced a lot of rich cats looking to get into good action. He would be just the type of worker that Gold Dawg would reach out to to book up his games.

"Yo, hold up," I call out to the boy just before he heads out the door.

"Yes, sir?"

"You wouldn't happen to know how I could find some action tonight?"

A smile breaks across the young man's face. "What kind of action would you like?"

The devil on the left gives me a mental high-five. "Looking for a game: Texas hold'em."

"I believe I can help you out with that."

27

Johnnie

"Fuck! Fuck! Fuck!" Harlem keeps swearing in a loop as he stomps his way back across the cemetery.

The anger radiates off him like sonic waves and it's all that I can do to try and keep up. Then I hit the same soft patch of dirt during our march back to the car, but this time, Harlem isn't paying attention and I pitch forward and hit the ground—hard.

"Ow!" My hands and knees immediately start aching.

Harlem keeps trudging off without me.

"HEY!"

He finally jumps and spins around. Beneath the strange moonlight, I can't tell whether he's shocked to see me on the ground or annoyed.

"Are you going to help me or not?" I snap.

When he sighs, I have my answer. He's annoyed.

I'm livid by the time he backtracks to me. Instead of accepting his hand to help me up, I struggle onto my feet alone. "Forget it."

"*Now* what the hell is wrong with you?" he snaps.

"Excuse you?"

"Whatever." His hands explode up into the air. "I don't have time for this shit!" Harlem spins back around and marches off again.

I'm left standing there, staring after him. Who the fuck is this brothah and what the hell did he do with the real Harlem? *Maybe this is the real Harlem?* That thought doesn't sit well with me. After all, I've just tossed my entire life into the garbage bin of history to be with this man. *Now* a wave of fear and regret slams into me, so much so that my eyes wet up, making it that much harder for me to see during our trek back to the car.

"Give me the keys," Harlem orders, beckoning me with his hand.

I ignore his rude ass and march to the driver's side. "*I'll* drive."

"C'mon, Johnnie. I ain't got time to stand here and argue with you."

"Then shut the fuck up and get in the car." I unlock the door and climb inside.

When he finishes staring a hole into the side of my head, he turns and marches to the other side of the car.

For a brief moment, I think about jamming on the accelerator and leaving his brooding ass right here. But I reluctantly dismiss the thought and wait until he climbs back into the car. "Where to now?" When he doesn't answer, I have to turn and look at him. "Well?"

"The fuck if I know," he swears. "I doubt that it even matters."

I don't know what to do with that answer, so I keep staring at him.

"What?" He explodes again. "Don't you get it? It's over. There is no plan B! Without that money, we're sitting ducks. My daughter doesn't get her surgery. My grandmother loses everything and you don't get your happy-ever-after. FUCK!"

Finally pulling my gaze away, I stare out over the gray, overcast cemetery with the backs of my eyes burning. "I have a little bit of money saved up."

"Ha! Too late for that. You think the government is going to let you get anywhere near that money now? Every single account you have has been frozen or seized."

"My parents—"

"Aren't going to risk their precious careers to help you run away with an escaped fugitive."

"Hey! Don't do that. You don't know my parents." I do and he's exactly right. "They'll do whatever they think is best for me," I add with less conviction.

"And you think your running off with me is what's *best* for you?"

Detecting that he was saying something else, I jerk my attention back to him. "What are you saying? You don't *want* me with you anymore?"

"Did I say that?" he challenges defensively. "I didn't say that."

"But you're thinking it," I toss back at him.

Silence.

I'm crushed.

"I don't fucking believe this." I shake my head as a way to ward off any tears from falling. "The first fucking bump in the road and you're ready to throw my ass under the bus?"

"This isn't a *bump* in the road, it's the *end* of the road. Why can't you get that shit through your head? The money is gone! We can't do jack without money!"

"Then let's get the money back," I shout.

"What?"

Yeah, what? "There . . . has to be some way to get the money back. He stole it from you, we'll just steal it back."

"Are you kidding me? With that much cash, he can be anywhere in the world right now—or gambling it away." Harlem cocks his head as his expression changes.

"What?"

"Nah." He waves whatever he was thinking off. "He wouldn't be so stupid. Would he?"

"You know the man better than I do."

Clearly, the thought circles back in his mind. "Even if he does decide to hit the tables, that still could be anywhere in the world."

"Where was his favorite place?"

"Well, he definitely wouldn't risk going to an open place like Las Vegas or Atlantic City. He never cared for the Indian casinos."

"So that leaves?"

"There was this cat in Atlanta that ran an underground thing. I don't remember his name."

After feeling like we were on a verge of something, my body deflates in disappointment.

"But I think I know some people in Atlanta that would."

I finally start the car. "So we're headed to Atlanta?"

Harlem glances at the dashboard clock. "Atlanta is like sixteen hours away from here."

"Fine. We'll drive in eight-hour shifts. We'll get there around noon tomorrow."

"But will he still be there?" Harlem wonders aloud.

"There's only one way to find out."

28
Harlem

Atlanta, Georgia

"Well, I'll be damned." Uncle Jonathan pushes his bifocals higher up his nose to take a better look at me. "Boy, if you ain't the spitting image of your momma, then water ain't wet. Get in here."

Relieved that the door hadn't been slammed in my face, I step across the threshold and allow the uncle I haven't seen in decades to wrap his impressively muscular arms around my neck.

"Look at you." Uncle Jonathan razzes the top of my head. "Big, strapping boy! Rawlo! Tremaine! Come see who's here." His gaze finally falls on Johnnie, who hangs back from the door. "And this must be Ms. Robinson. I hope you don't mind me saying, but you're a lot prettier in person."

Startled, Johnnie just blinks up at him.

"Well, you c'mon in here, too. We won't bite." He waves her in and soon as she enters the house, she receives a bear hug too, before he shuts the door. "I wish your aunt Sandra was here to see you, but she's over at Robyn's helping with the grandkids this week."

The floor shakes as a large man strolls around the corner. "What the hell are you over here hollering about?"

"Rawlo, take a look at who came to visit."

I stare back at the man, unable to square him with being the same man I remember from my childhood. This Rawlo looks as though he might have eaten the other one. The man has to be at least four hundred pounds, judging by how his belly button is racing to meet his knees.

"Aw hell," Rawlo groans, shoving his meaty hands into his pockets and then shoving some money toward Uncle Jonathan. "You win again."

Uncle Jonathan tosses his head back with a hearty laugh. "One of these damn days you're going to learn." At my confused look, Jonathan explains. "We've been following y'all escape on CNN. I thought you'd show up here and I was right."

"We're still on the news?" Johnnie groans.

"Around the clock. Got a special ticker and everything."

She looks faint.

"I'm sure it has a lot to do who your family is up north. Last hour they posted a million-dollar reward for any information or your safe return home."

Johnnie eyeballs him clutching the twenty-dollar bill.

"Oh no. This was just a little fun." He chuckles. "Trust us, we're the last dudes calling the police."

Rawlo's rumbling laughter joins in. "You can say that shit again."

"HEY! ARE WE PLAYING OR NOT?" another male voice shouts.

"Who's that?"

"Tremaine." Jonathan rolls his eyes. "He probably turned down his hearing aid again." He waves me forward until we reach the poker table they have set up instead of a normal dining room table.

When Johnnie and I follow behind my uncle and Rawlo, Tremaine finally glances up. "Oh. Why didn't you tell me that we had company?"

"TURN YOUR DAMN HEARING AID UP!" Jonathan shouts.

"What? Wait a minute. Let me turn my hearing aid up."

I crack the hell up until I remember that I came to these guys for help. *Damn. We're in serious trouble.*

"Wait. Aren't you Harlem?" Tremaine asks, late to the reunion.

"Hey, man. How are you doing?" We slap palms for a hearty handshake. The dude's hearing may be shot, but he can give Uncle Jonathan a run for his money in the strength department.

"Damn." Tremaine jams a hand into his pocket and comes up with another twenty and then tosses it over. "One day, I'm going to win one of these damn side bets."

"If you say so." Jonathan takes a seat. "Now where were we?"

Rawlo looks up at me. "Want to join us? Name of the game is Texas hold'em."

I wave off the offer. "Nah. It's not my game."

"No?" Tremaine laughs. "What is your game? *Grand Theft Auto?*"

The old guys share a laugh.

I look around. "Where is Mishawn?"

The laughter dies as they become fascinated with the cards in their hands.

"Bad news?"

Uncle Jonathan clears his throat. "He started having some memory issues. It was harmless for a little while until he started messing up his medication. When his niece found out, she came and stuck him in one of those godforsaken homes, where they leave you drooling in a corner with a diaper on." He shakes his head. "The shit ain't right."

"Well. We're all getting up there," Tremaine reminds the table.

They nod in agreement while I cut a look over at Johnnie. The look on her face matches what I'm thinking. *We're fucked!*

"So what brings you two jailbirds to my door?"

"Well . . . actually. I was hoping that you guys could help me find someone?"

"Oh yeah? Who's that?"

Feeling that we don't have anything to lose, I quickly catch them up to speed on what the jail break was all about and Isaiah beating me to my nest egg.

"You buried the money in a cemetery?" Rawlo asks after my long spiel. "That's sort of ingenious, isn't it?"

Uncle Jonathan appears more upset. "Why didn't Gloria come to me for help? I would have helped her out. I have some money . . . saved."

"You forget that she doesn't know about . . . certain things. She would never inconvenience you with our problems."

"That's ridiculous."

Tremaine tries to keep us on point. "So you're looking to find your ex-partner so you can get your loot back?"

"That's the plan." I reach over and grab Johnnie's hand. She's been quiet for a long time. It may be too much to hope that she's forgiven me for the blow-up back at the cemetery, but I'm hoping. "Isaiah has a gambling problem. He used to have a guy down here that arranged underground games for big players. I don't know if he still has his contact, but he may try to find his way into a hot game. I know that it's a shot in the dark, but . . ."

Rawlo shrugs. "I know a few cats like that. One dude, Gold

Dawg, deals with the really elite clientele. It won't hurt to put a call in and see whether your guy has shown up on his radar."

A seed of hope is planted. "Thanks. I really appreciate you checking into that."

Jonathan sets down his cards. "Once you find him, you'll find the money."

I nod.

"Any idea on how you're going to get the loot back?"

"Sort of flying by the seat of my pants on this one."

A huge smile breaks across Uncle Jonathan's face. "You hear that, boys? It sounds like we coming out of retirement."

29

Isaiah

"I got the money," I boast proudly over the phone to Kingston West. "I know that you had your doubts since . . . well, since I didn't get the chance to come through for you last time. But I'm ready to make things right."

At the heavy silence, I wonder whether the big man hung up on me. Then a deep baritone floats through the line. "Why didn't you come to me last night?"

"Last night?" I'm confused. "I just got into town last night."

"And yet you had time to buy into a high-stakes poker game."

"How did—"

Kingston chuckles over the line before he confesses, "I have eyes and ears everywhere. You should know that by now."

"My apologies—but like I said, I have your money. Give me the time and place and I'll be there."

"All right. But if you disappoint me again, there will be no third chance. Understand?"

"Completely." I grab the pen and hotel notepad by the phone and jot down the drop-off location. "Eleven o'clock. I'll be there with bells on," I joke.

Click.

"Hello? Mr. West, are you there?" When the dial tone comes over the line, I return the handset back to its cradle. Clearly, Kingston West doesn't have much of a sense of humor. I glance down at the clock on the nightstand and calculate that I have a solid seven hours before I have to meet Mr. West. That's plenty of time to squeeze in a couple of poker hands. At least to see whether I'm still hot. Last night had been like a fuckin' dream. I raked in an additional three hundred thousand before hopping up from the table. Ever since then, I can't stop thinking that I got up from the table too soon. I hadn't had a winning streak like that in years. It felt good that I could get up and walk away, but now? What if? What if I could have cleared another three-hundred thou—or a million? Those fat cats at the table were slinging chips around like money grew on trees. I used to be like that . . . until the money dried up.

I have plenty of money now. The devil on my left shoulder returns, *"You're still hot. You have plenty of money and plenty of time."*

I'm nodding my head and looking at the clock. Seven hours. That's plenty of time . . . just to see whether I'm still hot. I reach for the phone again; this time I have Gold Dawg's new number and I dial him up myself. "Yo, man. You got something I can get into?"

Less than thirty minutes later, I'm sitting in the back of a Rolls Royce Phantom being escorted to an underground game. It's a light crowd at happy hour, which suits me just fine while I pay my seventy-five-thousand buy-in. The moment I sit down, the half-naked waitresses are at my beck and call, with drinks, food, and most important, a smile.

Turns out, I'm still hot. The first two hours, the right cards are just coming to me like I'm God's favorite child. It looks like my life has finally changed for the better. It's about fucking time.

30

Harlem

"The Jackal is back in business," Uncle Jonathan crows and then looks at his watch. "But we're going to have to make sure that we're back before I have to put that pan of lasagna in the oven. Sandra will kill me if I forget again."

As Tremaine rambles around in his black gear, he seems to be unaware that his hearing aid is whistling.

Johnnie shoots me a look, asking whether someone should point that fact out to him. I would, but I'm too busy having a mild heart attack that I have to rely on this group of senior citizens in order to pull off this heist. I can't tell whether I've lost my mind or I'm simply desperate.

"Don't worry," Uncle Jonathan boasts, reading my mind. "We may be old, but we're still professionals."

"Yeah," Rawlo adds, stressing the hardwood floor. "We got this. Gold Dawg says that he just sent a car to pick up your man for another poker game. Clearly, this brother isn't the brightest light bulb on the marquee. His ass is a fugitive, too, but he's chilling the fuck out in a five-star hotel where there's cameras every damn where?"

"How much smarter can I be if I have to go into the same damn hotel to steal the money back?"

"Difference is that we're going to be in disguise." Rawlo grins. "So we better get going, if we're going to do this."

"Yeah. Hopefully, Isaiah hasn't lost all the money."

"That fast?"

"You don't know Isaiah like I do. He doesn't know how to get up from the table."

With no time to lose, the five of us pile into an old GMC van that rides as if it hasn't had a tune-up in the last decade. As far as the disguises, we're going in as plumbers. It was either this or pose as a set of electricians. I don't know why these retired cats have a costume closet, but I'm going to put that in the column of it not being any of my business.

"Are we ready?" Tremaine asks, his ears still whistling.

"Oh God. We're going to jail," Johnnie moans under her breath.

I'm thinking the same thing.

"Tremaine, fix your damn hearing aid," Rawlo barks before playfully punching his friend in the shoulder.

"Oh. Sorry about that." Tremaine flashes us his best reassuring smile.

However, we aren't much comforted as we ride out to Inter-Continental Buckhead Hotel. Gold Dawg was helpful with not only giving Rawlo the hotel information, but the room number as well. So entering the hotel through the back service entrance and finding our way to the right room is the easy part. Our challenge comes when it is time to lug the money back out of the hotel.

Rawlo, a master in his time, appears perplexed with the hotel's digital safe.

I'm more concerned about how small the safe is. No way twenty-five million dollars is in that little thing.

"Guys, you got to hurry," Johnnie coaches. "There's someone in the hallway."

Everyone freezes. Two excruciating minutes later, she gives us the all clear and the old guys go back to arguing about the make and model of the safe not being like the ones they'd mastered thirty and forty years ago.

While they argue, I start looking around the room. Then hit with inspiration, I get down on the carpet and look under the furniture. *Bingo.*

"Guys?"

Uncle Jonathan, Rawlo, and Tremaine are now arguing about how their arguing is wasting precious time.

"Uh, guys?"

Johnnie is the only one that is paying me any attention. "Did you find something?" she asks.

Nodding, I reach under the bed and pull out my trunk. It's not until I open it to reveal the stacks of cash inside do I finally grab their attention. Money has a way of silencing a crowd.

"Well, hot damn," Rawlo says, stomping over like the Jolly Green Giant to take a closer look. "I guess your boy really isn't the sharpest tool in the toolbox." He looks disappointed that his safe-cracking skills aren't going to save the day.

Judging by the look on Johnnie's face, she's as relieved as I am.

"Unless we want to be sharing a cell tonight instead of eating Sandra's lasagna we better get the hell out of here," Tremaine reminds us while fiddling with his hearing aid again. A second later, the damn thing is whistling again.

Uncle Jonathan pops him on the back of his head. "What's the matter with you? Don't you hear that damn thing?"

Tremaine twists up his face, but readjusts the aid to silence the whistling.

After everyone grabs a corner of the trunk, we rush back out of the hotel the same way we came. As we bolt away from the luxury hotel, I can't help but wish that I could somehow see Isaiah's face when he returns to the room. Karma is a bitch.

31

Isaiah

My hot streak is over. I don't know what happened. The first two hours, the poker chips were piled on my side of the table, making me look like a boss. Then I either got too cocky or these mutha-fuckas are cheating. I think they're cheating. All these shady-ass players are now hiding their eyes behind various sunglasses and winning with one miraculous river card after another.

When I'm finally the short stack at the table, I'm suspecting a damn conspiracy. Did Gold Dawg lure me back to the table today by making shit so easy last night? I wouldn't put it past him. Ain't no such thing as an honest thief no damn more.

"All in," I announce.

"I call," the only other player who didn't fold matches my bet.

"Two aces," I proclaim, standing up and tossing down my cards.

My opponent sucks his teeth and turns over his own cards. "Two jacks."

Maybe my luck is turning around. That notion is quickly dispelled when the dealer turns over the flop and another jack makes an appearance. Next comes the turn card: another ace. I'm back on top—but I still have to hold back my jubilation because the dealer has to turn over one more card. For the next five seconds, I'm holding my breath, certain that my opponent isn't going to be able to beat three aces. That is until the river card turns out to be the last jack in the deck.

Half of the table erupts in celebration for the winner and while the other half groans, sharing in my pain. I'm in shock.

"Better luck next time," Gold Dawg says, swatting me on the back.

Since I don't have any more chips, I know this is his polite way of telling me that I ain't gonna go home, but I either have to pony up more money or get the hell out of his card house.

I get up from the table, chuckling. "That's all right. You win some and you lose some." I remind myself that I have plenty of money back at the hotel. Once I pay off my debts, I can come back and turn this whole thing around. As I head out the door, I engage in another mental argument with the two devils on my shoulders on whether my returning is such a hot idea. After all, the last thing I need is to fall back into old habits. *But what's one more game?*

It's a short ride back to the InterContinental. I have an hour before I have to meet with Kingston West. After that, I should book a private plane and put Atlanta in my rearview. Ibiza is still calling my name—so says the devil on my right.

The argument continues as I make my way up to my room. However, the second I step into the room, I know that shit isn't right. I didn't leave the closet door open. *Did the cleaning crew come in this bitch after I left a "Do Not Disturb" sign on the door?*

I immediately rush over to the bed and drop to my knees. There's nothing there. "No. No. No." I swipe my hand across the bare rug as though my vision isn't trustworthy. There's clearly nothing there. "What the fuck? What the fuck?" I jump up and tear through the room like the Tasmanian devil. The money *has* to be here. It just has to be. After my sixth search around the room, I start grabbing fistfuls of my short-cropped hair and pulling. "This can't be happening. It can't."

Without thinking, I grab the phone and dial down to the front desk. I was just about to say, "Yes, I'd like to report a robbery," when my common sense kicks back in.

"Front desk."

Gritting my teeth, my grip on the phone tightens.

"Hello. Front desk."

"Uh . . . never mind." I slam the phone down and then take another sweeping look around the room. *I'm a dead man.* For the first time, the two devils on my shoulder agree with me. My heartbeat goes haywire as I struggle to come up with a backup plan. But the only option available to me is to get the fuck out of Dodge.

With nothing but the fucking clothes on my back, I race toward the door—only there's these two brick-building-looking muthafuckas standing on the other side.

"You must be Isaiah Kane," one of them says, grinning. "Kingston West sent us to make sure that you show up to your appointment this time."

Oh fuck.

32

Sam

"I might have something here that may fall into the category of shit you won't believe," Renee says, joining the team in our hotel lobby.

Taking a moment to stop rubbing my temples from a caffeine-induced migraine, I look up. "Oh. I don't know. At this point, I may believe any damn thing."

Renee hands over a stack of photographs. "Hot off the presses from the team working on the Isaiah Kane escape."

There, in bold digital color, are clear images of Mr. Kane entering a hotel, talking to a clerk at the front desk, and a few pictures of him waiting for an elevator. "Where and when was this?"

"At the InterContinental Buckhead Hotel in Atlanta. And they were taken last night. One of the agents from the other team decided to follow a hunch regarding Mr. Kane's rumored gambling issues. In the early 2000s, Kane was arrested a few times during illegal gambling raids in Georgia. It was enough to get them to wonder whether he still had the itch."

Greg looks as disappointed as I feel. "So they didn't come here to Laredo? We've swept through every backhouse, cathouse, and outhouse in this whole damn town. Could we have gotten the shit this wrong?"

"If Banks and Robinson were going to Atlanta, they were certainly taking the craziest scenic route I've ever seen." I hand the photos back over to Renee. "Maybe they weren't racing to the same location. Maybe one escape has nothing to do with the other."

"Or," Max interrupts, but then doesn't follow through with his thought.

"Or what?" I don't have time to try to read people's minds today. "Spit it out."

Max shrugs as if he doesn't believe his own hypothesis before he puts it out here. "Or . . . maybe . . . Isaiah won the race." He gestures to the pictures. "Where did he get the money to stay at a place like the InterContinental anyway?"

The rest of the team, mute, blinks up at him.

Now self-conscious, he shrugs and shakes his head again. "It's just an idea."

I look over at Greg. "Actually, it makes sense. We missed them somehow."

He nods, bolting up from one of the cheap upholstered chairs. "If Kane got to the money first, then no way Banks lets him ride off into the sunset."

"He'll go after the money," I agree.

The rest of the team hop out of our seats, each of us experiencing the same jolt of adrenaline.

"It looks like we're headed to Atlanta." I turn toward Max and pound him hard on the back. "Good job!"

"Thanks!" He puffs out his chest and then tosses a wink over at Greg as if to say he'd snatched the teacher's pet mug right from up under him.

Greg rolls his eyes. "Whatever, rookie. Let's go catch these damn thieves."

33

Johnnie

Back at Jonathan Banks's home, I stare wide-eyed at the open steam trunk of money. I've never seen so much cash at one time in my entire life. The idea of twenty-five million dollars is one thing; to actually see it is another. "You *stole* all of this money?" I hadn't meant to ask the question aloud, but when Harlem's head swiveled in my direction, I suddenly feel embarrassed by it. I try to cover by pinning on a smile, but I get the feeling that it doesn't work.

"Are you all right?" he asks, standing up from the trunk and moving over to me.

"Yeah. I mean . . . wow."

"Who wants a beer?" Rawlo shouts, still jubilant about their latest heist.

"I'll take one," Harlem answers and signals to him. "What about you, Johnnie?"

"Uhm, you wouldn't happen to have something a little stronger?"

Jonathan's smile doubles in size. "A woman after my own heart." He elbows Harlem. "You better hang on to this one."

Harlem nods as he keeps his gaze locked on me. "Don't worry, Uncle Jonathan. I intend to do just that."

"What's your pleasure, little lady?"

"Hmm. Bourbon, if you got it."

"One bourbon coming right up." Jonathan tosses me another wink before turning toward the living room's small bar.

Suddenly, I find it hard to keep Harlem's gaze. Waves of fear, regret, and doubt are now the size of tidal waves and I can't help but feel that at any moment I'm going to be crushed under them. But why? I'm the one who pushed for us to follow the money. I'm the one who refused to let him dump me in the middle of that cemetery. Now, I don't know what I want.

Still laughing and congratulating himself, Rawlo's heavy footsteps continue to stress the wooden floorboards as he crosses the living room to hand Harlem his beer. "Here you go, my boy. You definitely earned this one."

"Thanks, Rawlo." Harlem accepts the bottle with a stiff smile.

When he turns his attention back to me, I'm still doing a lousy job of pretending that I'm okay.

Meanwhile, Tremaine exits out of the kitchen with a bowl of chips and his hearing aid whistling again. "Hey, Jonathan, when are you supposed to put that lasagna in the oven? I'm starving."

"Amen," Rawlo growls before stealing a handful of chips.

"Aw, damn. I forgot." Jonathan hands me my drink before taking off toward the kitchen.

I, on the other hand, waste no time downing the strong drink in one long, burning gulp.

Harlem's beer bottle stops halfway toward his lips as he watches me. "Okay. Maybe we need to talk," he says.

"What? No. I'm fine," I lie. When it's clear to me that he's not buying it, I switch tactics. "You know, it's just been a crazy kind of day, you know?"

"A crazy couple of days," he amends, nodding in agreement. "You got to be exhausted."

"You have no idea. I could really use a nap."

"Oh. Okay." He turns toward the kitchen to yell, "Hey, Unc. You got a spare room for Johnnie to go and lay down?"

We hear the oven door slam shut. "What?"

"Spare room. You got one?"

"Oh, yeah. Tremaine, show them where the room is."

"Uh? What?"

"I'll do it," Rawlo says, rolling his eyes at his deaf buddy.

We follow Rawlo to the top floor of the house to a cute bedroom with twin beds on each side of the room. The pale pink tea roses are a nice touch.

"One of us will come knock when dinner is ready," Rawlo promises before leaving us alone.

Harlem's gaze searches for mine, but I turn away to test the firmness of one of the beds. "Are we really going to play this game?" he asks.

"What?" Even as the question escapes my mouth, I wonder if I appear as bad an actor as I feel.

He cocks his head. "Really?"

Finally, I give up the ghost with a long sigh. "Sorry. I just . . . I don't know. Seeing all of that money . . ."

"It finally hit you what I did for a living?"

"No . . . yes. I don't know." I jump back to my feet. "The police car chase and shoot-out should've brought that home. Then there was the car-jacking . . . and the grave robbing and a hotel heist." I sigh as my shoulder feels like it's getting heavier by the second and my low-grade headache is increasingly becoming an eye-twitching migraine.

"So . . . you're having second thoughts?" he asks, trying his best to wipe all emotion from his face. The problem is that it isn't working.

"Look. I really am just tired." *And I miss my family, my house, and my own bed.*

"I understand." Harlem nods as if he'd heard my private thoughts. "Maybe you should wash up and get some sleep. We're going to have to load up and leave in a few hours anyway."

"That sounds good," I agree eagerly. Anything so that I can get a few seconds alone. A bathroom is just across the hall and I have no trouble figuring out where the towels and toiletries are. When I'm finally beneath the hot spray of water, the tears flow. Suddenly, I'm not sure of anything. I love Harlem and I don't want to let him go—but can I really give up *everything?*

After washing and rinsing until my fingers turn into prunes, I exit the shower, towel off, and slip into a robe Harlem's uncle borrowed from his wife's closet. As I make my way back to the spare bedroom, I can still hear the men downstairs, joking, laughing, and playing poker.

Lying down, I think about all that I've been through the last three days. All of the action, all the emotions; it's left me drained. Maybe I will feel better after a quick nap. The second my head touches the pillow I'm out like a light. Hours later, I feel Harlem's lips grazing the back of my neck.

Moaning, I inch back so that he can have better access; that's when one of his strong hands slides inside of the robe. Instantly, my body comes alive and we make love. He has never tasted so good or felt so right. It's probably why my tears return, but it doesn't stop our flow. Hell, I'm not even sure how in the hell the two of us are able to fit on this small bed, but we make it work.

"Don't cry," he repeats. "I got you."

And I believe him. By the time we climax, I'm back to wondering how in the world I could ever think about letting him go. The past five years nearly tore me apart. I can't go back to that. I won't.

34

Harlem

Leaving Johnnie is one of the hardest things I've ever had to do in my life—but I know that it's the right thing. When we're together, there are sparks, fireworks—you name it. But it's not enough. It can never be enough. Life on the run would be harder on her than she realizes—or maybe she's already beginning to suspect it.

There's not a day I don't wish that I could just take my little Tyler into my arms and tell her how much I love her. I'm the one that should be by her side when she has her next surgery. I should be the one encouraging her to be brave—but I can and will never be able to do any of it.

My retirement will now be a life on the run. I can never look back—not even for Johnnie. When I creep downstairs, Uncle Jonathan is still up. He's in a pair of black pajamas and eased back in his La-Z-Boy. He has my number the second our eyes connect.

"I take it that you said your good-byes?" he asks.

My heart is so heavy that I can't even post up like everything is cool. "It's for the best," I tell him.

"Maybe." He nods. "Is that how she's going to feel about it when she wakes up in the morning?"

"To be honest with you, I don't know. Eventually, probably not tomorrow, the next day or maybe even a year from now, but one day she'll understand that I'm doing right by her."

"That's taking one hell of a gamble. Women are . . . complicated. I know. I had to lose Sandra and my daughter Robyn for a long time before I could win them back. Maybe the same will happen for you."

"You never had to deal with the US Marshals," I remind him. "I'll be looking over my shoulder for the rest of my life. Johnnie isn't built for that. She should be with a man who can give her and . . . her future children a real life in a nice house, a white picket fence and maybe even a damn dog if she wants it. I can't do any of that shit now."

"I hear what you're saying." Our eyes connect. "I'm proud of you. It takes a real man to be able to set someone you love like that free."

"Well, it definitely doesn't feel so good," I admit.

"No. I don't imagine that it does." He pushes himself up from his chair and for the first time in my life I allow another man to hug me good-bye.

When I step back, my eyes are wet and I force myself to go through with my new plan. We've already divided up the money. He'll make sure that the Tyler's surgery money will be funneled through Nana Gloria's church—so the payment will look as though the church had raised the funds. He'll also see to it that her bills are paid and that she'll never want for anything. I trust him. He knows how to move money around undetected. "Oh. And make sure you get that other money to this cat." I pull out a slip of paper with Goon's contact man written on it. "A man gotta pay his debts."

"Always."

"Is Rawlo downstairs?" I ask.

"Waiting on you with your *retirement* money." Uncle Jonathan grins. "He'll take you down to Jacksonville, Florida. He knows a guy who knows a guy that can get you on a private plane to anywhere you want to go. Fair warning: Rawlo can talk your damn head off. Just smile and nod to try to get through it the best way you can."

"Thanks, Uncle Jonathan. I really appreciate you looking out for me."

"Don't mention it." He walks me to the door. "In case our paths don't cross again, I love you and take care of yourself."

"Love you, too, Uncle Jonathan." We exchange another hug and then I'm out the door, pretending the whole way that my heart isn't breaking.

35

Johnnie

I wake up in a cold bed. When that reality sinks in, I bolt straight up and glance around a dark room. Harlem is gone. Reacting on nothing but a gut feeling, I scramble back into the clothes that I've been wearing for the last couple of days.

"Harlem!" I race out of the room, across the hall, and down the stairs, where I collide into Harlem's uncle Jonathan.

"Sweetheart, calm down."

"Where is he?"

He hesitates.

"Where?"

"He just left. He—"

Pushing Jonathan aside, I take off after Harlem. My heart is in my throat as I race out the front door. That old GMC van is backing out of the drive.

"Harlem! Wait! Harlem!" I run like my life depends on it. For a moment, I'm scared that Rawlo, who is behind the wheel, won't stop. But then he does.

I nearly weep with relief when the van finally stops and Harlem opens the passenger-side door.

"Johnnie—"

"I can't believe that you were just going to leave me like that."

"Trust me, this shit isn't easy—but it's the right thing to do. I know it—and you know it."

"Fuck you. You don't get to decide what's best for me without my having a vote." I swallow hard and then try to catch my breath. "I got scared, okay? But I know what I want—and I want you. I don't care that you're a thief or whatever. I just know that I can't go back to living without you. I tried it before. I can't do it again. Don't make me do it again. Please."

Tears pour down my face. I don't know what else to say to make sure that he doesn't leave me—but begging isn't out of the question. "Please don't leave me."

For a long time, Harlem just stares at me. "Once you get into this van, you can't turn back. You'll never see your family or friends again."

"*You* will be my family."

A smile splits across his face. "Deal."

I race into his arms and smother him with kisses—and love.

36

Sam

Atlanta, Georgia

Thirty minutes after my team touches down, we arrive at the InterContinental Buckhead Hotel and a chaotic scene. We expected our other team and local agencies to be here to catch their fugitive. We were hoping to get a few minutes alone with Isaiah Kane again so we can have some idea whether *our* guy is here, too.

However, I did not expect to find Isaiah's broken body being zipped up in a body bag. "What happened?" I ask the first guy I come across. It's not an agent but a paramedic. "The guy jumped."

"What?" That didn't sound right.

The paramedic shrugs. "It was either that or he was pushed."

I look up. "From what floor?" Not that it mattered.

"Don't know. You'll have to ask them." He gestures to the knot of US Marshals, Georgia Bureau of Investigation agents, and police officers.

I walk over and make my introductions. Again, no one is sure whether the ex-fugitive jumped or was pushed. Has Harlem Banks added murder to his résumé?

Unfortunately, the surprises keep coming. The hotel security team states that the cameras were offline for the entire day.

"But they were working last night," I counter, referring to the photos my team saw just hours ago.

"That was last night," the chief officer says. "Whoever punched those photos up for you guys must've knocked the system offline or forgotten to switch it back on."

The fact that that didn't make a lick of sense doesn't seem to bother the guy. That was the hotel's story and they were sticking to it.

"Smells like bullshit to me," Greg grumbles.

"I thought I was the only one who was smelling it." I take a deep breath. "Something was on those tapes."

"Yeah but . . . does our guy have the kind of juice to make something like that disappear?"

"Depends on what kind of money we're talking about."

I search out Agent Davis of the GBI and ask her whether her team recovered any money from Kane's room.

No money.

Greg tosses up his hands. "We're too late. He's in the wind. If he's smart he's halfway to some private island."

I'm afraid he's right. "Then I guess we better get busy trying to find which one."

"I don't know," Frank says, shaking his head. "I got a feeling this one is going to wreck your record."

I shake my head at my team's defeatist attitudes. "I'll find him," I promise them. "I don't know how long it will take. Maybe tomorrow. Maybe next year—maybe twenty years from now, but I *will* find him."

DON'T MISS

Her Sweetest Revenge
by Saundra

For Mya Bedford, life in a Detroit project is hard enough, but when her mother develops a drug habit, Mya has to take on raising her younger siblings. Too bad the only man who can teach her how to survive—her dad—is behind bars. For life. All he can tell her is that she'll have to navigate the mean streets on her own terms. Mya's not sure what that means—until her mother is seriously beaten by a notorious gang. Then it all becomes deadly clear . . .

Baby, You're the Best
by Mary B. Morrison

New York Times best-selling author Mary B. Morrison introduces her most seductive and vulnerable characters yet with the Crystal women, a family whose bonds are tested by love, lust, and the elusive quest for true happiness . . .

And coming in December 2015

Games Women Play
by Zaire Crown

Tuesday Knight is eager for a better way of life. That means getting out of the game her gentleman's club has been fronting. Her all-female "business" team has made a fortune using the club to attract, seduce—and rob—wealthy men. But in addition to being squeezed by a corrupt cop, an unfortunate incident has put Tuesday deep in debt to a ruthless gun dealer and is creating dangerous dissent behind the scenes . . .

Turn the page for an excerpt from these thrilling novels . . .

From *Her Sweetest Revenge*

Chapter 1

Sometimes I wonder how my life would've turned out if my parents had been involved in different things, like if they had regular jobs. My mother would be a social worker, and my father a lawyer or something. You know, jobs they call respectable and shit.

Supposedly these people's lives are peaches and cream. But when I think about that shit I laugh, because my life is way different. My father was a dope pusher who served the whole area of Detroit. And when I say the whole area, I mean just that. My dad served some of the wealthiest politicians all the way down to the poorest people in the hood who would do anything for a fix. Needless to say, if you were on cocaine before my father went to prison, I'm sure he served you; he was heavy in the street. Lester Bedford was his birth name, and that's what he went by in the streets of Detroit. And there was no one who would fuck with him. Everybody was in check.

All the dudes on the block were jealous of him because his pockets were laced. He had the looks, money, nice cars, and the baddest chick on the block, Marisa Haywood. All the dudes wanted Marisa because she was a redbone with coal-black hair flowing down her back and a banging-ass body, but she was only interested in my dad. They had met one night at a friend's dice party and had been inseparable since then.

Life was good for them for a long time. Dad was able to make a lot of money with no hassle from the feds, and Mom was able to stay home with their three kids. Three beautiful kids, if I may say so. First, she had me, Mya, then my brother, Bobby, who we all call Li'l Bo, and last was my baby sister, Monica.

We were all happy kids about four years ago; we didn't need or want for nothing. My daddy made sure of that. The only thing my father wanted to give us next was a house with a backyard. Even though he was stacking good dough, we still lived in the Brewster-Douglass Projects.

All those years he'd been trying to live by the hood code. However, times were changing. The new and upcoming ballers were getting their dough and moving out of the hood. Around this time my dad decided to take us outta there too.

Before he could make a move, our good luck suddenly changed for the worse. Our apartment was raided by the feds. After sitting in jail for six months, his case finally went to court, where he received a life sentence with no possibility of parole.

My mother never told us what happened, but sometimes I would eavesdrop on her conversations when she would be crying on a friend's shoulder. That's how I overheard her saying that they had my father connected to six drug-related murders and indicted on cocaine charges. I couldn't believe my ears. My father wouldn't kill anybody. He was too nice for that. I was completely pissed off; I refused to hear any of that. It was a lie. As far as I was concerned, my father was no murderer and all that shit he was accused of was somebody's sick fantasy. He was innocent. They were just jealous of him because he was young, black, and borderline rich. True, it was drug money, but in the hood, who gave a fuck. But all that was in the past; now, my dad was on skid row. Lockdown. Three hots and a cot. And our home life reflected just that.

All of a sudden my mother started hanging out all night. She would come home just in time for us to go to school. For a while that was okay, but then her behavior also started to change. I mean, my mother looked totally different. Her once-healthy skin started to look pale and dry. She started to lose weight, and her hair was never combed. She tried to comb it, but this was a woman who was used to going to the beauty shop every week. Now her hair looked like that of a stray cat.

I noticed things missing out of the house, too, like our Alpine digital stereo. I came home from school one day and it was gone. I asked my mother about it, and she said she sold it for food. But that had to be a lie because we were on the county. Mom didn't work, so we received food stamps and cash assistance. We also received government assistance that paid the rent, but Mom was responsible for the utilities, which started to get shut off.

Before long, we looked like the streets. After my father had been locked up for two years, we had nothing. We started to outgrow our clothes because Mom couldn't afford to buy us any, so whatever secondhand clothes we could get, we wore. I'm talking about some real stinking-looking gear. Li'l Bo got suspended from school for kicking some boy's ass about teasing him about a shirt he wore to school with someone else's name on it. We had been too wrapped up in our new home life to realize it. When the lady from the Salvation Army came over with the clothes for Li'l Bo, he just ironed the shirt and put it on. He never realized the spray paint on the back of the shirt said *Alvin*. That is, until this asshole at school decided to point it out to him.

Everything of value in our house was gone. Word on the streets was my mother was a crackhead and prostitute. I tried to deny it at first, but before long, it became obvious.

Now it's been four years of this mess, and I just can't take it anymore. I don't know what to do. I'm only seventeen years old. I'm sitting here on this couch hungry with nothing to eat and my mom is lying up in her room with some nigga for a lousy few bucks. And when she's done, she's going to leave here and cop some more dope. I'm just sick of this.

"Li'l Bo, Monica," I shouted so they could hear me clearly. "Come on, let's go to the store so we can get something to eat."

"I don't want to go to the store, Mya. It's cold out there," Monica said, pouting as she came out of the room we shared.

"Look, put your shoes on. I'm not leaving you here without me or Li'l Bo. Besides, ain't nothing in that kitchen to eat so if we don't go to the store, we starve tonight."

"Well, let's go. I ain't got all night." Li'l Bo tried to rush us, shifting side to side where he stood. The only thing he cares about is that video game that he has to hide to keep Mom from selling.

On our way to the store we passed all the local wannabe dope boys on our block. As usual, they couldn't resist hitting on me. But I never pay them losers any mind because I will never mess around with any of them. Most of the grimy niggas been sleeping with my mom anyway. Especially Squeeze, with his bald-headed ass. Nasty bastard. If I had a gun I would probably shoot all them niggas.

"Hey, Mya. Girl, you know you growing up. Why don't you let me take you up to Roosters and buy you a burger or something?" Squeeze asked while rubbing his bald head and licking his nasty, hungry lips at me. "With a fat ass like that, girl, I will let you order whatever you want off the menu."

"Nigga, I don't need you to buy me jack. I'm good." I rolled my eyes and kept stepping.

"Whatever, bitch, wit' yo' high and mighty ass. You know you hungry."

Li'l Bo stopped dead in his tracks. "What you call my sister?" He turned around and mugged Squeeze. "Can you hear, nigga? I said, what did you call my sister?" Li'l Bo spat the words at Squeeze.

I grabbed Li'l Bo by the arm. "Come on, don't listen to him. He's just talkin'. Forget him anyway." I dismissed Squeeze with a wave of my hand.

"Yeah, little man, I'm only playing." Squeeze had an ugly scowl on his face.

Before I walked away I turned around and threw up my middle finger to Squeeze because that nigga's time is coming. He's got plenty of enemies out here on the streets while he's wasting time fooling with me.

When we made it to the store I told Li'l Bo and Monica to watch my back while I got some food. I picked up some sandwich meat, cheese, bacon, and hot dogs. I went to the counter and paid for a loaf of bread to make it look legit, and then we left the store. Once outside, we hit the store right next door. I grabbed some canned goods, a pack of Oreo cookies for dessert, and two packs of chicken wings. When we got outside, we unloaded all the food into the shopping bags we brought from home. That would get us through until next week. This is how we eat because Mom sells all the food stamps every damn month. The thought of it made me kick a single rock that was in my path while walking back to the Brewster.

When we got back to the house, Mom was in the kitchen rambling like she's looking for something. So she must be finished doing her dirty business. I walked right past her like she ain't even standing there.

"Where the hell y'all been? Don't be leavin' this house at night without telling me," she screamed, then flicked some cigarette butts into the kitchen sink.

"We went to the store to get food. There is nothin' to eat in this damn house." I rolled my eyes, giving her much attitude.

"Mya, who the hell do you think you talking to? I don't care where you went. Tell me before you leave this house," she said, while sucking her teeth.

"Yeah, whatever! If you cared so much, we would have food." I got smart again. "Monica, grab the skillet so I can fry some of this chicken," I ordered her, then slammed the freezer door shut.

Mom paused for a minute. She was staring at me so hard I thought she was about to slap me for real. But she just turned around and went to her room. Then she came right back out of her room and went into the bathroom with clothes in hand.

I knew she was going to leave when she got that money from her little trick. Normally, I want her to stay in the house. That way I know she's safe. But tonight, I'm ready for her to leave because I'm pissed at her right now. I still love her, but I don't understand what happened to her so fast. Things have been hard on all of us. Why does she get to take the easy way out by doing crack? I just wish Dad was here, but he's not, so I got to do something to take care of my brother and sister and get us out of this rat hole.

From *Baby, You're the Best*

Prologue

Alexis

"Thanks for everything. I enjoyed serving you."

You? You? Not this shit again! That bitch waited on us for two hours. I'd kept my mouth shut when the "What would *you* like to drink?" was directed toward my man only. I had to interrupt with my request for a mai tai.

We'd adhered to their protocol by writing our orders on the restaurant's request forms, meaning there was no need to ask what we wanted to eat. The repeat for confirmation, "So you're having the fried wings, rice and gravy, and steamed cabbage and the vegetable plate with double collard greens, and fried okra?" was asked of my man as though he was going to eat it all by himself.

Now that the check was here, I was still invisible? *Aw, hell no!* I pushed back my chair, stood tall on the red-bottom stilettos my man had bought. The hem of my purple halter minidress was wedged between the crack of my sweet chocolate ass but I didn't give a damn. That working-for-tips trick was about to come up short.

I leaned over the table, pointed at the waiter, then said loud enough for all the people on our side of the restaurant to hear, "My man is not interested in you!"

James held my hips, pulled me toward my seat. Refusing to sit, I sprang to my feet, then told him, "No, babe."

Nothing was holding me back from the inconsiderate asshole that obviously needed customer service training. I stepped into the aisle. The only thing separating us was air.

"Not today, Alexis. Please stop," James pleaded.

I extended my middle finger alongside my pointing finger, and my nails stopped inches from the waiter's face when my man reached over the table and grabbed my wrist. I was about to put both of that dude's eyes out.

He posed, one foot slightly in front of the other, tilted his head sideways, put his hand on his hip with a bitch-I-dare-you attitude.

The room was cold. I was heated. The guests became quiet. A woman scrambled for her purse, picked up her toddler, then rushed toward the exit. I didn't give a damn if everybody got the hell out!

"One of these days, sweetheart, I'm not going to be around to intervene," James said. He handed the waiter a hundred-dollar bill.

I snatched it. "Give his ass whatever is on the bill and not a penny more."

James handed that jerk another hundred. This time the waiter got to the money before I did. He stuffed the cash in his black apron pocket, rolled his eyes at me, scanned my guy head to toe, then said, "Thanks. You can come anytime you'd like. Let me get your change."

He stepped back. I moved forward. I didn't have a problem slapping a bitch that deserved it. I swung to lay a palm to the left side of his face. His ass leaned back like he was auditioning for a role in the next *Matrix* movie.

"Don't duck, bitch, you bold. If you feeling some type of way, express yourself." I shoved my hand into my purse.

He screamed, "Manager! Manager!"

I didn't care if he called Jesus. "Say something else to my man. I dare you." If I lifted my gun and put my finger on the trigger, I swear he wouldn't live to disrespect another woman.

James swiftly pulled my arm and purse to his side, then told the waiter, "Sorry, man. Keep the change."

The waiter stared at the guests. "Y'all excuse my sister, she forgot to take her meds." A few people laughed.

"Take your lame-ass jokes to Improv Comedy Club for open mic, bitch. You weren't trying to be center stage before my man tipped you."

"I got you, boo." He pulled out his cell, started pressing on the pad. "You so bad. Stay turnt up until the po-po comes." He turned, then switched his ass away.

James begged, "Sweetheart, let's go."

Some round, short guy with a sagging gut, dressed in a white button-down shirt and cheap black pants, hurried in our direction. "Ma'am. Sir. You need to leave now."

The old lady seated next to our table said, "Honey, you're outnumbered in this town. You gon' wear yourself out."

I told my guy, "Walk in front of me."

Shaking his head, James said, "You a trip," then laughed. "You go first. I have to keep an eye on you."

That was the other way around. Atlanta was a tough place to meet a straight man who cared about being faithful. The ugly guys had a solid five to fifteen females willing to do damn near anything to and for them. The attractive ones had triple those options. The successful, good-looking men with big egos and small dicks were assholes not worth my fucking with. But these dudes boldly disrespecting me by hitting on my man, they were the worst.

"It's not funny, James. I'm sick of this shit."

I knew it wasn't my guy's fault that James was blessed eighty inches toward heaven, one hundred and eighty pounds on the ground with a radiant cinnamon-chocolate complexion that attracted men and women.

James opened the door of his electric-blue Tesla Roadster, waited until I was settled in the passenger seat. He got in, then drove west on Ponce de Leon.

As he merged onto the I-85, he said, "Just because you have the right to bear arms, sweetheart, doesn't mean you should. I keep telling you to leave the forty at home," he said, laughing. "I'm glad you like my ass."

"Nothing's funny. I don't understand how men hitting on you don't bother you."

"The way you be all up on my ass, what the hell I need a dude for? Soon as you finish your dissertation, I'm signing you up for an anger management course," he said. "You can't keep flashing on men because your father is the ultimate asshole. Let it go, sweetheart."

"That's easy for you to say. Your parents are still happily married. I bet if your dad disowned you, you wouldn't say, 'Let it go.'"

I was still pissed at that waiter. I had to check his ass. I was fed up with dicks disrespecting females. I'd seen my mother give all she had to offer and the only engagement ring ever put on Blake Crystal's finger was the one she'd bought herself.

James held my hand. "You're right, sweetheart. I know how much he's hurt you."

My father, whoever and wherever the fuck he was, was the first male disappointment in my life. Some kids cried because their daddy promised to show up but didn't. Mine never promised. Before I had a first boyfriend, my heart was already shattered into pieces by my dad. Staring out the window, I refused to shed another tear.

Continuing north on Interstate 85, James bypassed exit 86 to my house. "I know how to cheer you up. I'm taking you to Perimeter Mall."

"Thanks, babe," was all I said.

I was twenty-six years old and I'd never met my father. My birth certificate listed the father as unknown. Hell yeah, I was angry. My mama didn't fuck herself but in a way she had.

My way of coping with my daddy issues was to not allow any man to penetrate my heart or disrespect me. Every man I dated had to like me more. The second a woman liked a man more than he liked her, she was fucked and screwed.

"Sweetheart, I have a question."

"Don't start that shit with me today, James. Don't go there."

He let go of my hand. "If you answer, I promise, no more questions."

I knew he was lying. He always said that shit and didn't mean it. "What, James?"

"Have you had any other men in your house other than me?"

I could lie. Tell him what he wanted to hear. Or I could tell the truth. Either way it didn't fucking matter! My blood pressure escalated. "I'm not answering that."

He exited the freeway, parked by Maggiano's. "Cool, then I'm not paying your rent this month."

That's why a bitch kept backup.

From *Games Women Play*

The Bounce House was not one of those inflatable castles parents rented for children's parties. It was a small gentleman's club set in a strip mall on 7 Mile with a beauty supply store, a rib joint, an outlet that sold men's clothing, and an unleased space that changed hands every few years. In no way was The Bounce House on the same level as some of the more elite clubs in Detroit; with a maximum capacity of two hundred fifty and limited parking, it would never be a threat to The Coliseum, Cheetah's, or any of the big dogs. It wasn't big but it was comfortable and well managed, plus the owner was very selective in choosing the girls, so this had earned it a small but loyal patronage.

The owner, Tuesday Knight, knew that Mr. Scott, her neighbor and owner of Bo's BBQ, would be waiting in the door of his shop the moment her white CTS hit the lot. The old man had a crush on her and always made it his business to be on hand to greet her whenever she pulled in to work.

She frowned when she saw that someone had parked in her spot right in front of The Bounce House. The canary Camaro with the black racing stripes belonged to Brianna, and she was definitely going to check that bitch because she had been warned about that before.

Since all the other slots outside The Bounce, Bo's BBQ, and KiKi's Beauty Supply were taken, she had to park way down in front of the vacant property, and she speculated about which business would spring up there next. In the past five years it had been an ice cream parlor, a cell phone shop, and an occult bookstore. She wished its next incarnation would be as a lady's shoe outlet that sold Louboutins at a discount.

She shrugged the Louis Vuitton bag onto her shoulder then slid out of the Cadillac.

Up ahead on the promenade Mr. Scott was standing in front of his carry-out spot pretending to sweep the walk but really waiting for her. This was practically a daily ritual for them.

"Hi, Mr. Scott," she said, beaming a smile.

He did an old-school nod and tip of the hat. "Hey. Miss Tuesday, you sho lookin' mighty fine today." He always called her Miss Tuesday even though it was her first name.

"Thank you, Mr. Scott. You lookin' handsome as always."

He removed his straw Dobb's hat and was fanning himself with it even though the afternoon was mild. "Girl, if I was thirty years younger, I'd show you somethin'!"

"I know you would, Daddy! You have a nice day now, okay."

She strutted by him and since her jeans were particularly tight today, she threw a little something extra in her walk and made the old man howl: "Lord, have mercy!" Mr. Scott was seventy years old and had always been respectful of her and all the dancers so she didn't mind putting on for him. Plus the harmless flirting made his day and got her free rib dinners. When Tuesday reached the door of the club, she turned back to give him another smile and coquettish wave.

What The Bounce House lacked in size it attempted to make up for in taste. There was nothing cheap about the place despite being a small independent establishment. The design wasn't unique: a fifteen-foot bar ran against the far right wall, a large horseshoe-shaped stage dominated the center with twenty or so small circular tables surrounding it, booths lined the left wall and wrapped around the front, the entrance was where that front wall and right one intersected, and the deejay booth was next to it.

Before Tuesday had taken over, the entire place was done in a tacky red because the previous owner thought that it was a sexual color. The bar was a bright red Formica that was peeling, the stools and booths were done in cheap red leatherette, the floor was covered in pink and red checkered tile, and the tables wore hideous black and red tablecloths with tassels that made the place look like a whorehouse from the '70s

Tuesday had brought the place into the new millennium with brushed suede booths, a bar with a granite top, more understated flooring, and mirrored walls that gave the illusion of more space. She even gave it a touch of class and masculinity by adding dark woods, brass, and a touch of plant life.

When she came through the door, the first thing that jumped out at her was that the fifth booth hadn't been bused. There were half a dozen double-shot glasses on the table, an ashtray filled with butts and cigar ends, and a white Styrofoam food container that had most likely come from Bo's. She knew that it was her OCD that caused her to immediately zero in on this but before she could start bitching, one of the servers was already headed to clean it up. Everyone who worked there knew their boss had a thing for neatness so she shot the girl a look that said, *Bitch, you know better!*

Things were slow even for a Monday afternoon. There were only three customers at the bar with eleven more scattered throughout the tables and booths. Most of them were entranced by a dancer named Cupcake who was on stage rolling her hips to a Gucci Mane cut. Two more girls were on the floor giving table dances.

Whenever Tuesday came in, on any shift, her first priority was always to check on the bar. The bartender on duty was a brown-skinned cutie named Ebony who had started out as a dancer then learned she had a knack for pouring drinks. She took a couple classes, became a mixologist and has been working at The Bounce since back in the day when Tuesday was just a dancer.

Ebony called out: "Boss Lady!" when she saw her slip behind the bar.

Tuesday pulled her close so she wouldn't have to compete with the music. "Eb, how we lookin' for the week?"

From the pocket of her apron Ebony whipped out a small notepad she used for keeping up with the liquor inventory. "What we don't got out here we got in the back. We pretty much straight on everythang, at least as far as makin' it through the week, except we down to our last case of Goose."

Tuesday made a mental note to send Tushie to the distributor.

Ebony asked, "How dat nigga A.D. doin'?"

"He all right. Reading every muthafuckin' thang and workin' out. That nigga arms damn near big as Tushie's legs."

"When was the last time you holla'ed at em?"

Tuesday scanned the bar, quietly admiring how neat Ebony kept her workstation. "Nigga called the other day on some horny shit. Talkin' 'bout, 'What kinda panties you got on? What color is they?'" She did a comical impersonation of a man's deep voice. "Nigga kept me on the phone for a hour wantin' me to talk dirty to 'em."

Ebony poured a customer another shot of Silver Patron. "No he didn't!" she said, smiling at Tuesday.

"So I'm tellin' him I'm in a bathtub playin' with my pussy,

thinkin' bout his big dick. The whole time I'm out at Somerset Mall in Nordstrom's lookin' for a new fit."

"TK, you still crazy!" Ebony was laughing so hard that she fell into her. "The funny part is, he probably knew you was lying and just didn't care."

"Hell yeah, he knew I was lying. A.D. ain't stupid. But when I know that's the type of shit he wanna hear, I always tell 'em somethin' good."

"That nigga been gone for a minute. When he comin' home?"

Tuesday's smile faded a bit. She hated when people asked that question, especially when most of them were already familiar with his situation. A.D. was doing life and a lot of times people asked her when he was coming home just for the sake of gauging her faith and commitment to him. If she said "Soon," she looked stupid when the years stretched on and he didn't show, but if she said "Never!" it looked as if she'd just wrote the nigga off. Her and Ebony had been cool for a long time and she didn't think that the girl was trying to play some type of mind game but the question still bothered her.

As much as she hated being asked about A.D., it happened so often that over the years she had come to patent this perfect response: "He still fighting but that appeal shit takes time." This way she doesn't commit herself to any specific date while still appearing to be optimistic.

Ebony nodded thoughtfully. "Well, next time you holla at 'em, tell that nigga I said keep his head up."

Tuesday left from behind the bar agreeing to relay that message.

She was crossing the room by weaving her way through the maze of tables on the floor when suddenly: *whack!* Somebody smacked her on the ass so hard that it made her flinch.

At first Tuesday thought it was some new customer who didn't

yet know who she was, and just as she turned around ready to go
H.A.M., she realized that it was her big bouncer DelRay.

DelRay was six foot seven and close to four hundred pounds.
He was heavy but didn't look sloppy because it was stretched out
by his height. He also knew how to handle himself, possessing a
grace and speed rarely seen in men his size. DelRay could be very
intimidating when the job required it but by nature was a goofball.
While he had the skills to deal with unruly customers physically,
he had the game to get most of them out the door without making
a scene. This was what Tuesday liked most about him.

She said, "Nigga, I was about to flip!"

"We at four!" he yelled over the music. Lil' Wayne was playing
then.

She shook her head. "Hell naw, nigga, we at five!"

He used his thick sausage-like fingers to count. "Two Saturday
night, one Sunday before you got in your car, and one just now." He
grinned and rubbed his hands together like a little kid eager for a
gift. "I get to smack that fat muthafucka six more times!"

"Fuck you!" she said but with a smile. Actually she knew it was
only four.

He teased her. "Don't be mad at me, you should be mad at yo
boy Lebron! When it get down to crunch-time he always choke."

Tuesday was a diehard Miami Heat fan who swore that she was
going to suck Dwyane Wade like a pacifier if she ever met him in
person. At the time Miami had the second-best record in the east-
ern conference so when they came to Auburn Hills to play a struggling Pistons team, dropping a hundred on them seemed like a safe
bet. After the Heat lost in overtime, the bouncer asked his boss if
he could trade that bill she owed him for the right to smack her on
that juicy ass ten times. Tuesday had no interest in fucking DelRay
but they were cool like that, so she agreed.

"That's all right though," she fired back. "I still like Miami to win it all. Yo weak-ass Pistons ain't even gon' make the playoffs."

"Give us two more years to draft, we gon' be back on top again!"⤴

Changing the subject, she asked, "I saw Bree's car out front but is the rest of 'em here?"

DelRay nodded. "Everybody but Tush. Jaye in the locker room skinnin' them bitches on the poker. Bree and Doll in there with her."

"Tush will be here in a minute, I already holla'ed at her. But go tell the rest of them bitches I'm in my office."

"I got you, Boss Lady."

Just as she turned to walk away: *whack!*

She whipped around trying to mug him, but DelRay's fat face made one of those goofy looks that always melted her ice grill. "I'm sorry, Boss Lady, I couldn't help it. You shouldn't have wore that True Religion shit today. You in them muthafuckin' jeans!"

She jerked her fist like she was going to punch him. "Now we at five!"

"You wanna bet back on Miami and Orlando?"

"You ain't said shit, nigga, I ride or die with D. Wade! But if you win this time, goddammit, I'm just gon' pay yo heavy-handed ass."

DelRay lumbered off toward an entryway at the left of the stage and parted the beaded curtain that hung over it. That hall had three doors: one for a storage room where all the extra booze and miscellaneous supplies for the bar were kept; the second was the locker room where the dancers changed clothes and spent their downtime in between sets; the third, the door in which the hall terminated, was a fire exit that led to the alley behind the strip mall. DelRay went to the second door, knocked three times, then waited for permission to enter.

An identical hall ran along the opposite side of the stage, only this one did not terminate in a fire door. It was where the restrooms were located, and just beyond them was a door stenciled with the words: *Boss Lady*.

Her office was a modest but tidy space that was only fifteen by twenty feet long. It had a single window with only a view of a garbage-strewn alley. There was a cheap walnut-veneered desk holding a lamp and computer, a small two-drawer file cabinet, two plastic chairs that fronted the desk, and an imitation suede loveseat given to her by a friend. The most expensive thing in the office was her chair: a genuine leather high-back office chair ergonomically designed for perfect lumbar support, costing over fourteen hundred dollars; she had spent more on it than her computer. The office also came with a wall safe that Tuesday never kept any cash in. Other than the above mentioned items, there was nothing else in the way of furniture or decor. Tuesday didn't have anything hanging on the walls and no framed photos were propped on her desk to give it a personal touch. She stepped into her Spartan little space and closed the door.

Tuesday had spent twenty-one years at The Bounce House—ten as a dancer, four as a manager, and seven more as owner—but whenever she came in the office her mind always flashed back to that first time she stepped into it. She was sixteen years old, expelled from all Detroit public schools, a runaway crashing at a different friend's house every night and desperate for money. She had an older cousin named Shameeka who danced there but at the time the place was called Smokin' Joe's. Because Tuesday was light-skinned, pretty with green eyes and a banging body, Shameeka swore she could earn enough money for her own car and crib in no time. So led by her favorite cousin, a young and naive Tuesday was brought in and walked to the door of this office. Shameeka handed her a condom then pushed her inside like a human sacrifice to a sixty-two-year-old bony Polish guy, whose name, ironically, wasn't Joe. There was an eight-minute pound session in which he bent her over the very same desk she still had, then fifteen minutes after that, Tuesday's new name was X-Stacy and she was on the floor giving out lap dances for ten dollars a pop. The old man never asked her age, or anything else, for that matter.

She dropped her bag on the desk and sank into her favorite chair. She thought about what this place had given her, but mostly all that it had taken away.

She was snapped from her reverie when the door swung open. Jaye came in followed by Brianna, and Tuesday immediately cut into her: "Bitch, how many times I got to tell you to stay out my spot?"

Brianna responded with an impudent smirk. "It wasn't like you was using it. Shit, we didn't even know when you was gon' get here."

"The point of havin' my own parking space is so that I'll have a place to park *whenever* I pull up at the club. I don't give a fuck if I'm gone three weeks, when I roll through here, that spot right in front of the door is me! Every bitch who work here know that shit, even the customers know it."

Brianna took a drag off the Newport she was smoking, then flopped down on the loveseat. "Well, you need to put up a sign or somethin'."

"I don't need to put up shit!" Tuesday barked. "The next time I come through and you in my shit I'm a bust every muthafuckin' window you got on that li'l weak-ass Camaro!"

Brianna shrugged nonchalantly and blew out a trail of gray smoke. "And it ain't gon' cost me shit if you do. 'Cause like a good neighbor State Farm will be there . . . with some brand-new windows."

Tuesday pointed a finger at her. "Keep talkin' shit and see if State Farm be there with a new set of teeth!"

Jaye quietly witnessed the exchange with a smile on her face. She took one of the plastic chairs that fronted the desk.

Just then Tushie came in rubbing her ass, with a sour look on her face.

Tuesday laughed. "DelRay got you too, huh? Was it that Miami game?"

She poured herself into the second chair. "Naw, you know fucks wit dat sexy ass Carmelo Anthony," she said with her heavy southern drawl. "New York let da Celtics blow dem out by twenty."

Tuesday asked, "How many he got left?"

Tushie thought back. "He done got me twice already, he only got three left."

"You only gave that nigga five, he got me for ten! How my shit only worth ten dollars a smack and yours worth twenty?"

Laughing, Jaye said, "Maybe because she got twice as much ass!"

Tuesday shot back at her, "And I still got three times more than you!"

After sharing a laugh, she then said, "We can settle up soon as Doll bring her ass on." Tuesday looked to Brianna. "I thought she was with y'all. Where the fuck she at?"

"How the fuck should I know!" Brianna snapped back at her. "Just because the bitch little don't mean I keep her in my pocket!"

Baby Doll came in as if on cue and closed the door. She snatched the cigarette out of Brianna's mouth, dropped onto the loveseat next to her and began to smoke it.

Brianna said, "Ughh, bitch. I could've just got finished suckin' some dick!"

Baby Doll continued to drag the Newport unfazed. "Knowin' yo stankin' ass, you probably did. Besides, my lips done been in waay worse places than yours."

Baby Doll took a few more puffs then tried to offer it back to Brianna, who rolled her eyes and looked away. "Bitch, I wish I would."

Tuesday handed her an ashtray. "Well, now that everybody *finally* here, we can take care of this business."

This was the crew: Tuesday, Brianna, Jaye, Tushie, and Baby Doll. Five hustling-ass dime pieces with top-notch game who was out for the bread. Individually they were good but together they were dangerous. These were the girls who played the players.

Tuesday looked at Baby Doll. "You get yo shit up outta there?"

She butted what was left of the Newport and blew the last of the smoke from her nostrils. "The little bit I had being moved today. I only brought *what* I needed for the lick —just enough to make it look like home. It ain't like him and Simone spent a lot of time chillin' at her crib anyway. We either went out or was chillin' at his loft."

Code name: Baby Doll. She was only four feet eleven inches tall with hips and ass that stood out more because of her short stature. Her buttermilk skin always looked soft even without touching it. Delicate doll-like features had earned her name and made her age hard to place: if Doll told a nigga she was thirteen or thirty, he would believe either one. The type of men who typically went for Doll had low self-esteem and loved the ego boost she gave them; her small size and the helplessness they wrongly perceived in her made them feel bigger and stronger while that child-like naiveté she faked so well made them feel smarter. Baby Doll's greatest assets were her bright hazel eyes because she could project an innocence in them that made men want to protect and possess her. It was because of this that, of the five, Baby Doll was second only to Tuesday in having the most niggas propose marriage to her.

Tuesday asked, "What about Tank?"

"He don't think nothin' up," said Doll. "He done spent the last two days blowin' up that phone and leaving texts for Simone. Of course he thinking that li'l situation done scared her off. Same shit every time."

Tuesday nodded. "Good. Text his ass back and break it off. Tell him you thought you could deal with his lifestyle but after what happened you can't see being with him—"

She cut her off. "T.K. I know the routine! I ain't new to this shit."

"Make sure you lose that phone too," Tuesday reminded her. "How did he feel about that loss he took?"

Doll shrugged. "He wasn't really trippin' bout the money and he say he got insurance on the truck so he gon' get back right off that. He was just so happy that ain't nothin' happen to me."

"That's cause you his Tiny Angel!" Jaye said, teasing her. "'All right, I'll open the safe. Just don't hurt my Tiny Angel.'" She did a spot-on impression of Tank's pathetic voice that made them all laugh.

Code name: Jaye. She was five foot nine with a medium build. She wasn't that strapped but her face was pretty as hell; she had dark brown eyes, a cocoa complexion and big full juicy lips that promised pleasure. Jaye was not the stuck-up dime, she was the ultimate fuck buddy. She was that fine-ass homegirl you could hit and still be cool with. Staying laced in Gucci and Prada heels, Jaye was a girly girl but had some special tomboy quality about her that made a nigga want to blow a blunt or chill with her at a Lions game. She was cool, she was funny, and could easily make a mark feel at ease with her sense of humor. Her best asset was her personality but Jaye's secret weapon was her amazing neck game. She sucked dick like a porn star and the same big lips that got her teased in school were now her sexiest feature. Not too many niggas could resist a bad bitch who kept them laughing all day then at night gave them the best head they ever had.

"I know the type of nigga Tank is," said Tuesday. "He gon' be suckerstroking real hard about you." She looked at Baby Doll. "Lay low for a while and you might wanna do something different to yo hair. Trust me, this nigga gon' be stalkin' you for a minute."

While they spoke, Brianna just quietly shook her head with a look of disgust on her face. "I know having to get next to some off-brand niggas is part of the game, but god damn, Doll, you a better bitch than me. That fat, black, greasy-ass nigga with them big bug eyes; I don't think I could've pulled this one off." She jerked forward pretending to dry-heave then put a hand over her mouth. "How could you look that nigga in the eye and say you love him with a straight face? Just thinkin' about that nigga kissing and touching on me got me ready to throw up."

Doll looked at her sideways. "Bitch, like you said, it's part of the game, that's what we do. I'm playin' his muthafuckin' ass the same way you done had to play niggas and every other bitch in this room. I don't give a fuck what a mark look like, I'm about my paper!"

"Church, bitch!" Tushie leaned over so her and Doll could dap each other.

Brianna leaned back on the loveseat and inspected her freshly polished nails. "Well, I guess I just got higher standards than you bitches."

Code name: Brianna. She was six foot one with the long slender build of a runway model except for her huge 36DD's. Bree had that exotic look that came when you mixed black with some sort of Asian. Like the singer Amerie, she had our peanut butter complexion and thick lips but had inherited their distinctive eyes. Nobody really knew what Brianna was mixed with—Tuesday didn't even think she knew—but whatever she was, the girl was gorgeous. The type of men who were attracted to her were typically looking for a trophy. They liked rare and beautiful things and had no problem with paying for them. Brianna played the high-maintenance girl-friend so well because acting snotty and spoiled wasn't really a stretch.

Tuesday told the girls that they needed to work on their choreography. She felt that it didn't look real enough the other night when Brianna pretended to hit Baby Doll with the gun. "Y'all timing was off. Bree, you looked like you was just tryin' to give her a love tap. And Doll, you looked like you knew it was comin', you was already going down before she could hit you."

Brianna responded the way she typically did to criticism. "Why is you trippin'? The shit was good enough to fool him."

"I'm trippin', bitch, because we can't afford to make mistakes like that. Small shit like that is what could get us knocked."

"Watch this." Tuesday stood up and came from behind her desk. Tushie rose from her seat, knowing that she had a role in the demonstration.

The girls squared off then pretended that they were two hoodrats in the middle of a heated argument: they rolled their necks, put fingers in each other's faces and Tushie improvised some dialogue about Tuesday fucking her man. They pushed each other back and forth, then Tushie gave Tuesday a loud smack that whipped her head around. She held her cheek, looking stunned for a second, then came back with a hard right that dropped Tushie back into her chair.

She fell limp with her head dropped against her chest unconscious, but two seconds later she opened her eyes and smiled. "See, bitches, that's how it's done."

Code name: Tushie. This Louisiana stallion was five foot seven, and while she only had mosquito bites for breasts, her tiny twenty-four-inch waist and fifty-six-inch hips meant she was thicker than Serena Williams on steroids. "Tushie" was the only name that had ever fit her because by thirteen the girl was already so donked up that all her pants had to be tailor-made; by fifteen she was causing so many car accidents from just walking down the street that the police in her small town actually labeled her a danger to the community. Her Hershey-bar skin and black Barbie doll features made her a dime even without being ridiculously strapped. Despite having an ass like two beach balls, Tushie's best asset was really her mind. Many people had been fooled by her deep southern accent but she only talked slow. Tushie knew how to play on those who thought she was just a dumb country bammer and rocked them to sleep. Any nigga thinking she was all booty and no brains would find out the hard way that southerners ain't slow.

Jaye was impressed by the girls' little fight scene. The moves and timing were so perfect that it looked as if they had spent time training with actual Hollywood stuntmen. Jaye was only a foot away from the action, and even though she knew it was fake, she still thought that their blows had made contact. "Wait a minute," she said, curious. "I know she ain't really just slap you but I swear I heard that shit."

"What you heard was this." Tuesday clapped her hand against her meaty thigh. She explained: "Because I'm the one gettin' hit, you lookin' at my face and her hand. You ain't watching my hands! Me and Tush just got this shit down because we been at it longer than y'all."

"Well, I ain't gon' go through all that," Brianna said, standing up to stretch. "Next time I'm just gon' bust a bitch head for real!"

"And now can we wrap up this little meeting so I can get paid and get the fuck outta here. I got shit to do."

Tuesday went into her Louie bag and pulled out a brick of cash. She carefully counted it out into five separate stacks then began to pass out the dividends. As the girls took their individual shares,

Tuesday could see the disappointment on their faces. They were expecting more and she was too.

She passed two stacks to Doll, who took one then handed the other to Brianna. Bree made a quick count of the cash then dropped the sixty-five hundred onto the loveseat as if it were nothing. "What the fuck is this?"

Tuesday sighed because she knew this was coming and knew it would be from her. "Look, I know it's kinda short. Shit fucked up all the way around. I got twenty for the truck, seventeen for the work, and my mans said I was lucky to get that."

After doing two months of surveillance on Tank, Tuesday had put Baby Doll on him. It took another seven weeks of Doll's sweet manipulation to get everything they needed for the lick: personal information, alarm codes, copies of his house keys, the location of his stash, and a head so far gone that he wouldn't risk Doll's life to protect it. The girls had hoped for a big score but found out that Tank was not the hustler they thought he was. The scouting report said that he was heavy in the brick game and the team targeted him expecting at least a six-figure payoff, but when they opened fat boy's safe, all he had was forty-two thousand in cash and twenty-four packaged-up ounces of hard. Disappointed, the girls took his Denali even though it wasn't originally part of the plan. They split the cash that night but it was Tuesday's job to slang the truck and dope; now the girls didn't even get what they hoped for that. Minus what was due to their sixth silent partner, almost four months of work had only grossed them a little over thirteen racks apiece—if you factor in the expenses of renting a temporary place for Doll's alter ego Simone and the Pontiac G6 she drove, they actually netted a lot less. The team typically went after bigger fish, and while they only did about five or six of these jobs a year (sometimes having a few going on at once), they were used to making twenty-five to thirty stacks each, so a lick that only pulled seventy-nine total was a bust.

Tuesday leaned back against her desk. "Look, ladies, I know shit ain't really come through how we wanted on this one. That's my bad but I promise we gon' eat right on the next one." She took the blame because as leader of the group the responsibility always fell on her.

Code name: Tuesday aka Boss Lady. Tuesday was light-skinned five foot nine and thick. She didn't have junk like Tushie but her booty was bigger than average and had been turning heads since puberty. Aside from a pretty face and juicy lips, she had cat eyes that shifted from green to gray according to her mood. Tuesday had put this team together and was the brains behind it. She realized when she was just a dancer that clapping her ass all night for a few dollars in tips wouldn't cut it for a bitch who had bills and wanted nice shit. At nineteen she started hitting licks with A.D., and after he went away, she continued on her own. Over time she recruited Tushie, then slowly pulled in the others. Each of these girls had come to The Bounce just as broke and desperate as she was and Tuesday saw something in each of them that made her think they would be a good fit for the team. Tuesday's best asset was her experience. She had years on every other girl in the group and none of them could crawl inside a mark's head better than she could. She gave them all their game and therefore had each of their skills. She knew how to make a read on a nigga and adapt to the type of girl it took to get him. She could play the innocent square better than Doll, the cool homegirl better than Jaye, and the high-mainte-nance trophy bitch better than Brianna. She could play one role to a tee or blend a few of them together if it was necessary. Her strength was that she was not one-dimensional like the others. For Tuesday, her secret weapon was actually her secret weakness. None of the girls knew she suffered from obsessive-compulsive disorder. Her illness caused her to reorganize things over and over until they were perfect. Her nature to obsess over every little detail did make her a neat freak, but also the ultimate strategist. Tuesday had a way of seeing all the moves ahead of time and putting together air-tight plans that accounted for every problem that might arise.

"He only gave you twenty for the truck, rims and all?" Bree asked with some skepticism in her voice that everybody heard.

Tuesday nodded. "He said he couldn't do no better than that."

"You know that was the new Denali, right? That's at least a fifty-thousand-dollar whip."

Tuesday frowned. "It's a fifty-thousand-dollar whip that's stolen! You thank he gon' give me sticker price for it?"

Brianna shrugged and studied her nails again. "I don't know. Just seem like you got worked to me. Either that or somethin' wrong with yo math!"

That made Tuesday stand up straight. Every other woman in that room felt the sudden shift in the vibe as her eyes quickly changed from lime-green to icy gray. "Bitch, is you tryin' to say somethin'?"

Bree didn't retreat from her stare. "All I'm sayin' is that we done put in a lot of time for a punk ass thirteen Gs! If you figure it all out we basically got a little over three thousand a month. A bitch can get a job and do better than that!"

"The lick wasn't what I thought it was and I apologized for that." Tuesday inched closer to her. "But when you got to talkin' all this bullshit about my math, I thought you was tryin' to hint at somethin' else. So if you got anythang you wanna get off yo double Ds about that, feel free to speak up!"

Jaye and Doll just sat there silent because they both knew what Brianna had tried to insinuate and knew that Tuesday had peeped it.

Tushie was quiet too but she was more alert. She knew Tuesday better than anybody and she knew if Brianna said the wrong thing that Tuesday was going to beat her ass. The girl was just tits on a stick and Tushie figured Tuesday could handle that skinny hoe alone, but Doll and Bree were tight. Jaye fucked with Brianna too even though Tushie didn't know how cool they were. She was getting ready just in case she needed to have Tuesday's back.

The tension that swelled in the room seemed to have distorted time so after a second that felt much longer Brianna tucked her tail by looking away. She snatched up the money and threw the straps to her Fendi bag on her shoulder. "Well, if we ain't got no more business then I'm out." She pushed off the loveseat and started for the door. "Doll, if you wanna ride, you betta come on!"

Just as Baby Doll got up to follow, Tuesday called out to Brianna. She paused to look back just as she grabbed the knob.

"You done got you a li'l Camaro, a couple purses, and some shoes and let that shit go to yo head. You the same broke bitch who pulled up in a busted-ass V-Dub Beetle three years ago beggin' for a job; the same bony bitch who used to be out there on the floor looking all stiff and scared, barely making enough to tip out. I pulled you in, gave you the game, and got you together. Bree, don't forget that you came up fuckin' with me, you ain't make me better."

To that, all Brianna could do was roll her eyes.

"But if you ever decide that you don't like what we doin' in here, that door swing both ways." Tuesday looked around, making eye contact with each of them except Tushie then added, "And that go for everybody!"

"Is you finished?" Brianna tried to redeem herself from getting hoed out earlier by trying her best to look hard again.

Tuesday just waved her off. "Bitch, beat it."

Bree left out the office with Doll right on her heels. Jaye got up too but threw Tuesday a *we're still cool* nod before she dipped.

When Tushie got up and went to the door, it was only to close it behind them. She smiled. "I thought you wuz bout to whup dat bitch."

"I was. She did the right thang!" Tuesday went behind her desk and fell back into her chair. "I don't know where this bitch done got all this mouth from lately but she startin' to talk real reckless. If she keep it up, what almost happened today is definitely gone happen soon."

Tuesday dug into the inside pocket of her bag and pulled out a quarter ounce of Kush that was tied in a sandwich bag. She passed the weed to Tushie along with a cigar because her girl rolled tighter than she did.

Of the team, Tushie had been down with her the longest and been through the most shit. Even though she was five years younger, they were tight and if Tuesday were ever asked to name her best friend, there was no one else more deserving of the title.

Back in the early part of '05 that ass had already made Tushie a legend in the New Orleans strip clubs. Magazines like *King* and *BlackMen's* were calling her the new "It girl" and for a while rappers all over the south were clamoring to have her pop that fifty-six-inch donk in their videos. She had milked that little bit of fame into a brand-new house and a S550 Benz until Katrina came along and washed it all away.

Then she found herself living in Detroit and having to start from scratch. Tushie featured in a few clubs and because she still had a strong buzz, she was the most sought-after free agent since LeBron James. All the big gentleman's clubs were shooting for her and as bad as Tuesday wanted her, she didn't think she had a chance. She quickly learned that this country girl had a sharp business mind, because Tushie agreed to come dance at the struggling little spot that Tuesday had just bought, but only if she made her a partner.

Tuesday was leery at first but it turned out to be the best decision she ever made. When Tuesday took over The Bounce House it was losing money faster than she could earn it, but when Tushie the Tease became a regular featured dancer, all that turned around. She was like a carnival attraction as niggas from as far as New York came to see if she could really walk across the stage with two champagne bottles on her ass and not spill a drop or clap it louder than a .22 pistol. The club was packed like sardines whenever she performed, and within months The Bounce House was turning a decent profit. Tushie kept the place jumping for five years, until she finally hung up her thong and retired from the stage.

Single-handedly saving the club made her a good business partner but years of loyalty and her down-ass ways made Tushie a good friend. Tuesday trusted her so much that she put her up on how they could make some real money together: by robbing niggas who couldn't report the losses.

Tushie finished rolling the blunt, lit it, and took her first three hits. She was passing it across the desk to Tuesday when she spoke in a voice strained from the smoke in her lungs: "I already know you gon' talk to Dres bout dis shit."

Tuesday accepted the weed with a nod. "Hell yeah," she said in between puffs. "I'm on my way to do that soon as I leave here. I'm damn sure bout to find out why he sent us on this dummy mission."